"Readers are advised to remember that the devil is a liar."

C.S. Lewis

Ascended Guardians Series

BOOK TWO

HALO & HORN

MISTY HAYES

Halo & Horn by Misty Hayes

Books in *The Ascended Guardians* Series

Book One: *Shield & Shade*
Book Two: *Halo & Horn*

Books in *The Blood Dagger* Trilogy:
Volume One: *The Outcasts*
Volume Two: *The Watchers*
Volume Three: *Tree of Souls*

Dedication

Dedicated to Sherry Daugherty, Kung Fu Warrior Princess. Yes—I keep buying weird things for my sister at antique stores, like strange haunted dolls. Life would be boring without a bit of humor and horror. Love you!

1

LEO

The pain was unbearable.

The darkness was worse.

A shard, created by a demon and meant to kill angels, had pierced Leo while he had been in the demon realm. Now, its jagged edges churned inside him, creeping closer and closer to his heart. An extremely high fever was partly why Leo was making irrational decisions—or perhaps the slow, steady pull toward darkness was responsible for that. Either way, Leo believed he hadn't died because he was no ordinary angel.

He had been born of two archangels.

His body slowly succumbed to the relentless exhaustion dragging him under. He felt bone-weary. The shard would lead to his demise if he didn't find a cure.

Leo yearned for revenge against the Shades for what they had done to him—*and* for what they'd done to Corinth, and Corinth's brother, Peter. Leo's sister, Zoey, was not connected by blood but by the bond. She'd been seriously injured, but healed by angel grace. Alastair too.

Despite his increasingly pronounced limp and difficulty controlling his power, he needed more time.

Father, please give him more time, Leo implored.

The Son Doong caves, located under the Annamite Mountains in Vietnam, were occupied by a group of Shades who had been part of Ephrem's army. Ephrem, the demon who'd terrorized the Taylors, had created Shades. After that, he was banished to hell by Alastair Iszler and by—Leo admitted begrudgingly—the archangel Nakir.

Sunlight shone into the cavern's mouth as Leo quickly assessed his surroundings and decided which direction to take. The damp and gloomy grottos brought back memories of the demon realm, which made sense—it was where the Shades used to live.

Leo had been drawn here by a demonic entity. Unfortunately, he had no armor to protect himself from any threats. His armor had been ruined. He also knew that if his angel brothers and sisters found out he was here alone, they would try to drag him back to safety, against his will. Safety wasn't what he sought. He sought a battle, a task from which he knew he wouldn't return.

Leo knew that Corinth Taylor was unaware of the extent of Leo's injuries.

There was no point in anyone else getting hurt on Leo's behalf, so he'd cut himself off from the rest of the group. Now, guilt pressed down on him.

Leo!

Ikari's voice filled Leo's head as their telepathic link opened up. Their bond was so strong that he felt Ikari's emotions as if they were his own. Ikari was justifiably worried and angry. The feeling was so intense that Leo had to take a deep breath to calm himself.

The voice came again, more insistent.

What are you doing? Where are you?

Leo remained silent, resolute.

He had to do this on his own.

Didn't he?

Leo, please. Let us help you. I can feel the dark—

Leo cut their connection, mainly because his resolve was starting to waver. It felt like losing a limb. But he was determined—no one else would bear this burden.

He shuddered and stumbled forward, his body involuntarily tugged along as if being led on a leash.

The air was thick with the smell of mold, decay, and soil. As Leo staggered onward, he lost his footing and slipped. The temperature had dropped significantly, and a cascade of water from somewhere above drenched him, chilling him to the bone.

After mechanically lumbering along for hours, Leo stopped at a dead-end. A massive hunk of stone blocked his path. There was no way to progress any further by employing human travel. Yet here, the malevolence pulled at him the strongest, pressing in from all sides.

Leo's sword appeared in his grasp. The handle was unusually ice-cold as the blade emitted a brilliant electric hue against the pitch-black surroundings. *Brrrrr.* The cold was sapping. He sucked in a sharp breath, steeling himself.

Keep going. You have to do this. You want *to do this.*

Approaching the rock, Leo's heart pounded. His breath plumed before him as he placed his palm against the rock. He closed his eyes and listened. There it was—the unsettling presence.

Something dark and nasty ignited a yearning inside him to get to the other side.

A jolt of pain exploded from his rib cage and radiated

out to his limbs. He doubled over as the shard wriggled inside him.

Leo clutched his chest, struggling to shake the pain. This was a mistake. *Too late.* How did he even get here? He shook his headful of damp hair, trying to clear his mind. *He didn't know.*

What had he been trying to do? Kill Shades? Exact revenge?

Succumb.

As Leo decided what to do next, a dense cloud of black sulfur suddenly appeared out of the stone. The demonic tendrils engulfed him, choked him, and then devoured him whole.

Leo raised his sword, vaguely aware that he had been transported to a deep cavern behind the rock. His breath was visible in the chilly air, and his teeth chattered. He swung his blade in a mighty arc over his head, ready to face his opponent. He felt his vision failing, though. Dark shadows screeched and screamed in fright, darting to his left and right. Why couldn't he see in the dark like he used to?

As soon as Leo's hands crackled with portentous energy, another jagged pain ripped through his heart. He dropped to a knee, his blade clattering to his side, all the breath sucked from his lungs. Slowly, in agony, he took in his surroundings, and then he saw them.

Shades. A horde of them.

Surprisingly, Leo remained untouched as they skulked away from the angelic blade on the ground beside him. They seemed wary and frightened, some hissing while others vanished into swirls of thick black smoke.

Run, monsters, run.

Still on his knee, Leo shouted, "Come on! Fight me, cowards!"

The Shades probably knew Leo had reached a point of no return—or, perhaps, they sensed the evil force consuming him from inside and out. That was why he had to get them back for what they did to Peter; he had to kill every last one of them. It would be his final act of bravery.

However, unbearable anguish struck, stronger this time. He collapsed into a fetal position on the damp earth.

Gradually, the radiant angelic light dissipated, leaving Leo in pitch black. This frigid, lifeless hole was to be his final resting place, far from the comforting presence of his loved ones.

Corinth. He tried to open a link to his brother to tell him goodbye, but he only heard a deep crackling in his head.

Too late, brother.

Leo gritted his teeth and got back on his feet, swaying. What should have been an effortless task drained him of all his energy. He inhaled, struggling for air, his strength ebbing. The blade sputtered back to life, then flickered as it tried to stay ablaze. *Spark, sputter. Spark, sputter. Spark, sputter.*

Leo picked his weapon back up as a figure detached itself from the rest of the shadows. It moved toward him, its steps deliberate and confident. Despite the deadly crackling flame emanating from Leo's sword, the entity approached with a boldness that set it apart.

Notable and unnerving, Leo thought.

"I ... suppose you want to ... be the ... first ... first to try to kill me?" Leo spat.

The divine light of his sword flickered again.

"Not really," came a snide remark.

Leo glimpsed the ominous figure. It had black, oily skin, a bald head, and golden veins running up and down its neck. The Shade wore a ragged T-shirt with a white skull on the front. The fabric was torn down the middle, giving it the appearance of long, protruding teeth and a sinister grin—an omen of death.

Then the Shade backed off slightly. "*Leo?*" it said uncertainly.

The curiosity in its voice gave Leo pause, but it also angered him. "How dare you say my name, Shade," he snapped, his body flickering with uncontrolled energy.

The Shade threw a hand over its face, and Leo smiled inwardly at its pain.

Leo should have been curious about how the Shade knew his name in the first place. But his mind was in shambles, like a frayed string coming apart at the seams, and he couldn't concentrate.

"You don't look so hot," the Shade remarked coolly. "You're dying."

The thing dared extend its hand toward Leo, but Leo quickly swung his blade around, causing the creature to jump back and hiss.

The hatred was starting to feel … tolerable, enjoyable, and beckoning to Leo.

But he might still have enough energy to send a shockwave of grace into the sword and down into the earth, taking all the abominations.

And so, Leo snarled as he plunged the sword into the hard-packed earth, clasping the hilt tightly with both hands with the last ounce of strength he had left.

His legs went out from under him, and he collapsed.

The Shade barked out an amused chortle. "You

thought you'd come here and … what, Leo? Try to kill us all? Did you wish for a last-ditch chance for a cure or a fight?" Thin, delicate wisps of smoke emerged from its fingertips, swirling and coiling as they wound hypnotically in the air toward Leo. The wisps seemed almost conscious, as if they had their own mind.

Leo couldn't help but feel a sense of dread and … liberation, as they drew closer to him.

Succumb.

"A little of both," Leo admitted so quietly he wasn't sure it had heard him.

The black, ink-like vines moved in on Leo from all sides, the thick, sulfurous tendrils filling his nose and mouth. He coughed and shuddered as the shock and pain wracked his body in spasms—convulsing, twitching, dying.

Standing beside him, his sword gleamed like a star—a cross marking his grave. He closed his eyes, hoping for a swift and merciful end. His mission had been to serve God, and it was now complete.

"I was going to warn you about the danger of coming here." The Shade's voice was a low rumble in its throat as it crouched beside Leo. "But because you're only a few seconds away from certain death, it turns out it's a good thing that you did come after all."

The Shade inched closer, and its features became more discernible as it did.

Leo's mind raced as he tried to piece everything together, and when it finally came to him, he let out a sharp gasp.

Pete.

Peter Taylor.

Corinth's brother wasn't dead. Well, not exactly, anyway.

2

ZOEY

Going to school didn't seem as important to me as it once was. I wasn't into getting top grades or graduating early anymore. All I cared about these days was the supernatural—angels, demons, and ancient artifacts. The paranormal had piqued my interest, shattering any semblance of routine. Why have a routine anyway? Did working a nine-to-five matter? Everyday life, as people knew it, didn't exist.

Almost everyone walked around ignorant, with their eyes closed to the truth. A part of me wanted to spill it all and let them know they had been duped. But my rational side overcame that part, knowing no one would believe me anyway.

Economics was filling up, and the other students were taking their seats, chatting with friends, and catching up on the latest gossip. I, however, was lost in my own world, engrossed in the book I'd borrowed from the library: *Investigating Angels and Demons*.

I had become obsessed with learning everything I

could about angels and their unfathomable power. My oldest brother, Corinth Taylor, was a Nephilim. Leo, who claimed to be my half brother, was an archangel. And my brother, Pete…well, he'd gotten shafted by all of them. He'd turned into a demon for a brief period and then was taken from my family—a loss we would never shed.

Grief hit me like it always did, entirely out of the blue and in agonizing waves.

I laid my head on my book, hoping the cool, crisp pages would return me to the here and now. The darkness was a welcome relief from the chaos and noise of the outside.

My best friend at the time, Trevor, had pretended to be my classmate and had killed my brother right in front of my eyes. How does someone get over that? The answer is that they don't. No amount of grief therapy was going to make that image go away. None.

Ephrem

I leaned back in my chair, running my hand down the length of my braid as I tried to push away the familiar, creepy sensation clawing its way up my esophagus. *Go away*, I pleaded, trying to calm my racing thoughts. Although I was convinced that Ephrem was still trapped in the depths of hell, I knew there were ways for him to escape.

As I twirled the ring around my finger, I remembered it was a gift from Cor, made from the metal of his angelic blade—the bronze dagger. I hoped that this small piece would protect me when the demons came looking for me.

Again, there was a lot on my plate besides schoolwork.

I was so absorbed in my thoughts that I didn't even realize the lecture had started, until Mr. Woodcomb called my name ten minutes into the class.

"*Zoey ... Zoey ... Zoey!*"

I jerked my head up as he said, "Ah, there you are."

The kids around me giggled, and my face grew hot as Mr. Woodcomb asked me to answer the question on the board. I glanced up, reading the question silently: *Which of the following actions is an example of an improvement in human capital?*

Carlos hires three workers for his business.

Frank's Furniture trains employees to use computers.

Tasha applies for a job as an engineer.

The city of Upland builds a new nursing home.

I paused on C., *the engineer.* My stomach dropped. Pete had been trying to get his degree in engineering. *Peter.*

I knew the answer to the question—Frank's Furniture trains an employee to use computers—but I didn't care about getting it right. I shook my head and squinted at my open book, apathetic.

Mr. Woodcomb cleared his throat before saying, "Zoey, I know you know the answer, but I'm going to let it slide. See me after class, will you?"

I rolled my eyes.

Whatever. Great.

As soon as the bell rang and the room emptied, I propped my legs on an empty desk in front of me, hoping to finish a couple more chapters of my book before leaving. Who cared if I was late?

"Ahem," came a throaty voice.

I glanced up to see Mr. Woodcomb standing at the front of the classroom, waiting for me to finish. His expression was stern, his lips pressed tightly together, and his hands resting on his hip.

I packed my things, approached his desk, and paused before him.

"Zoey, I've noticed you seem increasingly preoccupied lately, especially regarding your grades. I understand that your family is going through a tough time right now," Mr. Woodcomb said, rubbing his balding head. He paused. "I can't even imagine what it's like not knowing about your brother. It must be truly awful …"

Mr. Woodcomb's voice suddenly distorted and then slowly faded away. My heart was pounding so loud that it was all I could hear. Pete had been reported as a missing person because there'd been no body to bury. My parents made it clear to the authorities that my brother had left of his own free will, which resulted in the police not putting in much effort to search for him.

He was just … gone.

Not vanished. Executed by Ephrem.

"As I was saying"—Mr. Woodcomb was still speaking—"I wanted to mention that your grades are slipping. I know that's not typical of you, so I wanted to help. If you'd like, I can arrange for you to speak with the school counselor—"

I shouted, "No!" and slammed my hands on the desk, causing him to flinch. The room spun. I tightened my grip on my backpack strap. "I don't need anything from you," I said firmly.

My teacher gave me a slight nod. He looked disappointed and sad.

A tight ache ballooned in my chest.

I didn't tell Mr. Woodcomb that I didn't intend to improve my GPA.

At that moment, I really missed Cruz Saldivar. He was the only person who truly understood what I was going through. He had experienced the same horrors I had when we were trapped in the demon realm. But despite the danger and fear, Cruz steadfastly refused to leave my side, offering me comfort and support. I felt grateful for our strong bond and knew I would never forget his help.

We'd texted back and forth since that terrible day, but I hadn't seen him since Corinth had taken him home to his mother. We'd both been trying to adjust—which for me meant disassociating—and my parents were still terrified about letting me out of their sight. It had been an all-out war between us for them even to let me go back to school. I only got their approval thanks to my ring and watch with GPS and a panic button.

I hadn't heard from Corinth or laid eyes on him in a while, so it felt like I had lost two siblings instead of one.

In the hallway, outside the classroom, I leaned against the wall, sucking in a shallow breath. I shook at the possibility of being targeted by the Shades for stabbing Ephrem.

I shut my eyes tightly, gathering the strength to move one foot before the other. The weight of my feelings was almost too much to bear.

"Hey," a voice said near me. "Are … are you okay?"

I opened my eyes, uncomfortable to have a witness to my meltdown. It was a familiar face: Keisha Tucker, a girl from my class. She had a dark complexion and light brown eyes that currently seemed to be dissecting me. I didn't want anyone's pity.

Annoyed and embarrassed at myself, I said, "Uh, yeah. I'm fine."

"I'm sorry, Zoey." Keisha offered her condolences, looking down. "I heard about your brother."

"Thanks," I said awkwardly.

She began again when I said nothing else. "Hey, I have an idea. A few of us plan to gather at the lake for a bonfire. Jordan's family owns a house right on the water. They're renovating it to sell. Since it's vacant, we thought we could use it for one night to let loose. You're welcome to join us if you'd like. It could be a great way to take your mind off family drama and spend time with … you, know, friends."

"Friends?" I said, lifting my brows. "I didn't think I had any."

"You do now," Keisha said like it was a done deal.

Part of me couldn't believe I wasn't shutting this down immediately. There were multiple reasons why going to a party would be a bad idea. It was unsafe. My parents were still enforcing a strict curfew. The last person I had trusted turned out to be a demon. I didn't want to endanger anyone else, which was a lot for someone my age to deal with. And I constantly felt on edge.

However, taking my mind off current events was also highly tempting.

As soon as I hesitated, Keisha put her hand out. "Give me your phone."

I tugged my cell from my pocket and handed it to her.

"No pressure, but …" Without hesitation, she entered her contact info and returned my phone. "Text if you change your mind," she added with a warm grin.

I watched my possible new friend walk away, thinking about inviting Cruz to the bonfire. I wanted to feel normal again, if only for a few hours.

3

CRUZ

Cruz Saldivar eagerly awaited the end of his shift at Sweets and Stuff. He only had fifteen minutes, and all he had left to do was take the trash to the dumpsters behind the building. Cruz closed the store by himself almost every night. He had volunteered to do it because he wanted a raise and didn't want to go home to an empty house.

His *madre* was making up for time lost, and she'd been going out almost every night.

Cruz's mom, Elena Saldivar, had made a miraculous recovery from a terminal lung disease. As a result, she resumed her position as the head librarian. This had brought in some extra income, which was a relief, but their top priority now was to pay off medical debts.

Cruz worked overtime and hadn't had much time to process the events from the demon realm or speak to Zoey, except through texting—they messaged each other a lot. But it just wasn't the same as actually being in her company. He missed seeing that stunning smile of hers in person.

Zoey's eldest brother, Corinth, had cautioned Cruz about the possibility of Ephrem coming for him. The mere thought of encountering that lunatic again made him shudder. Sometimes Cruz wondered if he was just being paranoid; if someone *were* to confront Cruz, it would be in a dimly lit alleyway at the back of a store ...

Maybe he wasn't *that* paranoid.

This was the worst part of his job. Cruz stepped outside, attempting to lift the two overstuffed and heavy garbage bags. He resorted to dragging them instead, determined to get them out in one trip. He didn't want to come back outside to this creepy alley. Struggling with the load, he grunted, his breath visible in the chilly air.

Finally, after an eternity, he made it to the dumpsters without ripping a hole in the bags.

Cruz had hoisted one into the bin, which was no small feat. Also, it really smelled like decaying garbage.

After finishing, he let out a deep sigh, wiped his hands on his apron, and turned back inside. But something caught his eye off the right, causing him to stop dead.

A red devil with horns or a bull on a man's body—

Macabre images flashed through his mind—demons and Shades—all things associated with darkness and malice and possessions.

Cruz grabbed the shield hanging from his neck, half-expecting it to be hot, but the metal was cool.

The holy relic he carried comforted him as he walked back toward the doors, warding him from evil. He tucked it under his shirt with a reverent kiss, trying to shake off the jitters. He rolled his shoulders, annoyed at himself for being overly anxious. He'd had too much caffeine.

A solitary light illuminated the back door while the

remainder of the closed-off backstreet lay shrouded in darkness. The space had mock surveillance cameras to scare off would-be burglars.

Cruz glanced at the digital screen on his smartwatch, which Corinth had gifted him. It had some pretty cool features, including a panic alarm that he had been warned never to use unless it was life or death. There were no visible signs of danger lurking nearby. However, the stillness in the air seemed to press down on him, causing a sense of foreboding.

Listen to your gut, his *madre* had always told him.

Cruz began to jog back to the store as a tall, dark form emerged from the shadows, blocking his path. He stopped and glanced down to check, but the shield didn't indicate demons or Shades. These were humans, and this human was big. He loomed over Cruz, obscuring the dim light from behind.

Cruz raised his fists, his heart rate skyrocketing as the guy spoke. "Cruz is taking out the garbage. Isn't that ironic?"

Two more hulking forms emerged behind the first one, stepping into the security light like the main actors in a theatrical performance. There was a jolt of recognition as he studied the group. They were not demons—although Daniel Cordova, with his raven-colored hair, dark eyes, and hostile personality, could be mistaken for one.

Cordova was built like a tank, with a square chest, jaw, and head. Even his haircut was a square. Cruz used to hang out with Daniel's gang before he decided to turn his life around. Although they were around the same age, Cruz was a little younger, he recalled. He had promised his mother that he was done with that life.

The two other guys, *Thing 1 and Thing 2*, positioned themselves to either side of him, ensuring Cruz couldn't pass.

Dumpsters and a fence trapped Cruz from behind, leaving him no way out.

Cruz locked eyes with each of them, his voice low and menacing. "Before you try to stop me from going inside, did Danny Boy tell you why I broke his jaw a few years back?"

The two guys exchanged a nervous glance, unsure whether to answer. Cruz's reputation might have preceded him. If they were smart, they'd know better than to take him for granted or goad him without taking precautions.

"Don't call me Danny Boy," Danny snarled, inching closer.

"Yeah, Danny Boy was drunk and obnoxious one night, bragging about how he'd cheated on his girlfriend and gotten away with it. When Debra"—Cruz scratched his cheek, shaking his head —"arrived, I told her in front of Danny that he'd cheated on her. That's why you're here, right?" Cruz turned to face Cordova. "To get even?"

Daniel rubbed his jaw as if the wound was still fresh. "Consider yourself fortunate that I'm allowing you to come to terms with your ass-kicking."

"Guys," Cruz said with a yawn. "I'm exhausted. Normally, I wouldn't mind taking you down a few pegs, but I don't feel like it tonight … Go home."

His blood hummed in his veins. His pacifism wasn't *entirely* honest—there was always a part of Cruz that itched for violence. Anger fueled him. It made him stronger. When it came to fighting people, Cruz was on equal footing. It was another thing to battle demons… he'd think twice about those things.

His feet moved forward of their own accord as he clenched his fists, reminding himself of his promise, but they were the ones looking for trouble.

Daniel laughed, probably misinterpreting Cruz's hesitation as a sign of weakness or fear. "Cruz, not in the mood for a fight? That's a first." He glanced at his two buddies; the one to his right had a black ball cap on. "It's funny you think you have a choice, Saldivar."

Cruz's heart rate spiked as they stepped closer; his muscles tensed. They closed around him, their faces twisted angrily, their chests puffed out.

Cruz's gaze shifted to his knuckles, which he brought up to his line of sight. They were lined with dozens of scars, some old and faded, others more recent and still healing. The scars were like knitting on a sweater, a patchwork of memories and pain that he wore like a badge of honor. Each one reminded him of a round he had won or a battle he had survived. Cruz's fists were more than just limbs. He knew his anger could be dangerous, but it was also the only thing that made sense to him.

The rush of adrenaline coursed through him, making him feel alive. "So, what's it going to be, Danny Boy?" he murmured, his voice laced with venom.

Daniel Cordova smiled. "I want to see you bleed."

"Three against one?" Cruz scoffed. "That's more revealing about your fear than my courage."

Daniel bit his lip and snapped, "What did you say, *pendejo*?"

"It means you're scared," Cruz goaded.

"That mouth always did get you into trouble," Daniel started to say, but Black Ballcap lunged at Cruz, trying to gain the upper hand first—a rookie mistake.

Cruz's world dimmed and slowed as the guy swung wildly at him. He dodged the fist, landing a powerful punch to the guy's gut. The guy doubled over, his face contorted in pain as he dry-heaved. Daniel and the other guy, whose name he vaguely recalled as Damien, were already moving in to help. As Cordova struck out at Cruz, Cruz instinctively lifted his arm to block the fist. He felt the rush of air missing its intended target.

Danny's heavy breathing and shoes scraping against the concrete were loud.

Cruz jabbed Damien with an elbow, causing him to stumble and let out a tormented cry. Then he delivered a blow to the black ballcap guy's cheek, the sound echoing through the frigid night air, leaving no doubt that the bone had shattered.

Something struck Cruz's jaw, causing a sharp pain that radiated to his ear, and then rough hands grabbed him around the waist. Someone else yanked him backward off his feet, and then the blows found Cruz's midsection. Once. Twice. Three times. He gasped for air as their grip prevented him from bending over to take deep breaths. The two at his sides brutally jerked Cruz upright, and he kicked out, connecting with a kneecap. There came a satisfying *crunch* followed by a string of expletives in Spanish.

"*You broke my knee!*" came a whine.

Something hard struck Cruz on his head, and his world plunged into black.

For a moment, in the darkness, he saw Ephrem leering at him, taunting him. *I'm coming for you.*

Cruz, thoroughly concussed, came back to the world in slow, blurry increments as he was hauled back to his feet. The next shock of pain found his ribs. His face. His torso.

Several more strikes to his head had him spitting up red. Salt and blood stung his eyes. He was dizzy and light-headed.

Danny was standing in front of Cruz, grimacing and favoring his knee. His nose was actively gushing. Cruz gave Danny an infuriating smirk when he saw Danny's distress.

He knew this: savagery, gore, and pain felt like greeting an old friend. A vicious wildness bloomed inside him, a caged animal waiting to be set free. He needed to release it, to tear them apart.

He liked this.

What was wrong with him?

Daniel panted as he pointed to the guy wearing the black cap. "Jay, check out that fancy watch on Saldivar." He wiped his mouth and spit. "Give it to me."

Jay pulled Cruz's watch off his arm and threw it to Daniel, who plucked it out of the air and said, "This is nice. I bet I can pawn this for some decent cash." He turned it over, examined it, and then tapped the digital face for a few minutes before the screen lit up. "I've never seen this brand before. It's strange. What does this red button do?"

"*Wait!*" Cruz growled, panic slicing through him. "Don't touch that!" Corinth wouldn't be happy if he found out what Cruz had done. He was also determined to see this through; he didn't want anyone's assistance.

Daniel hesitated, his finger lingering over the button while he glanced up at Cruz, flashing a knowing grin. "What's the matter? Does it call your mommy?"

"I wouldn't do that," Cruz wheezed, blood bubbling on his lips.

Daniel wiped his grimy face with his hand. "All right," he muttered before tapping the button and activating it.

Oh no.

"That was *not* a good idea," Cruz muttered, his lip rapidly swelling.

Daniel's face was illuminated in red as he peered at the watch. It beeped loudly and repeatedly flashed, demanding his attention. He gave it a closer look, trying to decipher its message. "Why does it show this address? ¡*Mierda*!" He spat. "The cops!"

"No," Cruz mumbled, his lip hurting. "Something much scarier."

4

CRUZ

Jay and Damien grabbed hold of Cruz's arms and forcefully dragged him toward Danny Cordova. Despite Cruz's efforts to resist, the two were too strong for him, and he was still feeling dizzy from the blow to his head.

"*Ándale*, Dan," Jay hissed. "Break his jaw and be done with it."

Cordova's knuckles made a cracking sound as he clenched his fists and sprang at Cruz—

Out of nowhere, a blinding light cut through the darkness, resembling a pair of supernatural scissors slicing the night sky open. The light was so bright that it felt like they were standing beneath a UFO. A swirling cloud appeared overhead, accompanied by wind and thunder.

Cruz might have passed out at the sight if he had not been ready.

Danny stopped in his tracks, transfixed, his eyes riveted on the streaks of lightning in the night sky. He paled as he struggled to comprehend what he was witnessing. It could have been extraterrestrials, apparitions, or dark spirits. The possibilities seemed endless and all equally terrifying. "*What—the—hell—is—that?*" he cried.

All three stood silently, staring up at the breathtakingly celestial sky. In their awe, Jay and Damien released their grip on Cruz.

"*Aliens*," Cruz said with wide-eyed sincerity.

Cruz shoved Jay back, causing him to stumble over a cement block, which was there to prop open the back door for deliveries. As Jay went down, he hit his head on a recycling bin, rendering him unconscious. At the same time, Cruz seized Damien by the scruff of his neck, hauled him down, and kneed him in the face, knocking him out cold before he even hit the ground.

Winded and concussed, Cruz locked eyes with Danny, who was staring at him as if he were a freak.

"You think it's a good idea to stick around to see what comes out of that cloud?" Cruz rubbed his eyes, and something hot and sticky leaked into them.

Daniel risked another glimpse at the strange, whirling mist above them before he chucked Cruz's watch and ran, leaving his two injured companions on the ground.

A figure sprang out of the vortex, landing gracefully in a crouched position. Their hands crackled with powerful, angelic energy.

Corinth Taylor.

Corinth's russet-colored hair was sticking straight up, and it looked like he'd hastily thrown some gold mesh chainmail armor over his black-and-gray flannel pajamas. His Converse were unlaced, and he was sockless. In his right hand, he held one of the deadliest relics in the universe— the holy Lance, otherwise known as the Spear of Destiny.

Corinth rapidly assessed the situation, his amber eyes

skimming the scene. Upon seeing the unconscious men splayed out on the ground, he gestured toward them. "Those guys aren't demons, Cruz. Are you okay? Were they trying to rob you?"

"Not exactly." Cruz gently prodded at his fat lip. For the briefest of moments, he considered saying yes. "Technically, they *did* try to steal my watch. But, no ... that's not the reason they were here." Guilt swirled in Cruz's gut. The angel would be livid with Cruz for bringing him out here in the dead of night. The guy had been either sound asleep or busy with something else. "What's with the pajamas?" he asked offhandedly.

"It's late, and I was asleep." Corinth's brows rose as he shrugged. "Your panic alarm woke me, and I didn't think; I just acted. Here—" Corinth stood to his full height, and suddenly, a flicker of lightning came down from the sky, striking Corinth and blinding Cruz. *Holy hell.* The next moment, when he blinked the light out of his vision, he saw Corinth was now wearing tactical gear—a holster strapped to his thigh that housed his dagger, boots, and fatigues. "Is this better?"

"You're still badass even in PJs." Cruz's eyes went wide as he nodded. "I'm just glad you came." The adrenaline was wearing off, and the pain was setting in, intensifying by the minute. He doubled over, grasping his knees as blood dripped off his forehead.

"You're hurt." Corinth was beside Cruz instantly, placing a firm yet gentle hand on Cruz's back.

A moment later, a comforting warmth flowed through Cruz's veins. He closed his eyes and left planet Earth— figuratively, not physically. The sensation was not new to him; it reminded Cruz of the sun's gentle kiss on his skin, spreading warmth from the inside out. As he surrendered to the soothing heat, the pain in his head, face, and stomach faded, leaving him renewed and whole once again. Angels had healed him before, but this time, it felt different. The sensation was potent, heady, and ethereal. As the high slowly dissipated, Cruz opened his eyes to see Corinth kneeling beside Jay, his hands emitting a bright energy that seemed to be affecting both Jay and Damien, who were still unconscious.

Corinth gave Cruz a critical squint before placing a finger on Damien's forehead. The swelling disappeared in moments, and Damien let out a contented sniffle.

Next, Corinth rose and walked over to check on Jay, who lay motionless on his back. Placing two fingers on Jay's neck, Corinth's hands blazed bluish-golden. At the touch, Jay let out a groan and began to stir. Gradually, his breathing improved, and his chest rose and fell steadily.

"They won't remember tonight's events," Corinth said, slipping his blade back into the sheath at his thigh and placing an elbow on a knee. "Judging by the dirty apron and overflowing dumpsters, I assume you were working."

Cruz nodded.

"Want to fill me in?" Corinth asked with concern, as he returned to his feet and met Cruz's gaze.

Cruz swiped at his brow, trying not to squirm under Corinth's accusatory frown. "First, I want to say this was not my fault. I got jumped by three—"

"Three? There were three?" Corinth looked around, his senses heightened. "Where's the third one?" His voice was heavy with disapproval.

"He took off right before you got here."

"*Great*," Corinth hissed, and then his gaze halted on

Cruz's watch, which was still lying on the ground. "What did the third guy see, Saldivar?"

Cruz screwed his face up, mashing his lips together before saying, "Well, he *might* have seen the cataclysmic giant hole in the sky ... but that's it, I promise."

Corinth swore under his breath. "Will that guy be a problem?"

"No," Cruz said, his voice hitching. "He shouldn't be. I mean, I don't think so."

Corinth snatched the watch off the ground, seemingly unconvinced. He pressed a button on the clock face, and it stopped flashing.

"The guy who ran away, we got into it awhile back, before all this demon stuff happened."

Corinth stared at the timepiece for a long moment, his eyebrows knitted. "So, they were looking for revenge? Was it for fighting?" There was a flicker of emotion in his eyes that Cruz couldn't discern—anger, regret, or disappointment. "Where's the shield, kid?"

Cruz lifted the gold chain around his neck and tugged the talisman from under his shirt, where he always kept it. Even in the dark, it seemed to shine brighter. It was made from part of the Spear of Destiny—Corinth's blade. "I understand if you want to take the watch back," Cruz murmured. "But please don't take this."

"Were you trying to show off? Or prove a point? If you need help, that's fine. I get it. This could have been a whole lot worse, though."

"I didn't *need* help," Cruz snapped. "They stole my watch and pressed the button. And nothing you say will make me feel worse than I already do." Cruz stared at the dried blood smeared on his hands and across his knuckles, feeling self-conscious and ashamed. "But it's like this urge to fight rises inside me no matter how hard I try to stop it. Trouble finds me." He licked his dry lips to bring moisture back to them. "I'm sorry. I guess this was my fault."

Corinth held the watch out to Cruz. "Trouble finds you because you go looking for it. That's what worries me the most, kid."

Cruz took the proffered timepiece and held it up, thinking. "If that's how you feel, why are you giving this back to me?"

"Don't make me change my mind," Corinth half-whispered, half-snarled.

"I—I won't. I swear," Cruz said adamantly.

Corinth lifted his hands, and blue flames shot out of them. Then, a rumble of thunder shook the ground beneath Cruz's feet, and he swayed a little.

"Are you going to be okay?" Corinth asked, turning back to him.

Cruz nodded.

Being this close to a portal felt more like an earthquake than magic.

"Be careful, Cruz," Corinth cautioned. "I may not always be around to help."

"Your brother, Pete," Cruz began. "How are you … you know … holding up? Zoey hasn't heard from you in weeks. She's worried. Have you spoken to her? How is she? Have you gotten any word about—"

"I appreciate your concern, Cruz, but stay in your lane and worry about yourself first."

A streak of lightning surrounded Corinth and devoured him whole, and he disappeared into the night in the blink of an eye.

5

LEO

Leo hovered somewhere between semi-consciousness and unbearable agony. Corinth's brother, Peter Taylor, was bent over him, and several other Shades held him down. Red fire emanated from Pete's hands.

They were killing him, which Leo thought was excessive since he was already dying. Leo's vision slid in and out of focus. He had no idea how many demons surrounded him. Or maybe they were turning him into something evil or wanting him to suffer more. Whatever the case, the shard twisted inside him, tearing at his insides. Leo let out an earsplitting bellow, fighting against their unyielding hold.

If these Shades were going to slay him, he wished they'd make quick work of it. He wasn't sure how much more of this he could endure. His chest felt like it was about to burst wide open.

And then, as suddenly as the agony had come on, it stopped. Leo could breathe again.

He slumped back onto the hard earth, breathing in the musty smell of dampness and rotten eggs. The Shades, except for Pete, finally let him go and drifted away, murmuring and whispering. The sensation that had wracked his body moments ago was gone, leaving only a feeling of liberation behind. The evil presence that had taken hold of him was no longer there.

In a flash, Leo extended his arm, lightning crackling around his hand as he gripped Peter's neck. Though the Shade flinched, he maintained a calm demeanor, his expression blank as he locked eyes with Leo. The cavern was filled with tense silence. Only Leo's breathing could be heard, as he gripped Peter's neck in a chokehold.

Peter Taylor opened his fist, revealing the burnt and black fragment that had just been inside Leo. "You're not treating your savior very well, are you?" he said, his voice a whispered rasp.

Leo closed his eyes and threw his shoulders and head back, electricity snapping across his skin. After taking several deep, reassuring breaths, he let go of Peter and flexed his fingers. The dazzling light faded, and the Shade stumbled back, grimacing.

Leo summoned his sword with a surge of energy that swept through the cave, and several creatures squealed in fright. The sword vanished in a swirl of electric fire, returning to its rightful place at his side. The realization that Peter was a Shade stirred a mix of emotions in Leo. Although he tried to suppress regret, sadness tugged at his heartstrings.

"*Geez*," Pete exhaled sardonically. "Turn that grace down, Leo."

"How … in the bloody underworld did you save me?" Leo demanded. "Better yet, *why*?"

Peter's voice was taciturn when he spoke. "We have the power to stop the change, just as we have the power to start it." His eyes, black as coal, gleamed as he dropped the splinter to the ground and crushed it under his foot. "As long as the shard hasn't overtaken your heart—which it had moments before this one pierced yours." He paused before continuing. "I don't like Ephrem, and anything I can do to disrupt his plans is *my* plan. The enemy of my enemy is my friend, so they say."

Leo noted Peter's lack of concern or inquiry regarding his siblings or parents.

"How are you still alive?" Leo finally asked. "I was told Trevor killed you in the demon realm."

Peter looked down at the ripped hole in his shirt, noticing the skull design that seemed to be laughing at him. "The demon failed. When I recovered, I discovered Alastair had banished Trevor back to hell. Amidst the confusion, I took the opportunity to escape before anyone could catch me."

"But you saved Zoey's life. Why leave? Why not tell your family that you're … alive?"

Peter's eyes were pitch black and devoid of emotion. He raised his arms, showing his skin, shiny as an oil slick. "Because I'm not alive," he hissed. "I do not have a beating heart. Do you really think I can go back to the way things were? It's easier to let everyone think I'm dead. I'm a traitor to my parents, Jimmy and Corinth. They will not forgive me, and I do not need their forgiveness."

"I don't believe you," whispered Leo. "Why bother about what your parents or brother think of you? By the way, they don't consider you a traitor; they believe you're a hero." Leo glanced at the other demons still circling him. "So, why did *they* help an angel, then?"

"When Ephrem met his demise, his followers were left

adrift. His Shades, who'd once had a purpose and a home, were now directionless. While some of his devoted disciples still anticipate Ephrem's return, a few have decided to follow me instead."

Leo arched an eyebrow. "You?" he asked, taken aback.

Peter gave a slight shrug that looked almost human. "They saw me rise against Ephrem. I took charge. My actions made me his successor."

Leo wasn't convinced that leaving the demons to their wicked ways was the right course of action. However, Peter had saved Leo's life, and he owed the Shade that much. Perhaps this meant that there was a way to reform the Shades for the better. Was there a possibility for a cure?

"Corinth will want to know you're still—"

"*No*," Peter snarled, his tone leaving no room for argument. "You can't tell Corinth about me."

Leo was in profound conflict, his loyalty to Corinth warring with his sense of duty. "Surely you do not expect me to keep quiet about this?"

"I demand it," Peter growled, his voice laced with an unyielding intensity. "You're in my debt now, and that's the price of saving your life."

Leo couldn't believe Peter was asking him to keep a secret while demanding a favor. He felt his frustration mounting. "I don't owe you anything," he retorted, his tone sharp and pointed.

Peter, not backing down, looked Leo directly in the eyes. "Keep my secret, seraph," he said, his voice low and firm. "And …" he paused, as if considering his words carefully, before adding, "I will owe you a favor."

"What makes you think I'll need a favor?" Leo felt a twinge of curiosity at what kind of favor Peter would be willing to offer him.

"When Ephrem returns, you'll need information." Peter's tone was matter-of-fact, as if it was a given that Ephrem would be back.

Leo tried to process those implications. He could feel the weight of danger upon Ephrem's return. The thought of Zoey or Cruz being hunted made him break out into a cold sweat.

He hoped Peter understood the gravity of their situation. "How can you provide information if you aren't on Ephrem's side?" Leo asked. "You'll be as much of a target as I am, Pete. You will need *my* help, not the other way around."

"I'd rather you call me Ari instead of Peter." He gestured toward the Shades behind him. "That's what they call me. And regarding your question about Ephrem, he's our creator. We're all connected. I can detect the presence of other Shades and contact those who claim to be part of Ephrem's inner circle. Leo, trust me, you'll need my help."

Leo pondered all the information Peter had presented to him. He realized it would be prudent to have a trustworthy ally within their circle who could inform him if Ephrem did escape hell. The situation demanded that they be ready to face any challenges, and having an inside source would be a significant advantage.

Finally, he gave in and nodded. "I'll keep your secret … for the time being … Ari."

6

ZOEY

The sweet melody of robins singing outside had finally lured me out of the house. I found myself sitting on the front stoop, completely lost in thought, reminiscing about Peter. I longed to revisit one particular memory, every detail etched in my mind like a vivid painting. Why was my grief so hard to put into words?

When I was seven, my family and I went camping. My parents drove their pickup while my younger sibling, Jimmy, lowered the tailgate, creating an open space for Peter and me to sit, our legs dangling. While preparing to take his permit test, Jimmy wanted to practice his driving, so we got chauffeured around the park. Peter and I whistled as we drove around, taking in the tranquil surroundings and enjoying the perfect weather. We had no electronic devices to distract us. It was just me and my brothers enjoying life's simple pleasures together.

I could feel Peter's presence beside me, so I glanced to my right, hoping against hope that it was him.

Instead, it was Jimmy beside me.

He had a magnificent crown of curls the color of a fiery sunset. It had only been three days since I last saw him, but his face appeared more fraught with sadness. There were deeper creases around his mouth. He used to be brawny, but had lost weight and muscle. It was obvious that none of us were eating or sleeping properly.

An intense pain filled my chest. I wiped at some errant tears and gazed ahead, focusing on a bird landing in the front yard. It was busy pecking at something on the ground.

Jimmy broke the silence after a few moments. "I miss him," he whispered with a heavy sigh.

I cleared my throat before responding, "Me too."

Staying in the present had proven difficult lately—the present was where my sorrow resided. "Are you okay?" I asked, but I felt like I was speaking from a far-off place.

Jimmy sat with his elbows on his knees, staring at the ground. "Are any of us okay?"

"Definitely not." I let out a small, sad laugh. "Have you heard from Cor?"

"Not since he left a few weeks ago. You?"

"I've tried calling, texting. I've even sent messages through the angels, but according to them, he's not responding or doesn't want to talk."

We sat silently, lost in thought, until Jimmy finally spoke again. "I can't bring myself to go back inside. Every inch of it reminds me of Pete. From the couch—with his permanent butt impression—to his untouched room and clothes. But Pete's gone …" He rubbed his nose and sniffed.

Intense pressure was building back up inside my chest. My rib cage was going to explode.

"I should have kept a closer eye on him," my brother whispered, his voice hitching as he choked up. "I never thought … I mean, I'm angry at both of them. Cor and Pete. Beyond angry, you know?"

I leaned against Jimmy's shoulder. His words trailed off, and his body started to shake with violent sobs. He was hurting just as much as I was, if not more. Jimmy and Peter had been inseparable.

I bottled up my fury, trying to keep my composure even as my brother cried beside me. There would come a time when I'd let it loose.

Back inside my room, I sat on my bed, thinking about Cor's eighteenth birthday and how he had been destined to become a soldier of God. Alongside his half brother, Leo, Cor had set out to save the world from a group of rogue angels calling themselves the Grigori. Leo had told me that Nakir had disappeared after leaving Alastair's body, but Nakir's piercing gaze still haunted me.

The memory was still fresh. Nakir had pulled me back from the brink of hell. I absentmindedly rubbed at my wrist, recalling the tingling sensation his fingers had left behind. It was implausible that I had been able to see the archangel's true identity beneath Alastair's face.

But miracles were also implausible, so there was that.

Usually, Biscuit would be lying right here beside me on my bed. I missed the little rascal, but he now kept Alastair company at the farmhouse. My cat had saved my life from a demon, but it was heartening to know Alastair had an emotional support kitty to aid in his long road to recovery.

Reading about heaven and hell, I tried my best to

digest everything. But I kept having to read the same sentences repeatedly. It was a lot—I couldn't find any mention of an archangel Nakir anywhere, and I'd read the Bible cover to cover twice.

The Catholic church highly regarded three significant archangels: Michael, Gabriel, and Raphael. However, other religious texts mentioned a plethora of archangels, including Uriel, Sealtiel, Jegudiel, Barachiel, Yerachmiel, Chamuel, Oriphiel, and Jerahmeel.

And then there was my personal favorite, Castiel from the TV show *Supernatural*. Just kidding, Castiel was fictional, but these other angels were not. I'd need to consult an authority on angels to learn more about them.

Leo, for instance, had lived for eons.

A sudden restlessness overtook me. I jumped out of bed, pacing.

I needed to talk to someone who knew about the supernatural world but wasn't a family member. It was already ten o'clock, but I knew Cruz Saldivar worked late and would probably still be up. So, I pulled out my phone, tapped the screen, and messaged Cruz to see if he had time to talk. I stared at my phone, waiting for the three text bubbles. When some time had passed without a response, I sighed, disappointed.

Why aren't you answering, Cruz?

Because he's too busy for you.

My phone buzzed as I pondered the best course of action to catch him before he left work. To my surprise, it wasn't a text from Cruz. Instead, I saw it was from Keisha. It read: *We're all at the lake right now. We'll be out here for a while. Come join. ☺ 4244 Lakeshore Way.*

What if it was a trap? A wave of emotions hit me—

apprehension, nervousness, exhilaration, and a tinge of fear. A part of me was hesitant to leave the house, especially at this hour. However, I did have my watch and ring, which made me feel relatively safe.

Determined not to let anxiety dictate my life, a foolish plan started to take shape in my mind, and my stomach somersaulted. If anything were to happen, Cor would be the one I'd turn to for help. I knew he'd been struggling to deal with his emotions since losing Pete, but he couldn't keep shutting out his family and friends. We'd all lost someone and needed to support each other through it. Jimmy relied on Cor; our parents depended on him.

Screw Corinth.

I didn't need him if he wasn't going to be there for his grieving family.

I could take care of myself.

Because it was a bit chilly outside, I grabbed a fuzzy sweater and threw it over my black T-shirt. After checking my appearance in the mirror, I felt relatively satisfied. My wheat-colored hair was hastily tied in a side ponytail. It flowed down my left shoulder in soft waves, and I ran my fingers through it to comb it out. I applied some lip gloss and took a final look in the mirror. The anticipation of doing something impulsive and reckless must have flushed my cheeks. The robin's egg-blue sweater accentuated my light brown eyes, and I matched it with brown leggings.

Last Christmas, Pete had gifted me a custom-designed pair of navy high-top Converse with tiny white stars all over them, mimicking the starry night sky.

This is as good as it gets, I thought.

Suppressing my growing guilt for disappointing my parents again, I invited Cruz to come out to the lake with me. As he was a night owl and might be free after work, I thought having him with me would be a good idea, especially since I didn't know Keisha well—safety in numbers.

I walked to the window and, with a gentle click, unlocked the latch and pushed it up.

As I leaned forward to peer outside, a sudden gust of chilly air hit me in the face, causing me to shudder. My hair stood on end, and goosebumps pebbled my flesh.

For a few seconds, I stood frozen, taking in the cold, crisp air and the dark, mysterious night outside.

Is this a bad idea?

Biscuit would tell me it was okay if he were here.

I nibbled on my fingernail. I knew it wasn't wise to sneak out, but I didn't want to miss out on living my life, especially after what happened to Pete. I would never have considered sneaking out last year, even before I knew that demons were after me. Bumping into the Devil at an ice cream parlor will do that to you.

"*Fine*," I growled, "I won't do it."

"Do what?" a voice said behind me.

I spun around so fast that my heart pounded in my ears, setting my nerves on edge. "Are you spying on me, Jimmy?" I hissed.

He blinked at me as if I had just said the most ridiculous thing he had ever heard. "Are you serious, Sprout? Do I have to remind you of the demon realm fiasco?"

I took my time as I turned my back to him to lock the window and conceal my disappointment. "I was invited to a party," I mumbled. "I just wanted to feel like my old self again. I don't expect you to get it."

As my mind raced with a million thoughts, I turned to Jimmy.

His face was a mask of indecipherable emotions, his eyebrows furrowed, his lips tightly pursed. What was going on inside that head? The minutes ticked by in strained silence.

Just when I thought I couldn't take it any longer, he broke the tension with a casual question: "So, where's the party at?"

Surprise colored my voice when I spoke next. "Lakeshore. About fifteen minutes from here ... why?"

He gave a tiny shrug. "I can take you *only* if you agree to a few conditions."

Without a second thought, I immediately replied, "What conditions?"

He glanced at his watch, like mine, and said, "It's 10:09 now. You have until midnight, not a second later. I'll drop you off and wait in the car nearby. As soon as you're inside, text me and let me know you're okay." I tried to speak, but he raised a finger. "You're not allowed to drink any alcohol, and that includes anything that someone gives you that you haven't seen come from an unopened bottle. You have to promise that you'll call me immediately if anything seems off, and that means *anything*. Do you understand?"

I was already nodding before he finished speaking, feeling my heart swell with excitement. "Jimmy, Cor would never have allowed me to do this," I gushed.

Jimmy chuckled. "I'm cooler than Cor ... and an easier mark."

7

CRUZ

As Cruz approached his apartment, the weight of the long and taxing evening pressed down on his shoulders. His clothes were stained with grease and sugar, and his body reeked of sweat and dried blood. Despite the physical wounds having healed, the mental scars still lingered, causing his muscles to feel tense and sore. All he could think about was taking a scorching hot shower, collapsing on the couch, and never moving again.

His phone buzzed in his pants pocket. After fumbling with the lock a few times, Cruz finally opened the door, slipped inside, and shut it firmly behind him.

Underneath his shirt, his shield talisman started to heat up and glow. Next to his skin, it pulsed like a second heartbeat, indicating the presence of demons.

As he turned around, his heart skipped. Cruz froze as his eyes fell upon a chilling sight. *Shit.*

Two shadowy figures, cloaked in black, stood by the slightly ajar window at the kitchenette's entrance. The potted avocado plant on the windowsill was lifeless, withered, and black. It had been thriving when he had left earlier in the day.

Cruz stumbled backward, colliding with the front door. With one hand, he reached for his shield and, with the other, grasped the doorknob at his back. He frantically turned the handle to flee, then paused.

Where was his mom? Was she hurt? Dead? He couldn't leave the apartment without knowing if she was there. He clasped the medallion tightly, its heat seeping through the fabric of his shirt. His earlier bravado vanished, leaving him clumsy and disoriented. *Please don't be dead.*

Corinth would know what to do. Cruz gave himself a mental shake. *Call for help, dummy.*

But the demon spoke before he could press the button on his watch. "Don't move, or your mommy dies." Its voice was dry and raspy.

Cruz went stiff, his eyes widening as he scanned the small living room, desperate for any sign of his mother.

The figure that had spoken moved toward the soft light emanating from the kitchen.

As it stepped closer, it pulled back the hood of its cloak, revealing its face. A Shade. Its features were striking: black polished skin, sharp cheekbones, and a chiseled jawline. But what caught Cruz's eye most were the silver veins throbbing beneath its skin, tracing intricate patterns up and down its arms and neck. The lines gave off an otherworldly glow, casting a faint, eerie light onto the low ceiling.

Cruz panted heavily, his terror escalating. Was this Ephrem's doing? If the demon *had* escaped the underworld, Ephrem would be here, gloating. Cruz was sure of it.

A dagger would be nice right about now.

Shield, transform into a weapon, he begged.

But his plea fell on deaf ears, and nothing happened. From where Cruz stood, he strained his ears to pick up any sound from the bedroom. Was she hiding? It was difficult to estimate how long the Shades had been in his apartment, and the uncertainty only added to his growing sense of unease. Cruz entertained the idea of charging at them, but fear consumed him as he worried that he might unintentionally cause harm to his mother. She had already battled lung disease, and now, because of his actions, she might die.

His stomach sank. Corinth was right. Cruz had acted foolishly, and now his family was in danger. *Is Zoey safe?* Had he missed a warning text? The weight of his phone in his pocket only added to his concern. If only he could reach for it now …

"What do you want?" Cruz asked, his breath hissing through his teeth. He tried to quell his rising fury, but it wasn't easy. "Where is my mom?" His voice echoed through the silent apartment. "*Mom!*" he called out toward her bedroom. "*¿Dónde estás?*"

Cruz turned his gaze back to the Shade, the silence ringing like tinnitus in his ears. One of its eyes was missing—a thick layer of oily flesh covered the skin around the empty socket.

"Remove that disgusting holy relic around your neck and dispose of it outside. Shut the door and lock it behind you. Don't forget to latch the chain. We wouldn't want any uninvited guests to barge in unexpectedly, would we?" The Shade's lips curved into a grin, creasing its face like a worn-out piece of leather. "Do it now, or Mommy dearest dies."

"Let me see her first, and I'll do whatever you want," Cruz negotiated.

"That's not how this works," the other Shade piped up, its voice scratchy and dry. "Do it now, or Mom dies."

Cruz considered throwing the shield at them as a distraction, but how far would it get him? Maybe the parking lot.

"I know what you're thinking, Cruz Saldivar, but don't do it, or we'll kill her … and then go after Zoey Taylor next. There's more of us than you think," the Shade whispered. "And they already have eyes on your little girlfriend."

His mother's life and Zoey's were at stake. Finally, Cruz drew the chain from around his neck and gave a grim nod.

"*Slowly.*" The creature hissed as if in pain.

Cruz lifted the relic over his head, thinking about Zoey's experience in almost the same situation in the demon realm. He now understood why she had discarded the dagger—she'd desperately wanted to save Corinth's life.

If the Shades caught even a whiff of an angel's presence, they would murder his mother.

Cruz struggled to twist the doorknob with slippery fingers as the shield thumped against his sweaty palm, emitting heat like a furnace.

A sudden burst of energy erupted from the relic, turning it from a small trinket into a thin, compact blade like a throwing knife. Cruz palmed the weapon, hoping to be able to use it.

At that moment, though, an incredible force slammed into him from behind. The knife slipped from his slick grasp and hit their welcome mat outside.

The sound of the door slamming closed in the empty hallway signaled the end of his only means of defense and protection.

That same demonic energy telekinetically hauled Cruz up and into the air and yanked him back into the apartment. His arms were held at his sides as he slammed onto the floor. Cruz rolled onto his side, coughing. Furtively, he clenched a hand over his watch, hitting the emergency alarm. It had only been an hour and a half since he'd last seen Corinth—the chances of him or any other angels showing up to aid him now were slim to none.

Cry wolf one too many times …

Of all the nights to be attacked by Shades.

"Nice try, kid." The stick-like Shade seemed almost extraterrestrial as it slithered close to Cruz's prone form. Its body language betrayed its unease—it appeared nervous and fidgety, constantly shifting its weight from one foot to another. "You were right." It turned to its comrade. "The human *did* try to fight. He had a knife."

"Fat lot of good it did," the other Shade snickered back.

Cruz assumed the more confident of the two was the leader. It slunk over to the two-person bar, pulled out one of the stools, and gestured at Cruz. "Come sit over here," it said as a dribble of saliva escaped its mouth. "Don't make me send Horace to get your mom."

With any luck, Corinth would show up to take the smartwatch back. Cruz would be totally okay with that; at least it would mean getting some backup.

Except, nothing happened. Corinth was probably asleep. Corinth's words echoed in Cruz's mind, haunting him: *I may not always be around to help you.*

"I'm doing it. Don't hurt her." Cruz shakily rose to his feet, eyeing the Shade—Horace—nearest him. He sat down, perching himself on the edge of the stool, his heart hammering and hands clammy. "Please, let my mom go. She has nothing to do with any of this."

The watch's display flashed, illuminating the one-eyed Shade. Fortunately, it seemed unfazed by the sudden burst of light. The thing emitted a pungent odor of burnt ash, smoke, and sulfur. Its arms and neck had bulging veins resembling swollen snakes.

Cruz flinched as its icy fingers grazed his skin. Horace pressed Cruz's hands down onto the chair's armrests. Then, zip ties were cinched firmly around his wrists and feet, binding them to the chair.

Don't freak out. Don't freak out. Don't freak out.

After Cruz was restrained, the one with a single eye entered the kitchen. It later emerged, clutching a piece of paper and reading what was written aloud: "'*Mijo*,' it began, '*I will be at Maria's for Bingo. Food's in the fridge. Don't wait up. Love, Mamá.*' Your mommy was never here," One-Eye said in a mock baby voice, laughing. "Twit."

Cruz sagged back.

Could he trust what they were telling him? Was his mom safe and not lying lifeless in her bedroom as he had been dreading? He tried to push that gruesome thought out of his mind.

"What do you want from me?" Cruz finally asked, his mouth bone dry.

The Shade fished something out from the depths of its cloak pocket.

At first, he thought it would be a shard—the kind used to infect humans and change them into Shades. Cruz recoiled, bracing himself for the worst.

Instead, he caught a flash of silver. It was not a shard; it was something else. A knife?

The Shade held up a metal keyring for Cruz to see, leisurely twirling it around its finger. The sound of metal jingling against metal sent shivers down Cruz's spine.

Those weren't just any keys.

They were *Cruz's* keys.

"Do you know where I got these from?" it asked slowly.

Cruz's eyes landed on the object One-Eye was holding. It let out a throaty chuckle, which sounded like the crunching of dry leaves. Its twisted, deformed face contorted into a mocking grin as it pointed to its empty socket.

A sudden surge of fear went through Cruz. A memory of his encounter with a Shade from the demon realm rushed back to him. He had driven a sharp key into the thing's eye to escape. Cruz vaguely recalled having to replace his keys when he'd returned home after the incident.

"So *that's* where I left those!" Cruz said nervously, trying to ignore the plastic pinching his skin.

"That was funny," One-Eye said. "It may not be so funny when I carve out your eye with this key, though."

Cruz swallowed.

Keep stalling.

"How did you find me?" he asked.

Where was Corinth?

Again, not coming.

"It wasn't easy to track you down after Ephrem's disappearance. Only a few of us knew of his fake identity as Trevor, which he used to get close to Zoey Taylor. It took us some time to figure out your workplace and follow you to this complex. We didn't want to draw attention, so we only accessed the unit at night, dressed in these hooded cloaks. We tried at least forty different apartments using each key on your fob until we finally found the right one. After that, it was just waiting for you to return home."

Moron, Cruz reprimanded himself. He never thought of replacing the locks.

Cruz's phone vibrated in his pocket. "If you followed me home from work, you could've grabbed me anytime. Why wait until now?"

Horace laughed. "Because seeing the look on your face with us standing in your living room was priceless. Also, we needed a way to get you to lose that angelic trinket. You're lucky we decided to wait until your mommy was away."

Cruz didn't say anything to that.

"Soooo," One-Eye hissed. "I'm here to collect something from you. Two somethings. Once I'm done, I'll finish the job Ephrem wanted us to do in the first place: To turn you into one of us." It picked out one particularly sharp-looking key from the others. It was the same one Cruz had used to ram into the demon's eye. He waggled it in front of Cruz's face. "Ephrem never said you had to be able to *see*. Which eye would you like to lose first? Right or left?"

"Let's talk about this." Cruz squirmed, slamming his eyes shut and wriggling to try and loosen the bonds, but the plastic only cinched tauter. How had he managed to make the amulet work last time? Cruz needed one more miracle. *Come to me, shield*, he thought. *Please.* Shouldn't the thing be breaking down the door? He knew it could do incredible feats ...

Rough hands seized Cruz's shoulders, and One-Eye pulled his head back by his hair.

Icy breath hit his face.

"No point in fighting this. If you don't open your *ojos*,

we'll wait until your mom gets home and pluck hers out, too."

A sinking sensation came over him.

Come on, shield!

The most important thing was that his mom was okay.

Cruz opened his eyes and glared at the asshat before him. "Just get it over with, leather face," he growled, gritting his teeth.

The one-eyed Shade hunched over him and laughed. "Stupid kid has a death wish."

Gradually and steadily, the key advanced toward Cruz until it occupied his entire field of view, appearing as nothing but a tiny sliver of silver.

His heart pounded fiercely against his chest, and he opened his mouth to let out a scream when—

One solid rap sounded on the front door, halting the thing from marring Cruz's face.

He expelled the air from his lungs and started to shout when the Shade slapped a frigid hand against his mouth. It felt like dehydrated meat and smelled like it, too.

"Don't say a word, or we kill whoever it is on the other side. Got it?" the thing said.

What if it was Zoey? But she wouldn't be here this late—not with her strict curfew.

A neighbor, possibly.

Cruz moved his head up and down.

"Go see who it is," One-Eye instructed its cohort. "Kill them if you have to. I'll keep the kid under control."

The whippet-thin Horace sped toward the entryway in a blur of black. As soon as it started to look out the peephole, an ear-splitting boom erupted around the apartment. The door was ripped from its hinges and hurled across the room.

A searing white light flooded the space, illuminating every corner with its intense radiance. The force of the explosion sent a shockwave through the air, rattling the windows in their frames. In mere seconds, the Shade was consumed by the blinding brilliance, disintegrating into ash under the onslaught of the overwhelming energy.

Cruz, thoroughly dazed, was thrown to one side, but he couldn't prevent his fall because his arms and legs were still strapped to the stool. His shoulder hit the carpet, followed by his head, and the ceiling spun like a dryer on a spin cycle as his vision filled with tiny golden comets.

One-Eye towered over Cruz as he struggled to catch his breath and not throw up.

Despite its dark, imposing presence, the creature appeared shaken; its remaining eye gazed off into the distance, transfixed by something only it could see.

Suddenly, its mouth fell open, and a swirling vortex of black dust engulfed it. The haze was so close to Cruz that the stench of sulfur constricted his throat from its acrid fumes.

And then the Shade disappeared.

Cruz smiled weakly to himself. A moment later, he saw feet approaching him—feet wearing purple Converse.

8

ZOEY

Jordan's parent's house was located right on the lake. After Jimmy had dropped me off at the front, I was greeted by a steady drone of frogs. The insects buzzing past my face were as big as Texas. The closer you got to any body of water, the bigger the bugs seemed to get. There were no fences bordering any lawns in this neighborhood. And it would have been super peaceful had it not been for the sound of music thumping from somewhere nearby.

I followed the rhythmic bass, which led me to a paved trail toward the backyard and, I assumed, the lake. The sprawling white two-story mansion before me looked like it belonged in a movie. Living in a house where you could enjoy some distance from your neighbors seemed idyllic.

As I strolled along the path, taking in the tranquil surroundings, I tried to call Cruz again to see if he could join me. It went straight to voicemail. Frustrated, I put my phone back into my pocket.

The plan was to slink in unnoticed and find the nearest chair to throw myself in.

The backyard was expansive, with towering oaks and velvety grass. I was struck by the lake, the jetty, and the scene ahead all at once—people living their best life. The dock was adorned with tiki torches, their flickering flames casting a warm, inviting glow. A group of kids were swaying in unison, their silhouettes appearing almost otherworldly. Their movements were fluid and graceful, as if lost in the music. Witnessing their abandon made me ache for that sense of freedom.

A boy took off running down the length of the pier, his arms and legs pumping. A whoop of joy escaped his lips as he flew off the end, plummeting into the lake's depths and vanishing from sight. My stomach pitched as I realized how brutally cold the water must be. And yet, part of me wanted to jump in, too.

Maybe I'd slough off some sorrow and guilt and … feel numb.

At the thought of the dark, my heart thumped harder.

Several people lounged in lawn chairs, surrounding a bonfire and listening to music from a Bluetooth speaker. An empty chair drew me in that direction. I wasn't brave enough to socialize yet; I had to work up to that. *Baby steps.*

A head popped out of the water in the distance, and the kids on the dock laughed as if they were having the time of their lives. Blue-orange flames licked at the night sky, sparks shooting toward the heavens to join the stars.

Thankfully, Keisha spotted me and waved me over to their group.

"You made it!" she exclaimed. "Everyone, look who's here!" Keisha turned to me and shouted, "*Zoey*, join us!"

I plopped down onto one of the empty folding chairs beside Keisha, flashing a quick thumbs up. *Awkward, Zoey.*

At least I was starting things off on the right foot … ugh. I was *not* good at dialog. My companions were books. I loathed introductions and attention. Most of the time, I preferred to just blend into a crowd and go unnoticed.

But maybe that's why I was here—to disrupt the routine, to step out of my comfort zone.

And boy, was I sure *un*comfortable.

"I'm glad you made it," Keisha said, with slurred speech and glassy eyes. A wine cooler sat in the cup holder of her chair.

Glancing timidly at the others around the fire, I said, "Me too." I tried to sink into the back seat. *Out of sight, out of mind.*

"That's Embrey," Keisha said, pointing to a girl with bright red hair and matching freckles. A pair of tortoiseshell, cat-framed glasses rested on the bridge of her nose.

"Hey," she said, giving me a two-fingered salute.

I nodded back in greeting.

"Hey, do you know Elias?" Keisha asked.

I'd seen most of these kids at school but didn't hang out in any of their circles. Well, technically, any circle, for that matter. Our school was big, and I'd always focused more on studying than making friends.

Anyway, the last friend I'd made, besides Cruz, had been a psycho demon.

Hoping to be sly about it, I took a moment to study Elias. He had striking features, black skin, an afro, and a thousand-watt smile. He leaned back in his chair, eyes closed, feet stretched out, contentedly holding a beer.

I retrieved my cell from my pocket and texted Jimmy, assuring him I was safe. He promptly responded with a smiley face to let me know all was okay.

Cruz had yet to respond to my earlier texts or calls. He was okay, right? I started to worry about him, but I pushed my concern aside. I was just being paranoid. Would I always be suspicious and afraid of going out? Would I always be lonely and unhappy?

I was tired of feeling this way.

"Do you want a beer or wine cooler? Soda?" Keisha broke me out of my mental fog.

I shook my head, remembering the deal I'd made with Jimmy. "No, thanks. Is that Jordan over there swimming in the freezing-cold lake?" I asked, changing the subject.

"Yup," Keisha chuckled, peeling off her bottle's label. "Elisha dared Jordan to jump in, and now they're all going in. You got here just in time." She winked at me as the song changed to *Crazy in Love* by Beyoncé.

Glancing back at the expansive two-story white villa, with its magnificent balcony overlooking the water, I almost shouted over the loud music, "So, Jordan's parents aren't home?"

"It's his grandparents' place, but they're vacationing in Italy. He's supposed to check in on the house—which he is *technically* doing. He planned to restock the adult beverages he took out of their fridge—"

"Sure, *that's* his plan," Embrey interjected with a snort. "You know what? I think I'll go join them in the water."

By now, the few on the dock were all pushing each other off the end.

Embrey got up, stretched, and grabbed Elias's hand, waking him up. "Come on, you're going in, too."

Elias shrugged, flashing white teeth as he shot to his feet. They took off toward the lake, giggling.

Once they were gone, Keisha reached over to her

phone and turned the music down on the speaker. "I'm glad you made it."

"Yeah, me too," I agreed. "This place is amazing."

"Jordan is super lucky," she agreed. "I would be here every day if my family owned property this nice."

"Are you two ... seeing each other?" I asked, hesitating.

Keisha grunted. "Uh, *definitely* not. We're just friends."

Sitting by the fire, I felt its warmth spread through my cold hands and knees. The sound of the wood crackling and popping soothed me. The night was peaceful. The stars were brighter than ever, painting the sky with endless sparkling lights. I was in awe, admiring the exquisiteness, reveling in the solitude and calmness of the moment. Suddenly, a bright green comet streaked across the sky. My mouth hung open in wonder.

"Stars are the street lights of eternity," Keisha whispered, glancing at the firmament. She slowly sipped her drink, clearly buzzed.

"That's ... beautiful," I said. "Where'd you hear that from?"

"The internet." Keisha shrugged. "So, intrusive question." She glanced at me as my heart rate spiked. "What was up with you and Trevor Malcolm? He left mid-year. You two were always hanging out, and he was super *smoking* hot. I mean, the *unreal* hot that looked fake as shit. I think every girl in school, except me, had a crush on him. People like that don't exist—and I heard he was *stinkin'* rich too." She paused, wiggling her eyebrows. "Trevor only seemed to have eyes for you. Spill the tea, Sis."

Ugh. The demon. Ephrem had pretended to be Trevor. Jerk. I hadn't even thought about how his sudden disappearance from school might be noticed. He'd been popular, I recalled. Rich and handsome got you far in life.

A flash of Ephrem's hand protruding from my brother's torso burst into my mind. I shuddered, feeling the blood drain from my face. The fire could not keep me warm as I imagined Ephrem emerging from it at any moment. *That would be my luck.*

Keisha sat up, suddenly appearing more interested and concerned. Maybe she'd interpreted the look on my face as something other than sheer terror. Or perhaps I couldn't hide my fear.

"Your relationship didn't end well, huh?" she presumed. "Sorry about that … that sucks. We don't have to talk about it."

I twirled the gold ring on my finger, a holy relic crafted from the remnants of Corinth's blade, and scrutinized Keisha more closely. Was she possessed? Was she hiding something about Ephrem? I didn't think so. I knew the ring was meant to shield me from any potential attack, but I still doubted people. Even so, I was pretty confident that Keisha wasn't a demon.

I didn't like feeling so suspicious all the time.

"He ended up being a major asshole, and I'm glad he's gone," I finally said.

"I knew something was off about that guy," Keisha remarked, shaking her head. "Never trust the hot ones. The good-looking ones are *always* the worst. We gotta look out for each other, you know?"

I appreciated her support even though she didn't know the entire story. "You have no idea," I added. "But thanks for saying that."

As I sat there quietly, lost in thought, Keisha leaned

over and extended her wine cooler toward me. "You look like you could use a sip."

I hesitated as I reached over to take the bottle from her. I knew she had been drinking from it, which should have reassured me that it wasn't tampered with. Nonetheless, a part of me couldn't shake off the paranoia and mistrust that had become so common in the world I now lived in.

It was so unfair that I constantly had to be on guard against potential dangers and threats.

I didn't want to think about Ephrem or Peter anymore, so I snatched the drink from her, taking a generous swig, and she smiled back at me warmly.

There goes my promise to Jimmy.

The flavor was fruity and sweet, just the right amount to appease my taste buds. The liquid felt tepid but not unpleasant as I took a sip, then another, enjoying the taste and the soothing sensation. I handed the bottle back to her, feeling lighter.

"That was the first time I've ever had alcohol," I admitted.

"What did you think?" Keisha asked.

"Got any more?" I said.

We were all gathered at the edge of the dock; everyone except me had towels wrapped around their bodies. The music played, and we swayed and danced, trying to stay warm. Clouds of white puffed out of everyone's mouths as they talked and sang. It was close to 11:30. I had drunk two and a half more wine coolers and felt great.

The moon reflected on the still lake, creating a

mesmerizing pattern of ripples. Captivated by the night's hypnotic, ghostly aura, the cold didn't bother me as much. I was lost in the gentle rhythm of the lapping water, and an intense desire to jump in struck me.

Take away the empty feeling. Take back control.

"I just ... jump?" I turned to face Jordan with an unsteady wobble. The dock was moving. No, wait, maybe that was just my head spinning. I felt giddy and alive.

Jordan put a steadying hand on my arm. "*Oh* no, you don't," he said, trying to gently guide me back down the pier toward the safety of land and the fire.

"You sound like my mom," I slurred, annoyed by his condescending tone. I flung my arms around, knocking his hand away. "Everyone else has done it, and they're totally fine. Why are you looking at me like I can't do this? You were all pushing each other in a second ago ..."

"Yeah, let her do it," Andrea whispered, her voice wavering from the cold. She was short, squat, and super athletic; she'd been out swimming with Jordan almost the entire time I'd been here, and her hair was wet and slicked back. A gymnast, that's what I remembered about her. Her nose was red, and she rubbed the sides of her arms with the towel. "I'm going to warm up by the fire. But you got this, Zo!"

A warm buzz went through me at her remembering my name. *No* one remembered my name.

"Zo's had too much to drink," Jordan insisted. "She'll sink like a stone if she goes out there."

"*I will not!*" I held up a finger in the chilly night air and wobbled. "I am a great swim-m-m-mer. And besides, I've survived worse." I removed my shoes, clinging to Keisha's arm to avoid tripping. She didn't object, but her expression suggested she was considering saying no. When my exposed feet hit the chilly planks, I gasped. "Wow, that's freezing!"

Embrey laughed, bouncing up and down on the balls of her feet. "Zoey, girl, you are *so* wasted. What do you think the water is going to feel like?"

"I'm *not* wasted—I'm just really enjoying the company of … people."

Everyone paused and turned to look at me, grins and smiles on their faces, and my cheeks flushed.

"Well, since you're enjoying yourself, I'm not gonna be the killer of fun," Keisha said. "But Zo," she turned back to me, "you don't have to prove anything to *anyone.* We're all cool. We can go back to the fire and talk shit about Elias. That's always fun." She winked at Elias as he stuck his tongue out at her.

"I'm just jumping in for a second, and then I'll swim right back." I patted Jordan's arm, giving him a crooked smile. "Besides, this guy can fish me out if I sink, right?"

"I'm going to have to nix this, Zo—" Keisha started to say, but I cut her off.

"I *have* to do this, Keisha." My voice broke, and then I couldn't speak.

No. Not the waterworks. I will not *succumb. Okay, Zo, you've had too much to drink.*

Oh, I felt good and numb, and I wanted to jump in.

Someone touched my shoulder, and I looked up to see it was Keisha. "Okay," she relented. "But don't go too far out. It's surprisingly deep, and we won't be able to see you in the dark."

This was probably a dumb idea, jumping into a cold lake at night. Alone. I should've been terrified. Who knows what kinds of creatures lurked out there—turtles, alligators, enormous man-eating catfish. Plus, Jimmy had warned me not to drink, and I had broken that promise. *And* I was typically scared of the dark, but not tonight.

Liar.

Some part of me was always going to be worried about demon attacks, but buzzed Zoey wasn't scared.

There was power in not being afraid or letting panic take the wheel.

Besides, I had a ring, my brother was out front in the car, and several strong swimmers were around me. I needed a break from the overwhelming emotions tearing me apart.

I shed my sweater, and a gust of bitter wind slapped me in the face. "*Holy smokes!*" Left with only a tank top and leggings, I figured they would serve as a makeshift wetsuit and keep me warm in frigid temperatures.

I stepped up to the edge of the pier, shivering, drew in a deep breath, and—

"Wait, wait, wait!" Keisha shouted, grabbing my waist and pulling me back. "Your watch. You're going to ruin it if you get it wet. Did you take your cell phone out of your pocket?"

I almost forgot about the smartwatch on my wrist until I glanced down at it. I quickly removed it and handed it to Keisha, relieved she had caught me in time. "*Phew!* That was a close call," I said, pointing to my sweater lying nearby on the pier. "My phone is in my pullover. Would you mind watching over it and my Converse like a hawk?"

Keisha made a cross over her heart. "*Girl*, you don't have to tell me that. I know how expensive our devices and shoes can be."

I paused to take in the serene view of the vast body of

water before me. After stepping back a few paces with all my might, I propelled myself off the dock and plunged into the lake.

9

CRUZ

Cruz woke to the sound of someone eating. Slurping, technically. At first, he thought it was his mother sampling food as she cooked. That thought left him feeling warm, cozy, and nostalgic. But then a nagging sensation of unease struck, and he knew that couldn't be right.

Something was wrong.

His brain was scrambled, his eyelids felt super heavy, and he found it extremely hard to wake himself up—like coming out of a drug-induced slumber.

And then his memory came rushing back.

Cruz sat up so suddenly that a bout of dizziness overcame him. Gently, he prodded his skull, expecting there to be a gaping wound, but there was no injury—only the lingering memory of hitting his head.

Craning his neck, Cruz peered into the kitchen. His mother wasn't there. Instead, he saw Corinth Taylor leaning against the sink, spooning soup into his mouth from a bowl. He was dressed in black tech pants and a gray T-shirt. He also had a custom black hi-tech-looking holster wrapped around his thigh, which housed his lethal blade. Even while eating, the Nephilim seemed threatening.

"I hope you don't mind me helping myself." Corinth held up the container for Cruz to see. It was labeled *Menudo*. "I've never had Menudo before. It's good."

"What happened?" Cruz asked, feeling sluggish.

"It takes longer for a mortal body to recover from a demonic attack, especially since I've already healed you twice tonight. You've been out of it for a while. I got hungry."

The smell of sulfur remained, along with the reheated food. Cruz also noticed an overpowering floral scent permeating the cramped apartment. His stomach roiled against the vastly different aromas as he staggered to his feet. He grabbed the side of the sofa, his knuckles going white and then slumped back onto the couch. "My mom ..." Cruz gulped, licked his lips, and tried again. "Wh-h-here is she—?"

"She's fine. She's all right." Corinth placed the bowl on the kitchen counter, coming out of the kitchenette and into the living room. "Take it easy, kid. She came home and saw the damage, and you tied to a chair, and she flipped out—so, I had to compel her. She's back at her best friend's house. Maria, Miranda, or something like that. I didn't want her staying here tonight, to be on the safe side."

An overwhelming sense of relief and blame bloomed inside Cruz as he ran a hand through his disheveled hair. Almost losing an eyeball . . . or two . . . had shaken him. The demons were gone, and the apartment door was back on its hinges, good as new. No dust or wood littered the carpet; even the barstool he'd been secured to back in its original spot. Cruz assumed Corinth had taken care of the skinny Shade when the door had exploded. The only remaining evidence of the dark presence was the dead, brittle avocado plant on the windowsill.

"Did you ... kill it? The one-eyed Shade?" Cruz asked carefully, not really wanting to know the truth.

Corinth pressed his lips together into a firm line before saying, "I took care of *one* Shade. But the other, I *think* it had only one eye ... managed to get away in a cloud of sulfur, which you inhaled. That's why you blacked out. *Muy mal*," he added in Spanish.

"*Oh no*," Cruz breathed. He patted his chest and looked down, expecting to see something there. "Am I going to die?"

Corinth tilted his head to the side. "One day, but not today."

Cruz sighed in relief, and then his eyes went wide as a troubling thought hit him. "We have to find Zoey." His voice was almost a rasp; his throat was dry and itchy. "She's in danger."

"My sister is okay. Jimmy is with her," Corinth reassured him. "We need to talk."

Cruz's heart rate spiked. He waited nervously as Corinth pulled something out of his pocket and sat beside him. Why were his palms so clammy? He scrutinized the intricate design on the couch's fabric and the way the security light outside shone through the window. This was it. Would Corinth obliterate his memory or something, or take away Cruz's relic?

All the while, Corinth remained silent, his expression unreadable.

Finally, he held Cruz's chain out, the one with a golden shield and his patron saint charm. The object seemed to shine even brighter in Corinth's hands. "If you lose this again, I'm keeping it," he said before handing it back to Cruz. It felt cool as Cruz slid the chain over his neck, where it belonged. A part of him had been returned, and he could inhale again.

"When I saw your alarm go off and the shield blazing on the ground in the hallway, I knew something was seriously wrong. I didn't want to put your mother in any more danger if she was home, so instead of portaling inside your apartment, I knocked first."

"Thank you. *Again*, I mean." Cruz shifted his gaze from Corinth's, feeling humiliated that he had to be rescued twice in one night. "I didn't think you'd come because of earlier …"

"Look at me, kid."

Cruz glanced at Corinth, resolutely staring back at him, his brown eyes large.

"I know I give you a hard time," Corinth said firmly, evenly, "but I will *always* answer a call for help. Got it?"

Cruz's eyes welled up, and then they spilled over. Annoyed at himself for showing emotion, he nodded in gratitude and swiped at his face.

"What did they want from you?" Corinth prodded gently.

"My eye." Cruz spoke barely above a whisper, feeling completely drained and exhausted. It had been such a long, crappy day. Who had to deal with such things? In what messed up world did this happen to people? Let alone, teenagers?

"Your eye?" Corinth sat up straighter, the curiosity and disgust evident in his voice. "In heaven's name, *why*?"

"Back when we were all trapped in the demon realm, I

got attacked by a Shade. I managed to stab it in the eyeball with my house key and escaped. But it tracked me down out of revenge ... and also to complete the task Ephrem had started in the first place. They wanted to turn me into one of them." He put his head between his hands. "Those things had my apartment key this entire time. My mom could've been killed ... they could've made multiple copies. What if this wasn't the end of Ephrem's plan? They know where I work. We can change the locks, but they also know where I live now."

The sudden hush was so deep it seemed to reverberate off the walls, leaving the air thick with apprehension. Cold and unyielding, a pervasive stillness descended upon Cruz, wrapping him in an icy grip.

"I know." Corinth exhaled. "You're going to continue getting into trouble, aren't you?"

Cruz shrugged.

"I will probably regret this," Corinth continued, "but how do you feel about spending the summer in Scotland? You asked me to train you. Supposing that's what you still want—I can make that happen. Finish out the school year and come to Scotland with me. Alastair and Larna are there; he's still recovering. They can train you and Zo. I'll tell your mother you were accepted into a gifted and talented program abroad. I'll figure it out."

Cruz's heart raced with excitement as Corinth's words sank in. The prospect of traveling to Scotland and learning to fight alongside Zoey was a thrilling departure from his usual routine. Spending an entire summer with his best friend filled him with a sense of adventure he hadn't felt in a long time.

"Yes, please," Cruz managed to choke out.

Maybe change wasn't all bad.

10

ZOEY

The frigid lake water slapped against my face, shocking my senses awake. My brain's commands to my lungs went unanswered, and I felt the burn of water filling my throat. I coughed, desperately trying to draw in air. The sensation was like a surge of electricity, every nerve in my body on high alert.

Breathe, Zo, I urged myself. *You can do this.*

The distant sound of shouting reached my ears, urging me to swim. I felt numb and on fire, a strange combination. Taking a deep breath, I extended my arms and kicked with all my might. The bottom was out of reach, but determination propelled me forward. The cold began to fade, and despite my fear of the dark, the pitch-black of the water no longer held the same terror for me.

Or maybe it was just the alcohol clouding my judgment.

My leggings and tank top expanded, acting like an anchor more than a wetsuit. It had been ages since I had done any physical activity, and my limbs felt heavy and uncooperative. It seemed like my body had forgotten what it was like to move.

The opposite shoreline was visible, and it appeared to be roughly halfway across the water. I wasn't concerned about getting lost because it was a short distance. If I got too tired, I would head in that direction. A dense thicket of trees outlined the other side of the lake, and there were no nearby lights or houses. This area was shaped like a horseshoe cove, and the water was as smooth as glass. The depths beneath me were utterly obscured. For the first time in what felt like forever, I felt free.

I could see Jordan in the light of the tiki torches, still whooping and hollering while everyone danced.

"*YOU OKAY?*" he shouted, his hands cupped around his mouth.

I waved to let him know I was okay, and he waved back.

Allowing my body to go buoyant, I flipped onto my back, gazing at the nearly full yellow moon. A gray cloud hung over it like a curtain, while brighter stars twinkled in the sky above.

My mind felt as light as my body.

I zoned out because when I started swimming again, I realized I'd drifted farther from the dock and my friends than I'd intended. It didn't take long for me to begin quivering. It was time to head back in. After all, I'd achieved my goal.

Suddenly, I heard splashing nearby.

A bit alarmed, I stopped paddling and glanced around, listening, trying to figure out if something was heading toward me. A monster. A gator. A snake.

"Who's there?" I couldn't see anything. "Jordan?"

Someone was messing with me.

Still, my pulse raced as I turned to face the lighted dock. No one could see me. Swimming back toward land, I took long strokes, kicking frantically.

A sharp, knifelike pain seized my left calf—a cramp. Involuntarily gripping my leg, I tried to flex my foot as my head went under. It happened quickly. I didn't even get a chance to shout for help. I opened my mouth and sucked in the lake.

And I sank.

The pain was too much. I tried to swim back to the surface, but my body wouldn't listen. My nose and lungs burned, and I descended lower, unable to distinguish where the surface was any longer. All around me was gloom, which made me panic even more. I convulsed, my body's every fiber screaming for oxygen.

An arm wrapped around my neck, and another hooked me around my middle.

I clawed at the hand curled around my stomach, panicking, still underwater, choking, dying. And then a strange, comforting warmth enveloped me, turning the black lake into light. Divine. Holy. I was no longer drowning. I could breathe … *fully submerged. No way.* The cramp was gone; even as miraculous as that was, the man before me held *all* my attention. Curly amber hair floated around his head like a halo. Even in the murky water, I could tell he had the most arresting green eyes I'd ever seen in my entire life— beyond striking.

I knew that face. Nakir. The archangel who'd saved my life in the demon realm.

We stared at each other, our ghostly hands suspended beside us. *Whoa.* My brain and lungs told me I shouldn't be able to breathe underwater. The moment was ethereal, otherworldly, and beyond belief.

Nakir nodded reassuringly at me, reached out, and placed two hands on my shoulders.

And then, the next instant, I was on dry land, flopping onto my belly, coughing and spitting. *Holy crap.* My clothes were sopping, and a blustery wind had me shivering like mad. I slid in the muck; my hair had come out of the braid and was hanging half in my face.

The archangel bent over me and gently helped me to my feet. At that moment, the moon peeked from behind the clouds, illuminating his face and casting a trail of light across his features. Droplets of water trickled down Nakir's nose and traced a path along his lips. The damp fabric of his clothes clung to his form, accentuating the well-defined contours of his shoulders, biceps, and arms. His hair was slicked back, with longer locks on top, and those bright eyes seemed to reflect the light of the heavens themselves. In his own skin, he appeared timeless but also ancient.

"Are you okay?" he asked.

A strong wind cut sharply through my clothes, making me shiver. The shoreline was a blurry mass of thick foliage.

"I breathed water." I wrapped my arms around myself, trembling, still out of sorts and in shock. My hair was a mess, hanging in my face like a wet towel. "You saved my l-l-life."

Nakir looked around the dark woods, furrowing his eyebrows. We were on the opposite shore from where I'd jumped off the dock, away from prying eyes. "Is it usual for humans to swim in freezing temperatures in the dark?"

"Uh-h-h," I said by way of answer.

Nakir moved to stand inches from me, causing me to inhale sharply.

Up close, I could smell lake water and flowers emanating from him, and his lips had a blue tinge. As Cor had mentioned, the cold affected all angels negatively, dampening their angelic grace.

"You're shaking," he said.

I couldn't seem to get my lips to work right. It felt like they'd been stung by a dozen bees.

"Your core temperature is too low," Nakir went on.

"*You're* the one who's shivering," I said stubbornly—because he was.

"I—I am not." Despite his physical state, his voice conveyed a hint of warmth and a flicker of fire, which made me wonder if he was upset at the prospect of being cold.

As his skin brushed against mine, a subtle yet intense energy emanated between us—a mist of charged particles suspended in the air around us, looking like tiny fireflies. My heart fluttered. It reminded me of the moment Nakir had first clasped my hand, preventing me from plunging into the pits of hell. Gradually, I was infused with a warm radiance that drove away the chill and brought feeling back to my limbs, fingers, and toes.

Genuinely curious, I asked, "How did you find me?"

"Alastair," he said thickly, his lips still bluish. "When we were connected, our thoughts got intertwined, tangled. I still have access to his whenever I choose it."

"How does Alastair know where I am?" I asked, incredulous. "Isn't he in Scotland?"

"We all keep tabs on you, Zoey Taylor," Nakir clarified, holding my confused gaze with such intensity that it made me look away. "I was following you when I saw you go underwater."

I pursed my lips, glancing around. "So why are you still

here? You could have magicked yourself away as soon after you pulled me from the lake …"

Before he could respond—I wasn't sure if I was angry at the intrusion or relieved—I heard footsteps thundering through the forest, coming in our direction.

Nakir twirled around, blading his body, partially blocking my view as two people burst through the tree line to stop before us, panting.

Jordan and Elias.

To prevent any harm from coming to them, I quickly stepped between the archangel and the boys, extending my arms. Nakir dropped his hands by his sides, relaxing his posture as I said, "Whoa, whoa, whoa. Everything's okay."

Jordan's gaze fell on Nakir, whom he eyed suspiciously. "We were worried you might be in trouble. We saw a strange flash of light over here. Did you see it? Do you know this guy, Zo?"

"Um …" I glanced at Nakir.

Jordan was still breathing heavily, and Elias was standing right behind him. They glanced between me and Nakir.

"There aren't any houses on this side of the lake. What are you doing out here?" Elias asked, a hint of doubt creeping into his voice.

"I got a c-c-c-cramp," I finally said. "He saw me struggling in the water and … jumped in to help." It wasn't a lie.

Nakir nodded and stepped forward, offering his hand to Jordan and Elias. "My name is Nik," he said smoothly. "Do you think you could take Zoey somewhere to get warm?"

Jordan finally seemed to relax as he shrugged off his

robe. "Oh, right." He handed it to me hurriedly. "My place is around the corner."

"Thank you for this, but you won't freeze in just your swim trunks?" I asked Jordan hoarsely, fumbling to put on the fluffy robe.

"I'm fine," Jordan said.

"That was way cool of you to jump in and help Zoey. Why don't you join us to warm up by the fire? And then you can tell us all about yourself, Nik," Elias piped up.

It had to be close to midnight, and I knew Jimmy would kill me if I were late. I needed to know precisely why Nakir had been following me. I wouldn't let him out of my sight. Maybe he felt the same about me. He could have portaled away or made Elias and Jordan forget he existed in the first place.

If Nakir was back, did it mean Ephrem was, too?

After marching back to Jordan's house, my hands and feet were half-frozen again. I went inside to dry off as best as possible, since I had around eight minutes before my brother came hunting me down. If he found out about my jumping into the lake and almost drowning, he'd never let me go out again.

At the fire, I wrapped myself in an oversized blanket and retrieved my phone to let Jimmy know I was all right.

Nakir was bathed in the flickering light of the fire. He was extraordinarily tanned, like he'd spent most days basking under the sun. He looked like a Greek god, like a deity from ancient mythology—or perhaps it was just the appearance he chose to adopt. I tried to picture him with wings and was struck by a mental image of his glowing skin, merman-like, under the water. I shivered. It wasn't from the cold but the profound sense of peace I'd experienced being near him. Chestnut-colored locks curled around his cheekbones and the shells of his ears. When Alastair had been Nakir's vessel, I thought his eyes were more feline and golden.

My heavy, damp hair was twisted into a bun to keep it off my face and neck. I watched as the wood crackled and popped, and showers of sparks glided high into the night sky. Flames twirled and flickered, casting enchanting shadows on the ground.

Enchanting indeed.

Keisha sat beside me, examining Nakir as if he were a piece of artwork, her sour expression suggesting she didn't like what she saw. Perhaps she thought I was a hypocrite because he was good-looking, and we'd just had this conversation about not trusting hot people. If she only knew she had been in the presence of both a demon— Ephrem. And now an archangel—Nakir.

I was sure Elias or Jordan had already informed her about what had happened while I was drying myself off inside.

"Hey, *Nik*," Keisha drawled, her lips twisting to the side. "So, you were just chilling in the woods, minding your own business, when you spotted Zo struggling in the water? Sounds a bit … rehearsed and creepy, don't you think?" She couldn't hide her mischievous grin. "Were you two having a secret rendezvous?"

"Seriously, Keisha?" I said, flabbergasted. "We were *not* hooking up! I almost died …"

Nakir glanced down at his soggy gray socks, his face

blank as my cheeks reddened. Did Nakir even know what "hooking up" meant? Without his shoes on, at least he seemed less *biblical*. His black boots were drying by the fire. I knew he could use his angelic grace to dry off, but he didn't. He was trying to fit in for a reason. Maybe he wanted to stay close to me to get to Ephrem, which was a chilling thought. Perhaps he wanted to check out my friends to ensure they weren't possessed. Even more chilling.

"We met last month," Nakir explained. "Zoey offered to show me around since I'm new to town." He shrugged. "She invited me to your party, but I took a wrong turn and got lost. Then I saw her struggling in the water and jumped in."

Andrea snorted. "Sure … that's what happened."

I shot Andrea an annoyed glare, trying to convey that she should shut up.

Nakir's green eyes met mine, and he raised an eyebrow, tilting his head slightly. "Nah, anyone would have done it," he said eventually, clearing his throat.

My watch buzzed, making me jump. I glanced down at it, knowing full well who was calling.

Jimmy. Time to go.

11

GABRIEL

Gabriel Stanton recently acquired a new office space on the 49th floor of One Vanderbilt Tower, located in the heart of Manhattan. His company, Stanton Capital, was registered under this address. The office was magnificent, with its spacious interior, fifteen-foot slab ceilings, and column-free floors. He had access to multiple corner offices, each with breathtaking views of the surrounding cityscape. In addition to his office space, Gabriel also owned a penthouse on the 68th floor of the same building. It had a panoramic view of sprawling New York, including Brooklyn and Jersey.

He stood at the high-rise window, gazing out at the skyline. The sunset sparked off the glass of the neighboring building, blazing the color of a solar flare. He took a long, slow pull of his Scotch, savoring the smoky flavor at the back of his throat as he pondered.

Immortality. That's what he'd possessed, until Corinth Taylor and his do-gooder gang took it away from him.

He could see his reflection in the glass. A day's worth

of salt-and-pepper stubble lined his jaw. His hair was more salt than pepper now, and he was in a terrible mood. Aging was abhorrent. Plus, his back hurt. How many more chemical peels, Botox, and lasering could his skin take?

"*Sir.*" A mousey voice spoke behind him.

Gabriel remained unmoving. He was on his own time. He had to show people his power. They obeyed him—not the other way around.

Someone cleared their throat. Even mousier.

Gabriel stirred his drink with his pinkie finger and then licked it. He knew they wouldn't go away until he addressed them.

Finally, he turned to see a short, stocky kid wearing a white coat. The kid had sandy blonde hair and black-rimmed glasses and stood there awkwardly. He held a silver tray in one hand, on which sat a capped syringe with a whitish-colored liquid inside.

"Is that sample sixty-seven?" Gabriel asked Mr. Mouse, perking up immediately.

"Yes, sir," the lab tech said. His name tag read Seth. "The latest prototype."

"How many people has it been tested on?" Gabriel asked softly.

Sweat dripped down the tech's forehead, betraying the fear he felt in the presence of his superior. "Four hundred and thirty," he explained.

Gabriel relished the visceral reaction he elicited from his subordinates. He took another swig of his drink before saying, "Results."

"Out of 430 subjects who received the serum, 47 developed cysts after more than two weeks' exposure. Unfortunately, 70 of them had an immediate allergic reaction, which resulted in death. Another 212 people developed a rare skin disorder, causing permanent disfigurement of their faces. However, the remaining 100 subjects who received the injections for two months experienced younger, tighter skin—fewer wrinkles were reported."

"I'm making progress," Gabriel hummed, his excitement increasing. "Have the families of the unsuccessful candidates been compensated?"

Seth gave a stiff nod, uncomfortable. "All subjects signed nondisclosure agreements and contracts acknowledging the possible side effects, including a high mortality risk, sir. They were compensated generously. There should be no issues arising from those participant's families."

"How much of Corinth Taylor's samples do we have left?" Gabriel inquired.

Gabriel—well, technically, *Sarah*—had stolen Taylor's blood long ago, when the kid was still a Nephilim-vampire hybrid.

The tech cleared his throat again and averted his eyes from Gabriel's intense gaze, his face flushing. "We don't have any more samples from Mr. Taylor," Seth squeaked, "but we do have the ones from Angela and Ephrem before their passing, if that helps."

Gabriel's temper started to rise to an unbearable degree. "*Bollocks.*" He plucked the syringe off the tray, uncapped it, and slammed it into Seth's neck, pushing the plunger down. *That felt fantastic.* He yanked the syringe back out and set it on the tray in the tech's hands. Surprisingly, Seth was still standing. A moment later, Mr. Mouse's eyes widened, and his face turned pale before he collapsed, foaming at the mouth.

Of course, Gabriel thought. *It didn't work.*

If Gabriel had gone through with his plan to inject that one dose, he would most likely have been poisoned. Considering how much the Fountain of Youth was worth to him and the risks he was willing to take to attain it, it was interesting.

Everything.

"*Idiots*," Gabriel swore under his breath, stepping over the still-convulsing body. "I need *better* idiots working for me."

12

ALASTAIR

A lastair Iszler leaned on one crutch, staring apprehensively at the 400 square meters of open floor space ahead. He could do this. It wasn't long ago that he'd effortlessly run marathons, but now he struggled to walk even a few steps. His injury had caused extensive nerve and ligament damage, and the recovery process had been far from easy.

Today, Alastair's goal was to reach the opposite wall without assistance.

The dojo was adorned with three Japanese suits of armor, all belonging to Ikari. They were respectfully showcased at the center of the far back wall. The floor, walls, and doors were all covered in bamboo, creating a light and airy atmosphere.

Light and airy was not how Alastair felt. More like sad and dark.

Alastair drew in a deep breath and let go of the crutch, which made a loud *thump* as it hit the floor. He stretched his leg out and set his foot down. A sharp pop of pain went up his injured ankle to his thigh. Despite the twinge, he soldiered on, wincing.

Biscuit, the red-furred Maine Coon who belonged to the Taylors, eyed Alastair doubtfully from the open doors. Alastair had reluctantly accepted the feline from Zoey, but it seemed like Biscuit was the one who had grudgingly taken in Alastair. He seemed to like angels, too. The cat's face seemed to say, *You're going to fall.*

It licked itself and watched him with haughty indifference.

"Some emotional support cat you are," Alastair grumbled as he took a hesitant step forward, bracing himself for the pain he knew was coming. *Keep walking. You can do it.* Two more light hops and Alastair was panting. As he made his way across the room, it became apparent that he had been relying on the wheelchair for far too long— nearly two months. His muscles had all but atrophied.

Alastair gingerly took a step forward, gritting his teeth. Immediately, his ankle gave out, causing him to collapse and fall. He pounded the mat in frustration, clutching his throbbing foot, angry and frustrated. "*Dammit!*"

"What did the floor ever do to you?"

Alastair lifted his gaze and saw his wife, Larna Iszler, standing in the open doorway. She watched him with a familiar expression—a mix of exasperation and fondness. Her blue scrubs clung to her athletic form, a testament to many long hours in the gym. He couldn't help but feel guilty for relying on her. Alastair knew how much it took for her to juggle work, fitness, life, and caring for him. Looking at Larna, he realized how lucky he was to have her by his side. She was supportive, brilliant, fierce, and always ready to lend a helping hand. Oh, how he loved her.

"I'm pretty sure I told you to rest *after* PT," Larna chastised, stepping into the training circle onto the mats. "As I've often said, you're not ready for this."

Biscuit lagged behind Larna, his tail high as if to say *I told you you'd fall.*

Alastair let out an angry growl as he sat up, grimacing and grasping his foot. Biscuit stopped beside his leg, purring softly. Despite the discomfort, Alastair felt reassured by Biscuit's furry presence.

Larna dropped down in front of Alastair, crossed her legs, and gently stretched his ankle back and forth, trying to improve the blood flow.

He hissed.

"I just heard back from Cor," Larna announced. "He says we should expect guests over the summer, if not sooner. I'm unsure what to expect, but it should be interesting."

"Corinth *always* keeps things interesting," Alastair said with an exasperated sigh. He leaned back and scratched Biscuit's ear. "Did he give you any more information to work with?"

"Nope." Larna shook her head. "Cryptic as usual."

"Shouldn't you be back at the hospital, checking on your patients?" Alastair whispered. "I truly appreciate everything you're doing for me, but I don't want you waiting on me hand and foot. I've got this. I know the exercises."

Larna pressed on his ankle, and Alastair winced. *Ouch.* "This *doctor* is only focused on one patient right now," she murmured.

"That's the problem," Alastair grumbled. "We need someone to look in on the house, and you need to keep your day job. I've got the angels here to look after me, and you've taught me enough therapy—"

"Your inability to rehab *properly* is the problem. You're pushing too hard." Larna gently placed Alastair's foot back on the floor. "Besides, I'm on paid leave, and the hospital is aware you were in a serious accident. Vinson will check on the house, so we've got everything under control. What's really bothering you?"

Biscuit hopped onto Alastair's lap and stretched out across his legs.

Alastair didn't want Larna to witness his raw emotions—anger, depression, and hurt. "This new dynamic of being infirm is not a good look on me." He couldn't bear to gaze at his wife in such a state of vulnerability.

Larna scooted over to him and gripped his hand in hers. "Look at me."

Alastair met her concerned hazel eyes. They were steadfast and determined and not filled with pity.

"I need you to know that you will *never* be a burden. You are my *husband.* This is exactly what I signed up for—helping you get through the tough times *and* the best. Do you hear me? That's what we do for each other, right?"

Alastair nodded. It was all he could do; suddenly, his throat was too constricted to speak.

13

ZOEY

Cruz and Corinth were in my bedroom well past midnight when I got home. I didn't tell them about nearly drowning, or about seeing Nakir. Mainly because when I'd entered, Cruz had immediately thrown himself at me, hugging me in a death grip.

They launched into the story about Shades attacking Cruz, which made me feel sick. Guilt swirled through my gut. I should have made a better effort to contact him earlier. I must have asked him a million times if he was okay. He looked exhausted, with his tousled, dark, wavy hair and half-moon circles under his eyes. A crumpled duffel hung off one shoulder, weighing him down.

"I'm exhausted," Cruz muttered, collapsing onto my bed and dropping his bag. "I thought they would come after you … I thought the worst …"

A sudden wave of compassion surged over me. I crossed my arms over my chest and turned to face my brother. Corinth had been away for weeks, leaving us to face our grief alone. "And where the *hell* have you been?" I demanded.

"Trying to protect you," he said, rubbing his eyes. "You're not making it easy by sneaking off to parties."

"First of all, I didn't sneak off; secondly, I only attended *one* party, not several. Jimmy was my ride. He dropped me off, picked me up, and even texted you to tell you I was safe. So, can we please leave it at that?"

"Fine," Corinth said in acquiescence. "It's late, and I don't want to argue. Look, Cruz is going to stay here tonight. I've already briefed Mom, Dad, and Jimmy."

I arched my eyebrow at Cruz. "What's going to happen to your mom? What is she going to do?"

Corinth said, "Cruz's mother is safe. You two get some rest. I'll fill you in about what's going to happen in the morning."

I recognized the moment when it was best to avoid pushing Cor's buttons, and this particular instance was one of them. But I didn't care. "You owe me answers ... not tomorrow. Now, Cor."

Corinth was already on his way out of my room, dragging Cruz with him. Cruz gave me an apologetic shrug. I followed them.

"Are you staying in Pete's ..." My voice cracked. "Room?"

"Absolutely not," Cruz interjected, grasping the patron saint of healing and the golden shield on his necklace. His face contorted in anguish before he spoke again. "That's Peter's room, and I don't want to overstep. I'm happy to crash on the couch."

Every thought in my head exploded to a pounding white. A crushing wave of sorrow struck. The thickness charged the room; I knew Cruz and Corinth could feel it, too.

"Do you plan on staying the night?" I asked Corinth as we locked eyes. Mine brimmed over.

"I'm taking Pete's room but will be up all night, standing guard." He nodded gently. "Get some rest."

I retreated into my bedroom, softly closing the door behind me. As much as I wanted to check on Cruz again, I knew we both needed rest and a clear head to face what would come next.

The following morning, I hurriedly scrambled out of bed. I slipped on my comfy slippers and headed into the living room, rubbing the sleep from my eyes.

Cruz stood by the couch, folding the blanket he had used the night before. He looked tired, and his clothes were wrinkled, as if he'd slept in them. The house was quiet except for a gentle ticking of the grandfather clock in the dining room. No one else was awake.

"You look like you didn't sleep," I remarked.

"I didn't." Cruz shrugged. "There are new shadows here. I kept staring at them, half-expecting them to turn into a Shade. It's all my fault. I believed I could leave everything behind—all we went through in the demon realm. But it seems like it won't ... go away."

His voice was heavy with sadness, and the weight of his words resonated with me. He'd gone through hell and back, too. I ran my fingers through my hair, and it dawned on me that I hadn't brushed my teeth or combed my hair in my hurry to meet him.

"No, it doesn't," I replied.

"I'm sorry about your brother, Zo. I should have been

there for you more these last few months." Cruz slumped down onto the couch, looking frail. "Everything's been a blur since the ... you know, *incident*."

I joined him on the couch, shifting a leg beneath me. I reached out to hold his hand without looking at him. Cruz's fingers squeezed mine in response, and we both went quiet. We didn't have to say anything. The silence spoke volumes.

"Do you want something to eat?" I finally asked. "Or coffee or tea or something else?"

"Coffee and eggs sound great." Cruz flashed me the faintest of smiles—a shadow of his usual self. "But I can fix it."

"How about we both fix it?" I got up but turned back to him. "About last night, I keep asking, but ... are you sure you're okay?"

"There's nothing okay about a Shade trying to take one of your eyeballs. Of course, I did take one of its."

"Well, when you put it like that." I thought about how strange our conversations were.

Cruz followed me as I entered the kitchen, and I flipped on the lights. The bright bulbs made me squint. The microwave clock read 6:00 A.M, much earlier than I'd thought. Although my parents were early risers, they were not up this early.

"Could you grab a couple of mugs from the top cabinet?" I gestured toward a cupboard behind him.

Cruz opened the cabinet and pulled down two mugs— one for each of us.

"Is light roast okay?" I asked, starting the coffee maker. There wasn't much to do, as it was set to come on at 8:00 A.M. every morning anyway.

"Anything is fine," Cruz muttered, coming up beside me. "Do you need help?"

"Nah. I've been making coffee since I was in diapers. I could probably brew it in my sleep."

A low chuckle escaped Cruz as he sat at the kitchen table. "But you don't drink it?"

"I never acquired a taste for it," I confessed, leaning against the counter and tapping my fingers on the granite. "My brothers, conversely, can't get enough of it ..." I paused because it was dangerous territory to continue talking about my brothers ... brother. Pete. "Do you plan on staying here for a while?"

"Corinth mentioned going to Scotland for the summer. He told me to pack *all* my clothes, especially the winter stuff. It never gets that cold in Texas, so I only own a coat and a parka."

The aroma of freshly brewed coffee filled the air. Even though I wasn't a coffee drinker, I realized I'd need something more substantial to help me shake off the grogginess.

"Plans got moved up," Corinth said as he swept into the kitchen, fully dressed and ready to go. "We're leaving for Scotland today." His russet-colored hair was heavily moussed and styled to stick straight up. What caught my attention was that he wasn't wearing his holy blade—or at least, if he was, I couldn't see it. Despite this, I knew he wouldn't leave without it. Maybe he'd disguised it using his grace?

"When you say *we*, you mean you and Cruz, right?" I said slowly, giving my brother a stern scowl up and down. I was still upset with him.

The java had barely stopped dripping into the pot before Corinth started helping himself to a cup. Then he came around and poured some into the empty cups in front of Cruz and me, who I noticed was about to fall asleep sitting upright in his chair.

Corinth leaned back against the counter, picked up the steaming coffee, and blew on it briefly before taking a tentative sip. My brother was a notorious coffee snob. He had a refined taste for drip pours, cold brews, and coffee presses, which he took very seriously.

The expression on his face changed in an instant. It was one of disgust. He immediately spat it back into the cup and grimaced. "What in the muddy water is *this* crap?" he exclaimed, glancing at me over the rim.

"It's a light roast, and if you don't like it, maybe you should have stuck around to stock up on the good stuff."

After a beat, Cor whispered, "I didn't *want* to leave, Zo. I *had* to."

I picked up my mug and gave him a questioning frown as he refused to explain.

Corinth glanced at Cruz, leaning back in his seat. I think he was trying to anticipate his following words.

"You two are in immediate danger," Corinth said without sugarcoating. "The threats are escalating, which means you both have to be relocated to the safehouse in Scotland earlier than planned."

"Excuse me!" I blurted out, slamming my cup on the table like a gavel.

The mere thought of leaving school and moving away made me anxious. I'd finally started to make friends. And what about Nakir? I knew he could transport himself anywhere, but would he know I'd left? My parents? My studies? Although that was lower on the list these days. "We can't just pack up and leave. I only have a few months left of this school year. Cruz has a job and his mom to take care of. Besides, I'm already behind on projects. Absolutely not."

Corinth rolled his eyes to the ceiling, his arms crossed over his chest. "Why must you *always* give me a hard time, kid?" The furrow on his forehead indicated how frustrated he appeared. "Look, I know you're eager to graduate, but you can't do that if you're dead." He sounded stern but sympathetic. "We'll figure out the school stuff, but right now, my top priority is to keep you both alive."

"This is my home. It was … it was *Pete's* home, too. I don't want to be scared anymore, but if I go now, it will feel like I'm running away. Cruz, what do you think about this? Weigh in here."

Cruz gulped down his coffee and placed it on the table, his hands shaking. "I think we should leave." I gave him a look that I hoped conveyed my disappointment. He shrank back before adding, "I have to protect my mother. The Shades were after her because of me. I'm tired of being scared, too, Zoey, but I want to regain control. Corinth promised to train me—"

"Actually, it won't be me," Corinth corrected him. "Al and Larna will be at the cottage."

Cruz's gaze caught mine, and his face lit up. "We'll have the entire summer to learn how to defend ourselves. Zo, come with me. When I wasn't sure if you were okay, I thought they might have come for you too. I can't do this without knowing you're all right. Besides, once we learn how to fight, we can take the battle to them."

As my eyes flickered over to Corinth, he gestured with his hand, signaling Cruz to halt. "Cruz, seriously? Let's not get ahead of ourselves. We're not taking on any battles anywhere. We aim to equip you with the skills to protect yourself, and that's all. Do you understand?"

Cruz's expression turned serious. His eyes narrowed, but he paused and nodded, albeit somewhat reluctantly.

"Let me finish school before the summer break," I pleaded.

Corinth, leaning against the counter, pushed himself off it and took a step forward. "I'm sorry, Zo," he said, looking at me with a pained expression. "I promise you I'll work it out. But for now, we need to leave. Please trust me."

"How can I trust you when you disappear?" I asked.

14

CRUZ

The kitchen felt like a pressure cooker about to explode, as Zoey struggled to accept the idea of leaving.

A cold, sharp stab of panic gripped Cruz. The terror he had experienced last night was still fresh. He didn't want to leave his mom, but he knew with absolute certainty that that was precisely what he had to do.

Enough was enough.

Zoey trailed after Corinth as they left the kitchen, their conversation still audible.

"Let Cruz stay here, and you can stay in Pete's room if you're worried about us. It's not fair that we have to uproot our lives over this! Can't you be reasonable, Cor?"

"This *is* me being reasonable!" he snapped.

Cruz would have eavesdropped a bit longer, but Jimmy entered the kitchen, his hair disheveled. He was still wearing his flannel pajamas, which hung loosely off his hips. It appeared as though he had lost weight.

Jimmy raised an eyebrow and tilted his head toward

the living room, where the raucous shouting was still coming from. "How long have they been at it?"

Cruz scratched his head. "Too long," he muttered.

"Yeah, they woke me up. If you haven't noticed by now, Zoey's pretty headstrong," Jimmy said with a laugh.

"You want breakfast?" Jimmy asked Cruz.

"Yes, please." Cruz nodded eagerly. "I'm starving but didn't want to start digging around in your kitchen."

With keen interest, Cruz observed Zoey's brother pluck two bowls from a cabinet, pick up cereal from the top of the fridge, and pour some into the dishes. He took out milk and spoons, placed them on the table, and sat down.

"It's not gourmet, but it does the trick," Jimmy said.

"I'll take anything that doesn't run from me," Cruz added, picking up a spoon.

Jimmy snorted. "You seem to have a good head on your shoulders, Cruz. I appreciate you taking care of Zo. I didn't get a chance to thank you. It was … brave, what you did."

Cruz felt his cheeks grow warm at the compliment. He sipped his lukewarm coffee, avoiding Jimmy's penetrating stare. "I—I didn't really do anything except run. Anyway, I did what anyone else would have done." Accepting compliments was never his thing. Cruz's mother always praised him because he was her son, but that was different— she had to.

"No, you didn't," Jimmy refuted.

Cruz savored the silence, while Jimmy got busy with a pack of bacon, tossing some slices on the pan. The delicious aroma of sizzling meat made his stomach growl, reminding him that he was famished.

"Do you need any help?" Cruz asked.

"Nah, I got it." There was a beat of silence. "But I will ask you a favor," Jimmy said.

Cruz was least familiar with Jimmy, among all Zoey's brothers. Curious, he said, "Sure, name it."

"Could you promise to watch out for Zoey when you're in Scotland? We're all heartbroken, and I'm worried about her. She needs this break more than she realizes …"

"So, you know about Scotland?" Cruz asked.

"We all do."

Corinth had spread the word quickly.

"Yeah, of course. I'll always keep an eye on Zo—I mean, not in a weird way …" Cruz cleared his throat, annoyed at his awkwardness. "I promise."

Someone cleared their throat loudly from behind.

It startled Cruz, causing him to spin around. Zoey casually leaned against the doorjamb in the open doorway. She gazed at him, amused, as if to say, *You'll do what, now?*

Cruz felt his cheeks light up like a Christmas parade float.

One side of Zoey's mouth quirked up.

Corinth had joined Zoey, appearing solemn and lost in thought.

"I'm capable of taking care of myself. But," Zoey paused, considering her words as she glanced at her eldest brother, "maybe you're right. Maybe a change of scenery would be beneficial. But I want to be clear: *if* I decide to leave, it will be *my* decision, and no one will force me to stay. Do we have an understanding?"

"You got a deal," Corinth agreed.

Cruz finalized his packing in the Taylor family's living room. He made sure to grab his passport—even though he was traveling to Scotland with Corinth through lightning, which was an unconventional way of traveling. Next, Cruz searched through his belongings to find his parka. Knowing Scotland was infamous for its rain, he didn't want to get caught off guard by a sudden downpour. While digging through his bag for the fourth time, Cruz paused when he heard yelling coming from Zoey's room.

He drifted toward her cracked-open bedroom door. After hesitating, he knocked lightly.

A soft shout of "*Come in!*" came from inside.

Cruz poked his head into Zoey's room.

She was using her entire body to shove clothes into the luggage piled high on her bed. Her long sandy hair was in disarray, strands falling across her face. The tips of her cheeks were flushed bright red, which only served to accentuate her freckles and lend her an air of charm and whimsy. Whenever he looked at Zoey, he felt an invisible force robbing him of his breath, leaving him weak-kneed, like he was on the cusp of something meaningful and life-changing.

Cruz cleared his throat, trying to suppress his emotions. "Do you need help with that?"

"I just"—Zoey huffed and puffed—"need to get this … zipped up."

Cruz slid the rest of the way into her room and came to the opposite side of the suitcase. He dove over it, shoving the lid down with all his weight. "What do you have in here?" he asked, gasping for breath. "An entire library?"

Zoey managed to zip the first half; she paused, wiping hair out of her eyes. "I have to make sure I have everything for school—and then some."

A few of Zoey's clothes popped out of the suitcase. Cruz stuffed them back inside and then zipped it up. "We have laptops and tablets for that," he said. The top of her luggage was bulging, bursting at the seams, but at least it was securely fastened.

"Thanks," Zoey said, still winded. "But I prefer real books."

"How's that going?" Cruz asked, sitting down on her bed.

When she gave him a quizzical head tilt, he added, "School. I remember you saying you wanted to graduate early."

"I don't know. I don't like it as much anymore," Zoey said from the other side of the luggage. Frowning, she tucked one leg underneath her. "I got off track for a while, but maybe I can compensate for lost time. It just doesn't feel the same."

"*Pfft.* Imagine that," Cruz retorted, giving her a teasing look. "It's not like we had life-altering stuff happen that shook us to our very core or anything."

"You can say that again," Zoey agreed, blowing out a raspberry. "It feels so good to talk to you about all this—with someone else who went through ... what we went through."

Cruz responded to her statement with a hint of sarcasm. "Trauma?"

Zoey nodded. "That's exactly what I'm referring to."

"Have you thought about what you'll do after graduation?" Cruz tried tactfully to steer the conversation in a new direction. "Are you still planning to study abroad in England?"

She shrugged. "I guess so, except now, after everything that's happened, it feels ... so empty. Like I'm just going through the motions. Does that make sense? There's so much more out there to explore."

"Do you have to have it all figured out right away?" Cruz whispered. "I think that's normal—testing the waters. You know, getting that education is part of exploring and leveling up."

"I always had a path picked out for myself." Zoey sighed. "But after what happened to Pete, I feel lost. I don't know where to go from here."

"Welcome to the club." A smile tugged at the corner of Cruz's mouth. "Maybe we can walk that path together, and it won't be so lonely."

"Sounds good to me." Zoey giggled. "Your patron saint medallion, it's cool. I did some research on it. I mean, I've been researching everything, including reading the entire Bible twice."

"That's very studious of you." Cruz pulled the gold necklace out from underneath his shirt. The gold shone like a secret, a shared moment just between them. "And wise, probably."

"Saint Raphael the Archangel is revered as the patron saint of healing, known to mend people's bodies, minds, and spirits," Zoey said. "Also, he's recognized as the patron saint of young people, love, travelers, and those seeking protection from nightmares."

"You're like Zoeypidia." Cruz arched an eyebrow at her and smiled, impressed. "Are you studying angels or Catholicism?"

"I study what I fear," Zoey whispered. "Angels *and* demons."

"But your brother is one of them … a *Nephilim*," Cruz pointed out, emphasizing the word. "You're not afraid of angels, right? They're the good guys. They've saved us countless times."

"Not *always*—they've also put us in grave danger." Cruz and Zoey went quiet, contemplating that before she went on, picking at a fingernail. "After witnessing my brother's possession, angels almost terrify me more than demons do."

Cruz recoiled at the thought. Maybe she was right, but he trusted angels more than demons. "Not me," he muttered. "Demons and those zombie Shades—they give me the absolute *creeps*." He shifted his gaze, unable to bear Zoey's piercing brown eyes any longer. The mere notion of sharing feelings made him cringe.

After a beat, Zoey asked, "Can you keep a secret?"

Cruz furrowed his brow. "That sounds ominous." Although he had been making more promises lately, he didn't hesitate this time. He would always say yes to her. "Cross my heart," he added, signing the cross over his chest.

"Okay, so last night at the party I went to, I saw Nakir."

Cruz's heart rate increased. "Like the archangel who almost *killed* Alastair?"

Zoey's head bobbed up and down, and her complexion seemed to have lost some color. The soft lighting in the room could have contributed to that, but Cruz didn't think so. Something had happened to her.

"Are you serious?" Cruz's chest constricted as he relived the terrifying memory from the demon realm. "Were you in danger last night, Zoey? Why wouldn't you say something to Corinth?"

Zoey shook her head. "Not in the way you're thinking … no …"

"Oh my gosh." Cruz felt his eyes go wide as he rubbed his forehead. "I knew it. What happened?"

"I might have almost drowned—and Nakir saved me."

"What the heck?" Cruz hopped up from the bed, his pulse racing as he ran a hand through his hair. "How?"

"I was at that party and decided to swim in the lake but got a cramp. Somehow, he showed up before I drowned and portaled me out."

Cruz thought about that for a moment, blinking slowly back at her. "You went swimming? At *night*?"

Zoey shrugged. "I'm exploring, remember?"

"Alastair was seriously injured. Was he using someone else's vessel? This can't be good. Has he managed to track down Ephrem? Wasn't that what he threatened to do?" Cruz rapid-fired the questions.

When Zoey spoke next, her voice sounded raw. "No. Nakir was in his own body. He didn't say it because we got interrupted, but I think he wanted to warn me about Ephrem returning—or maybe that's why he's been following me."

"Ephrem returning?" Cruz gulped. The mere thought of encountering that monster again made his anxiety spike. "Why do you want to keep this a secret from the people who can protect you?"

"I don't want Corinth to worry any more than he already has. He's whisking us away to Scotland … imagine how much he'd be breathing down my neck if he knew Ephrem might return. Corinth is making me abandon my home, school, and whole life because *he's* scared."

"For good reason, don't you think?" Cruz pressed. "Those zombies are skulking around our homes. This is grave—"

Zoey let out a long sigh. "You sound exactly like Cor. If we have to let him know, I'll tell him. But for now, can we please keep this between us?"

Cruz, though hesitant, eventually nodded. "I have a feeling that this might come back to haunt us," he said, "but okay. I won't say anything for now."

15

NAKIR

Nakir, a mighty warrior who had once flown in heaven, found adjusting to the mortal world extremely challenging.

After descending from the celestial realm, he was disheartened to discover that his physical form was no longer as resilient as it used to be. His muscles had weakened. He felt a constant ache in his bones—gravity. Earth felt like slogging through muddy water. But the worst part was losing his wings. Without them, Nakir was permanently earthbound—unable to fly. The memory of soaring through the clouds, the wind beneath his wings, was a painful reminder of what he had sacrificed. This was what it felt like to be human. Weak. An experience Jesus had already been through—which was why Nakir had obeyed top orders. Always.

Despite Nakir's frustration, he was determined to adapt.

Here, though, the cold sapped him of his grace.

When he'd dived into the lake to help Zoey, he'd

instantly felt drained. Although he still possessed angelic abilities, he wasn't at his best. It had been part of the deal when he'd signed on. To make matters worse, his armor and weapon were gone. When Nakir had hastily left Alastair's vessel, the armor and weapon had been ripped away from him and scattered across the planet. His helmet, greaves, breastplate, and *Stronghold*, too. It had been worth saving Alastair's life, but tracking his gear proved more complicated than he imagined. And worse, if anyone else encountered them before he did, demon or human, they could be used for devastating and destructive purposes.

Then there was the greater demon who'd escaped hell.

Nakir *needed* his armor to defeat it. He had two responsibilities: to ensure the demon was thrown back into the pit and to guard Zoey Taylor. Corinth Taylor sure did have a lot of supporters in heaven. Orders had come straight from the top.

The kid better be worth it, he thought.

Nakir enjoyed the view of the Hudson River from far above at night. It was as close to flying as he would get for now. Manhattan's skyline was obscured beyond the wall-to-wall windows of Gabriel Stanton's condominium. People looked like ants from this height, walking to and from work. Tiny boat lights dotted the distance while the bright city dimmed the stars above. It was a marvel of God's creation at its finest. Nakir now understood why people fought over spoils like land and material possessions.

Gabriel Stanton knew angels had specific abilities. When Alastair had been Nakir's vessel, he had experienced everything Alastair had, as their emotions and memories had been entangled. Nakir was still connected to that bond. Alastair did not trust Gabriel Stanton; his mistrust had bled into Nakir.

Behind Nakir, the door opened, allowing a thin light to penetrate the room's darkness. Nakir's shadowy figure remained concealed, barely visible in the faint illumination. The silence was only interrupted by the soft sound of the door clicking shut.

A tall, thin silhouette entered.

And then there came a startled voice. "Who's there?"

In response, the illuminations flickered on, revealing a tense Gabriel Stanton, his hand firmly gripping a gun aimed directly at Nakir.

The mortal was fast, but Nakir was faster. He teleported behind Stanton, grabbed the scruff of his white sports coat with one hand, snatched the pistol out of his hand, and sent him sprawling to the floor in a wounded heap.

Gabriel Stanton looked up at Nakir, his expression steely and calculating. After a measured beat, the man sat up. "Have we met?"

"Yes," Nakir answered, effortlessly snapping the weapon in half, causing the metal to disintegrate and fall to the ground.

Gabriel adjusted his tie and smoothed the wrinkles out of his pants as he stood back up. His hands trembled. "What do you want, angel?"

A slow smile spread across Nakir's face. "I am Nakir, an archangel of the Lord."

"Didn't I just say *angel*?" Gabriel paused, shooting him a contemptuous scowl. "So, this is how you look without possessing Iszler. You appear younger than I thought you would. It's an improvement from Alastair. Angels have the best skin: tight, toned, and bronzed. They never get old. I'm envious of your immortality." Stanton's voice was practically dripping with jealousy. "Do you think you could lend me some of that? I need a little blood sample for a test … I can pay handsomely—"

"Our grace is not meant for mortals," Nakir said vehemently.

"*All right,*" Stanton said, his lips pressed tight as he raised his arms. "Then why have you come, Nakir?"

"You change your loyalty as frequently as your outfits. I'm aware that you've been conspiring with demons. Ephrem will come for you first, you know that, right?"

"Will he, though?" Gabriel said, a hand on his chin. He moved to the corner of the room and picked up a goblet at the bar top. Stanton poured a brown liquid into the glass and chugged it in one gulp. "We all know who the demon will come for first, and it's not me. It's the girl."

Zoey. Nakir lunged forward, seizing Stanton's shirt. The glass slipped from Stanton's grip and rolled underneath the counter. Nakir's gaze was unwavering as he met Stanton's eyes, letting his angelic power flow through him. Despite the moral objections of some, Nakir knew that his duty demanded he find the truth. No matter what the cost. It was a compulsion, some would say. "Did you assist Ephrem? Have you found my armor and sword? I know you have the capability and money to find it."

Gabriel struggled, but was trapped in Nakir's divine gaze and iron grip.

"*Answer me,*" Nakir snarled.

But to Nakir's surprise, a knowing grin spread across Gabriel's face.

"What?" Nakir let Stanton go, stunned that compulsion hadn't worked on him.

"Sword and armor?" Stanton leaned forward with interest. "How *intriguing.*"

Nakir's plan had failed. "You ... *how* did you do that? Are you *not* mortal? No human can fight an angel's compulsion." He'd handed Gabriel valuable information.

"I am thousands of years old, archangel. And I prefer the term Ascended Being. Do you think I have not mastered control over my mind after all this time?" A muscle in Gabriel's jaw feathered. "Throughout the years, only one person has been able to compel me, and it wasn't an angel." His eyes narrowed. "It was a teenage girl."

16

GABRIEL

The stakes were high. Gabriel knew the world was in peril, threatened by the combined might of angels and demons. They both sought to destroy it. But not on his watch.

Still, going up against such daunting adversaries was no small feat. Gabriel needed every possible advantage he could get, including angel weaponry. Bargaining. Trading. Fighting. He could name a thousand different advantages of possessing holy relics.

Nakir was dressed in black fatigues and boots, his fingers crackling with the same energy Corinth possessed. A crease had appeared on the archangel's forehead.

Gabriel Stanton enjoyed seeing the confusion on his face. He resented that Nakir possessed eternal youth, while his own had been ripped away.

"So, who was this girl who could compel you so easily?" Nakir asked slowly, sounding doubtful. "She must have an angelic lineage. Is it Zoey Taylor?"

Hmmm. Zoey Taylor. She was about as ordinary as they came. *Wasn't she?* Perhaps Gabriel should have paid closer attention to the Nephilim's half-sister. Nakir might know something about her that Gabriel did not. He filed this information away to meditate on later.

"I assure you, this girl didn't compel me easily," Gabriel snapped. "She fought hard and emerged victorious." He paused. "But I possess information you do not. Knowledge is power, and I have it in spades. What are you willing to trade for it?"

"Says the self-proclaimed philanthropist," Nakir shot back. But he sounded like he was on the hook. The angel needed him.

"You're not completely clueless," Gabriel all but purred. "You've bypassed my security. If you work for me, I might consider providing the information you seek."

"Security? I fried all your electronics and cameras instantly. I can also teleport in the blink of an eye. And work *for* you?" Nakir leaned closer to Gabriel threateningly. "As far as I know, Zoey Taylor doesn't have angelic ancestry. Corinth's father, an archangel, only passed on his divine legacy to him."

Nakir balled his hands into fists by his sides. Steam practically shot out of the dolt's ears, Gabriel noted. Gabriel finally shrank back only when the archangel's hands turned into twin balls of flame, and a twinge of fear prickled his spine.

"Are you claiming ignorance, human?" Nakir snarled. "You have *no* idea where my armor is? Because if I find out differently, you won't have to worry about Ephrem finding you first."

Avoiding questions about Zoey Taylor, check.

"No, I don't," Gabriel countered. "But if I come across your ... gear, how would you like me to contact you?"

"Don't worry, Stanton, I'll find you."

With a brilliant flash of light, Nakir vanished into a swirling tunnel, and the air got sucked out, the building shaking from the force of the vortex closing. Gabriel's bones all but vibrated. He couldn't help but think that any more pressure might have caused his insides to implode.

Oh, how he despised those uppity celestial beings. Arses. All of them.

Heavy footsteps thundered down the hallway outside his penthouse.

A second later, the double doors swung open. Gabriel's security team rushed inside, guns drawn and ready as they checked every nook and cranny for threats. The security team was the cream of the crop—ex-Navy seals, battle-hardened mercenaries, and specialists from less conventional fields. Gabriel had spared no expense in hiring the best.

So much for that.

"*Now* you show up," Gabriel muttered. His legs felt unsteady as the building finally stopped swaying.

Gabriel's head of security, Kiefer, approached him cautiously, sharply scanning the skylight above.

"Are you all right, sir?" Kiefer asked. "What the hell was that?"

"Another pissed-off angel." Gabriel felt a headache starting to form. "I have a task for you. I need a team that can travel light and fast. We need to find armor and a sword ... and fast."

This powerful blade could give its possessor an edge against the demonic and angelic forces threatening their world. Whoever found it first would hold the key to victory.

Of course, Gabriel had his reasons for wanting the weapon. If he could get his hands on the sword, he could use it to force Nakir to do his bidding.

Or, he could even turn the sword against him and his nemesis—Corinth Taylor.

17

ZOEY

It was three o'clock in the afternoon. Corinth, Cruz, and I stood together, while my parents and Jimmy looked on from the other side of our living room couch. My family appeared moody and on edge. Jimmy, in particular, looked a little thinner and paler every day—a mere shadow of his former self. His hands were buried deep in the pockets of his navy joggers, and I couldn't help but feel concerned for him.

As I prepared to leave, a mix of emotions swirled within me: nervousness, eagerness, and trepidation. My parents were sad to see me go, but they knew our safety was paramount. They no longer opposed Corinth's advice. Jimmy would watch over them while we were away, so I didn't feel as bad about leaving.

Cruz, on the other hand, couldn't contain his excitement. He was practically jumping up and down with anticipation. Despite his eagerness, I couldn't ignore the nagging feeling that I was running away from my problems instead of confronting them head-on.

Technically, it wasn't my fault—leaving wasn't *my* choice. That was the real reason why I felt so unsettled. But maybe that wasn't such a bad thing? Perhaps I needed time to clear my head and gain perspective.

Yeah, right. The regret you're having right now is that you didn't get to say goodbye to Nakir.

My gaze landed on the couch, still infused with the musky scent of Pete's cologne. A tear trickled down my cheek. I quickly wiped it away, frustrated that I couldn't control the onslaught of random emotions.

My mother, sensing my distress, leaned into my shoulder. "Fresh air and nature can be an amazing cure for grief. You have to keep an open mind. Journaling will help, too. It's what I've learned from my support group."

Mom and Dad were both taking grief counseling.

"Open mind? What's that?" I laid my head against her shoulder and smiled. Her short, cropped hair had more gray in it these days. Losing Peter had taken a toll on all of us. Dad especially. The hollows in his cheeks and the shadows under his eyes were more pronounced.

My voice wavered as I said, "I prefer smog and congested traffic to sheep poop and clean air any day of the week, but I promise I'll try, Mom."

"I love you, bug." She pulled me into a tight embrace and held me. I didn't draw away. We both needed close contact. I sniffed, and her arms enfolded me from all sides.

Dad put a supporting hand on my shoulder. "Enjoy Scotland, okay?"

I clutched my luggage and nodded.

Corinth reached out to lay a hand on top of Jimmy's shoulder. "I'm counting on you to care for the family while I'm gone."

Jimmy gave a solemn nod. "I've got things handled here. You take care of the angel stuff and our little sis."

"Call me if you need anything," Corinth added.

"You got it, brother," Jimmy said, and they embraced.

It was nice to see everyone finally getting along.

After we said our goodbyes, Corinth placed one hand on my arm and the other on Cruz's shoulder, and my parents stepped back.

Jimmy gave me a quick wink before we were swept up into a portal Corinth had conjured. We vanished into thin air in a split second, leaving my household behind.

When we arrived at the cottage, a quiet eeriness filled the place. It was dark. The six-hour time difference left me disoriented, and a bout of dizziness overcame me. I clutched one of Corinth's arms for support as we entered the small living room.

"Are you okay, Zo, Cruz?" Corinth asked, glancing between Cruz and me. "It'll pass, I promise."

Cruz struggled to keep his balance, rubbing his eyes and dropping his over-stuffed duffle. "I don't think I'll ever get used to that," he whispered, looking around and squinting. "It's nighttime, and we just came from daylight. So weird …"

I glanced around. Not much had changed since my last visit. It was a cozy yet dim setting: muted colors, hardwood floors, faded coffee-colored couches, and hand-me-down furniture. In the corner of the room, wood burned in a free-standing stove, welcoming us.

Biscuit bounded into the room, his fluffy tail swishing

back and forth. He landed between my legs with a graceful leap, purring and rubbing his head against my shins.

I bent down to rub his ears, happy to see him. "Hey there, buddy," I cooed, my voice softening. "Did you behave for Alastair? I missed you bunches, little man."

"Behave?" Alastair chuckled softly as he limped into the room using a cane. "That cat doesn't know how to behave. The beast has been good company, though."

I stood up, taking in Alastair. Corinth had shared the details about what had happened to him after the demon realm debacle, but seeing him standing here now seemed like nothing short of a miracle. Blonde hair poked out from underneath a black beanie. He had on loose-fitting sweats and leaned on a walking cane. Had he lost muscle mass? *Maybe*, I considered, *but not much.* Something told me he was pushing himself harder to recover faster. Because, of course, it was Alastair, and he didn't have a half-speed. The healing process had been arduous for him; the circles under his eyes were a testament to that.

"Admit it, Alastair, you love Biscuit as much as I do," I said in a mock-baby voice as I scratched my cat's head.

Biscuit had saved my life, and I loved him dearly. Letting my fur baby stay at the cottage in Scotland instead of at my house had been hard. Still, I knew Alastair needed his companionship more than I did. Besides, Biscuit loved the angels, especially Leo.

Corinth walked over to Alastair and hugged him tightly, placing a fist at his back. "It's great to see you, Bro."

Alastair winced and pulled back. "Easy, Cor. Your angel strength is crushing me. Or maybe I'm scrawnier … either way, *ouch.*"

"Oh, sorry, Al! Let me ease some of that pain for you."

Corinth's hands glowed blue with grace, but when he moved to touch him, Alastair backed up even further, lifting a hand in protest.

"You're the only pain—in the neck—I have," Alastair teased, tilting his head in irritation and amusement. "You know it hurts you when you try and heal me. You've punished yourself enough. I'm good, Cor." He pointed at me with his cane, adding, "And don't worry, I can handle two teenagers without needing superpowers."

I bristled, hearing Alastair say, *handling teenagers*. I had endured more hardships than most grown-ups ever did in their entire existence.

Alastair's intense blue eyes bore into mine before turning to Cruz. "I hear you two have been getting into your fair share of trouble."

My cheeks flushed, and the blood in my ears thumped louder. *Stop it, Zo.* Ugh. You do *not* still have a crush. Despite my, shall we say, "effort" to move on from Alastair, it wasn't proving easy.

"Technically, that was Cruz," I muttered, barely audible, knowing full well that I had almost drowned. I wasn't going to tell Alastair that.

Alastair seemed to struggle to stay awake as he yawned. "Cruz." Alastair nodded. "I heard about the attack."

Cruz breathed deeply, as if saying *understatement of the year*.

Alastair limped toward the stove. When his pant leg rose from behind, the soft, flickering firelight illuminated a scarred patch of pale skin just above his ankle.

"Where's Larns? I was expecting the wife to be here to welcome us," Corinth said, genuinely disappointed. She was his best friend.

"Despite many objections, I convinced Larna to check in on her patients, who should be the priority, not me. She'll be away for a few days."

"Okay, well. Since you've got this handled, I'm going to leave you to it, Al," Corinth said, clapping his hands.

"You're leaving?" I turned to my brother. "I thought you were supposed to protect us?"

Corinth pursed his lips before saying, "I have unfinished business to take care of, but don't worry, you're in good hands. This place is secure, and more angels stay in the guest house nearby."

"Unfinished business? What does that mean?" I asked. "And you better tell me the truth, Corinth Taylor."

He sighed. "Angel stuff."

"That's not an explanation," I huffed.

"Yet it's all you're getting for now." Corinth turned to Cruz. "For now, Cruz, focus on self-defense. You have one job, and that's to train. Don't worry. I'll try to pop in and out whenever possible to check on y'all."

"If you get news about the One-Eyed freak, you'll tell me?" Cruz asked.

"*Later*," Alastair said firmly. "Right now, let's settle in. We have a lot of work to do."

18

CRUZ

Cruz couldn't believe he'd been transported to another country in only seconds—and now he was sharing a room with Zoey. They were roommates because Alastair had taken residency downstairs. Their communal bedroom was upstairs, on the cottage's southeast side. The cozy two-story home featured only three small bedrooms and a staircase so narrow that Cruz's head nearly grazed the ceiling when climbing them. This cottage was where Peter had been taken before becoming a Shade. He shivered at that thought, trying to dispel the image. This would be a fresh start.

Tamp the doom and gloom back down, Cruz.

The house was old and creaky. A sudden gust rattled the windows in their frames. He glanced around, unsure if to unpack his things or leave them crammed in his bag. *That's tomorrow's problem*, he thought. Except Cruz wasn't tired at all. The instant six-hour time difference was royally screwing with him.

A nightstand separated two twin beds. A small beige

dresser was in one corner, closer to the bed Zoey had claimed. Cruz's bed was closest to the connecting bathroom. He hoped things wouldn't be awkward between them.

Cruz also couldn't shake the worry he felt being away from his mother. Corinth promised she would be safe, and he had to take that promise at face value, but he missed her terribly. He wasn't exactly the best in trusting people, but Corinth had proven himself more times than he could count. So, for now, he would make himself stop worrying so much.

The sound of Zoey's automatic toothbrush came from the bathroom.

He'd never had a sleepover before. How did this work?

Cruz took the opportunity to change into his pajamas, quickly tugging on his shorts and removing his shirt. As he did, he felt the shield thump preternaturally against his bare chest, reminding him of its presence. The holy relic felt cool against his skin. Cruz curled his fingers around the charm, whispering a silent prayer, grateful for its protection.

He must've been in a trance. The next thing he knew, Zoey had swept back into the room, and Cruz realized he was still shirtless.

Crap.

She stopped dead in her tracks at seeing him in a half-state of undress, and a flurry of butterflies erupted in his stomach.

"Sorry, Zoey. Sorry—" Cruz stammered incoherently as he threw on a white T-shirt he'd laid out. "I thought you were going to be in there longer."

Color formed in Zoey's cheeks. She cleared her throat, turning around. "No worries," she said after a beat. "I've got three brothers, remember …?" her voice trailed off and faltered.

Oh man, she was thinking about Peter again. How could she not be?

"I'm dressed," Cruz told Zoey, noticing how long her sandy blonde hair had gotten. Tiny water droplets trickled down the sides of her neck, and she was wearing pink pajama bottoms and a matching V-neck shirt. A sweet fragrance of peaches and cream filled the air as she drifted to her side of the room.

"I think we should have a bathroom schedule or something. We will be stuck in this house together all summer." Zoey wiped the water off her forehead.

"Sure. Yeah—of course," Cruz agreed quickly.

Zoey noticed Cruz's shield and the patron saint hanging from his neck. She lifted her hand and fiddled with the ring on her finger, its red jewel sparking. It was divine, just like his charm.

"I still can't believe how you got that small amulet to turn into a life-size shield. Have you been able to change it again? Like you did before?" Zoey asked.

Cruz nodded. "Yeah, it turned into a knife when those Shades attacked me, but I can't seem to control it very well—the thing burns my skin when it goes off."

She nodded. "The jewel on my rings flashes. Wow, it's impressive that it changed for you again. I'm just happy you're okay."

"Thanks to your brother. I couldn't fight them off. Those zombies have telekinesis. They're too strong." After a brief pause, Cruz shrugged and added, "You joining me to train? I'm excited to start learning self-defense."

"Remember, this wasn't my idea. I'm not as excited about being here as you are." Zoey sat on the bed she'd chosen and shrugged. "Exercise has never been my strong suit. I'd rather use mind over muscle. But more power to you, I guess."

"Brawn *and* brains don't have to be mutually exclusive." Cruz twisted his mouth into a half-grin. "You showed badassery when you stabbed Ephrem."

Zoey raised an amused brow, but then her face dropped. "For all the good it did."

"You hurt a *demon*, and you saved my life." Cruz understood the pain of loss, as he had been mentally preparing himself for his mother's passing. But his mom had received a second chance at life, which bolstered him. Cruz owed Corinth everything. "That's why we train. Through practice, you learn how to kill the bad guys."

"You sound so cavalier. These are real stakes, Cruz. Real death." Zoey picked at a fingernail before going on. "I—I don't want to be placed in a position where I have to *kill* anyone. This was forced upon me, and I resent Cor for it." Zoey wrapped her arms around herself.

"I get that." He nodded, looking down at his duffle. He started pulling out workout clothes for tomorrow morning. "Don't put so much pressure on yourself. We can start fresh. Take a deep breath and relish some time away from your busy schedule."

"Okay," Zoey replied. "I'll try and give it a shot."

19

ALASTAIR

Zoey and Cruz's room was shrouded in darkness, with only a faint glow from the nightlight plugged into a socket. Alastair remembered Zoey disliked the dark, and the light was for her. The kids were fast asleep, their bodies sprawled out on their beds.

As Alastair burst into their room at 6:00 A.M., they were still in a deep slumber, unaware of the chaos that was about to unfold. He flicked the lights on and off several times and bellowed, "Wake up! It's time to start training."

Neither of them moved. However, a faint groan escaped from Zoey's bed. Eventually, Cruz sat up, yawning and stretching his arms. His hair was all over the place, piled high on his head, and his eyes were still closed. But he seemed excited when he flung the covers off himself.

Zoey stayed wrapped in her comforter, disregarding Alastair's presence. He knew they'd had a late night. Adjusting to the time difference was going to take a few days. But he was determined to get Zoey on board with training ... eventually.

Corinth had been quite apathetic when he'd first begun training, too. For now, Alastair knew that Zoey had been through a lot. Grief was all-consuming.

Cruz moaned. "Is it still the middle of the night?" he mumbled.

Alastair's voice boomed loudly. "Get dressed and meet me in the training room in ten minutes, Cruz."

Cruz rubbed his eyes and jumped up to get ready.

Ten minutes later, Saldivar strolled into the dojo, stretching his arms to his sides. He was dressed in athletic gear and tennis shoes.

"Where's Zoey?" Alastair asked, already knowing the answer.

Cruz shrugged in response.

The gym was decked out with bamboo mats. At one end of the wall were training weapons like swords, knives, daggers, and staffs made of wood, rubber, or graphite to minimize the risk of injury. Cruz would be taught the fundamentals of sparring and handling each weapon.

The actual armaments were on the other side of the sparring room. On the opposite wall of the dojo was a punching bag, gloves, and a Wing-Chun wooden post.

Excited and intrigued, Saldivar looked like he'd just been handed the keys to heaven.

Alastair held twenty black belts and aimed to teach Cruz different techniques from around the world. Thanks to his long life—which lasted one hundred and fifty years before he became mortal again—he had perfected most martial arts styles.

"That sword looks so cool," Cruz said, looking around with his mouth agape.

Alastair limped on his cane toward the training wall, nodding. "The Suburito. Good choice."

"A burrito?" Cruz asked, sounding confused. "I like burritos."

"A *Sub-u-rito*," Alastair corrected, picking up the blade. "It's a Japanese sword designed for solo practice and cutting drills. It's heavier than a bokken or katana. Training with this sucker will help you build upper-body strength. By practicing with it, you can gain greater control, which makes transitioning to lighter swords easier."

"Bad—ass," Cruz said, as Alastair directed Saldivar's attention to the training tripod. "What's that thing?"

"That's a Wing-Chun dummy. It's used for practicing Chinese martial arts. Do you see the arms protruding from it?"

Cruz nodded.

Alastair continued, "It has that configuration to enhance your skills and chi. The wooden slats on the *muk yan jong* make it similar to fighting against a human opponent, which allows you to practice absorbing energy into your stance."

"So," Cruz turned toward Alastair with a huge grin. "When do I get to start hitting it?"

"When you're ready," Alastair said evenly.

Cruz's expression fell.

"We're going to work on cardio as much as strength training and martial arts. Everything equals out, or you cause injuries. I've seen you run." Alastair paused, thinking. "How fast is your kilometer?"

Cruz shrugged. "I'm not sure about a kilometer, but I

think I can run a mile in six minutes. I've never actually timed myself. When I played soccer, I ran five miles a day."

"Let's start with two miles and see how that goes. I need your baseline to know how hard I can push you. Buckle up, Saldivar. It's going to be an intense summer."

Cruz hesitated as he looked longingly at the swords and other weaponry again, clearly not wanting to run.

Outside the dojo, Alastair said, "Head toward the Zen garden, then continue through the grounds until you reach the rock wall marking the end of the property line. From there, run until you hit the road leading into town, then return. I will time you so we can see what your pace is."

"Understood," replied Cruz, jogging in place.

"It's, *yes, Sensei* during our training sessions, okay?" Alastair added.

"Yes, Sensei," Cruz echoed as he took off at a breakneck pace, leaving Alastair in awe of the kid's speed.

Alastair wished he could join him. He hadn't realized how much he'd missed it until it was gone.

Drenched in sweat, Cruz panted and slumped down onto the stone walkway outside the dojo, beat. It was 59 degrees Fahrenheit and sunny. Alastair knew Saldivar wasn't playing much soccer these days because his time could be improved.

"Not bad," Alastair noted. "Two miles in fourteen minutes and forty-seven seconds. You could be faster. I'll add hill training to your routine, which will help improve agility and endurance. Grab some water and join me at the dojo in ten."

Cruz returned to the gym ten minutes later, his hair damp and curling at the back.

Alastair wore his karate gi, and his black belt was tied around his waist. "I will get you a gi, but wear your workout gear for now. No shoes on the mats."

"Yes, sir," Cruz said, stepping out of his shoes and leaving them at the door.

"It's sensei, not sir," Alastair corrected.

"Sorry. I knew that." Cruz shook his head, seemingly annoyed at himself. "Yes, Sensei."

The kid had so much to learn. Memories of the challenges of training Corinth flooded Alastair's mind.

Alastair gestured to the center of the room, where the bamboo mats were neatly laid out. As Cruz stepped forward, his expression betrayed his lack of confidence.

"Do you know what katas are?" Alastair asked.

Cruz shook his head. "No, Sensei."

Alastair turned around, realizing he'd left his cane by the open doors. Shoot. He didn't need it anyway, but this would be an adjustment. An intense pain started in his right ankle and went up his thigh. Alastair gritted his teeth and took slow, deep breaths. "*Kata* is a Japanese word that means form," he explained, grimacing. "Katas are intricate movements that involve extensive footwork and breathing techniques. Mastering form and posture are the keys to getting it right." He took a couple of hops toward Cruz, trying to baby his ankle so he could show Saldivar the proper footwork. "Katas help develop muscle memory and generate power from your hips and core instead of relying on your legs and arms." He widened his stance and lowered his center of gravity. After performing several complex movements, Alastair lunged forward—and went down hard.

Dammit. He did need his cane.

Cruz rushed over to help, but Alastair waved him off. How was he supposed to train Cruz when he was in so much pain? *One day at a time, that's how*, he chastised himself.

"I'm okay." Alastair massaged his ankle. "But since I'm already down here, let's try Judo breakfalls first instead of katas."

"What are breakfalls?" Cruz joined Alastair on the ground. He crossed his legs underneath him, making it look easy as he added, "Sensei."

"Falling safely so you don't injure yourself. I'll also teach you how to get to your feet faster by doing kick-ups."

"Falling safely?" Cruz asked, clearly puzzled. "I didn't know there *was* a safe way to fall ..."

Alastair tried to suppress a grin. "The world is full of banana peels. So, avoiding a fall is job one. And knowing how to *take* a fall by landing softly is another."

"That makes sense," Cruz said, looking encouraged.

"You ready?" Alastair asked.

Cruz nodded, and then they got down to business. Alastair alternated between showing Cruz breakfalls, katas, and proper striking techniques. Although Saldivar already knew how to throw a punch, Alastair wanted to ensure he knew how *not* to break his hand in a fight.

The sun lowered as the day drew to a close, casting a wintery, golden light over the Zen garden.

Cruz appeared as exhausted as Alastair felt, but it was a productive fatigue. They'd been at it for over ten hours. The kid had followed Alastair's instructions to the letter and completed every task without ... well, *mostly* without complaint.

"Let's call it a day and grab dinner. We'll start tomorrow morning again," Alastair suggested, the aches and pains overtaking him. He needed ice and pain reliever stat. This was going to be a long summer, indeed.

20

CRUZ

Cruz was in agony. Alastair had worked him over. It felt like every muscle in his body was screaming concurrently. A scalding shower sounded like heaven, but he couldn't move his arms without feeling … *everything*. Sweat had dried on his T-shirt, leaving behind unsightly stains. His forehead was covered in tiny granules of salt. All he could do was lie on his bed and moan.

Eventually, when Cruz finally got motivated enough, he went downstairs into the kitchen. Zoey was seated at the table, engrossed in a biology book, while Corinth was busy cooking something delicious-smelling on the stove. The atmosphere between the two didn't feel as awkward or tense as Cruz anticipated. Zoey and her brother had been having issues lately, but maybe they had sorted things out while Cruz had been training.

He was too tired to ask if Corinth had found the one-eyed Shade yet. Maybe he didn't want to know.

As Cruz gingerly lowered himself into one of the vacant chairs beside Zoey, he let out a soft "Ouch." He allowed his head to rest on the table's surface, sighing deeply.

"That bad?" Zo asked, coughing slightly. Her voice sounded like she was trying to hold back laughter or say, *I told you so, Cruz.*

"That …" He mumbled into the table. "That bad."

"I trained with Alastair—expect to be sore for life," Corinth told him, emphasizing Alastair's physical prowess. "Consider yourself lucky the guy isn't at a hundred percent, Cruz. You'd really be hurting. He's a force to be reckoned with, and he'll get you into shape quickly, regardless."

Cruz's head shot up, his eyes narrowing in disbelief. The thought of Sensei not being *at a hundred percent* was inconceivable. "I'm starting to question my decision to train. It sounded incredible, but now, not so much."

Corinth chuckled. "I can get almost any groceries or takeout anywhere in the world. Remember, we have to pay for this stuff, and it's not cheap. So no caviar from Russia or anything fancy like that." Corinth grabbed a pot and set it on the table. "Tonight's cuisine hails from the USA—sloppy joes." He placed a pack of hamburger buns and a tray of fries on the table.

"Fine by me," Cruz said. Without further thought, he reached into the bag of buns, grabbed one, and started piling the sauce onto it. He pressed it down and devoured it in one breath. Cruz chewed loudly, breathing in satisfaction, then saw Zoey and Corinth staring at him.

"What?" Cruz said between bites. "I'm *starving.*"

"No doubt." Corinth leaned back against the stove.

Clad in black fatigues, a snug T-shirt, and sturdy black boots, Corinth's attire suggested he had just returned from a mission.

Okay, it was too much. He had to know. "Did you find that Shade yet?" Cruz asked between bites, his voice filled with anxiety and hope. "You're back after only a few hours away. Tell me you have good news?"

"I might have word soon," Corinth answered, his tone serious. "Ikari is working on something. I'm about to meet him. In the meantime, if either of you want local cuisine, you can bike or run into town to check it out. Shepherd's pie is good. The city is about ten kilometers from here, in any case. Two bikes are against the back shed near Vinson's place. Also, stay away from Vinson. He doesn't like people. Also, also, I don't need to remind you two to have situational awareness. There's no reason to think any demons will be looking for either of you here—but make sure you have your shield, Cruz, and your ring, Zo, if you go anywhere. And don't be gone long, *capiche*? Rest assured, this is a safe place," Corinth reiterated.

"Sure," Zo chimed in as she helped herself to some food. "So what's around here? I can't even remember the name of this village at the moment."

"Crieff," Corinth reminded her. "We're in Scotland, kiddo."

"I know we're in Scotland," she said, shooting her brother a dirty look.

"There's an art gallery and an ice cream shop in town, perfect for a little adventure. Glen Turret, a path that runs up into the hills, takes you to the Loch Turret Reservoir. It's the starting point for several high-level inclines, a challenge for running and deep meditation," Corinth finished.

Zo's eyes lit up at the mention of the ice cream shop, and the high-level inclines piqued Cruz's interest. Cruz filed all that information away for later. Right now, all he wanted was to eat and sleep.

"Oh, and the weather can be temperamental, so dress accordingly," Corinth added.

"Noted," Zoey said, taking a bite of her sloppy joe. "Rainy days are the best days to stay indoors and read anyway."

Corinth stood behind an unoccupied chair, his hands resting on it. "Zo, it's crucial that you learn at least some self-defense. My blade responded to you and Cruz. I believe we can recreate that effect and, maybe, learn how to control it. Your ring and Cruz's shield are integral components made from the Spear of Destiny. I want you to meet me tomorrow afternoon for your first lesson in the dojo," he said, underlining the importance of their safety.

"Yes." Cruz perked up at hearing that. "*Magic school.*"

Zoey popped a fry into her mouth. "I can get on board with that kind of training. It's like Hogwarts without the funding."

"Don't stay up late. I'll catch you tomorrow," Corinth said, seizing a fry on his way out.

After Cruz had taken a shower, he fell face-first onto his bed. From the corner of his eye, he noticed Zoey had switched to a different book from the one she was last reading. Her finger delicately traced the words as she mouthed something she read. Cruz found it captivating. He wished he had that sort of attention span. Cruz lifted the covers, sucked in a sharp breath, and groaned as he flipped onto his back. Everything hurt, especially his shins and thighs.

"You sound awful," Zoey murmured without taking her eyes off her book.

"I *feel* awful," Cruz agreed with another grunt.

"What have you been doing all day?" she asked, her brown eyes curious as she turned to him.

"Mostly falling," he mumbled, his words trailing off.

Zoey cocked an eyebrow. "Falling?" she prompted. "Tell me more."

Cruz shifted onto his side, taking in the sight of his friend. There was a slight smirk on her lips. Her wheat-colored locks were gathered in a haphazard bun, a streak of yellow highlighter smudged on her chin. "Alastair is showing me the art of falling," he confessed. "I know, sounds odd, but it's true."

"Shouldn't he be teaching you how to *fight?*" Zoey asked as she closed her book.

Cruz shrugged under the blanket. "I'm learning katas—fighting forms. And supposedly, the falls help me recover quickly, get back to my feet, or transition to ground grappling if needed. Honestly, it's all kind of a blur right now." His eyes drooped closed again.

"Do you … like it?" she asked, hesitating. "Do you think you'll get anything from it?"

"Ask me tomorrow," Cruz mumbled, passing out into a well-earned slumber.

21

ZOEY

The morning began with Alastair energetically waking up Cruz, like he'd done the day before. I got out of bed, dressed, and had breakfast an hour and a half after they had already left.

Corinth arranged for me to have a tablet to submit schoolwork online, and Cruz was supposed to do the same. It was anybody's guess if Cruz was submitting any work. Luckily, this was his senior year, so it was more of a coast for him. Junior year was an absolute nightmare. I had to submit a few assignments and had already sent in an exam.

My thoughts were drawn to the enigmatic realm of demons, angels, and Nakir. I pondered his current activities, a puzzle I was eager to solve. There was a persistent feeling that the archangel would stage an unexpected entrance at any given moment.

Stepping outside, I lost myself in an audiobook, leisurely strolling through the grounds. The urge to explore the town tugged at me, but the thought of going alone held me back. I contemplated inviting Cruz to join me if he was free, but I doubted it.

Leo's occasional abode was the guest cottage, half a mile from the main house. I wondered if he and the other angels—Samyaza, Tamiel, and Ikari—were lurking nearby. Intentional or not, the uncertainty of their presence regarding the Ephrem situation piqued my curiosity. A part of me was tempted to snoop and uncover their secrets.

As I ventured outside, I was immediately enveloped by the serene beauty of this place, a sanctuary for angels. The tranquility was alluring. The vast green pastures and open terrain offered a sense of privacy that the bustling city could never provide. Heavy with moisture, the clouds promised rain, yet the air was crisp and damp. I savored the cool, gray weather, grateful for the foresight to pack my backpack and don a hoodie before setting out.

A paved path led to the small guest cottage on the edge of the property, but the sound of children's laughter got my attention before I got to it.

There were kids around here?

Intrigued by the source of the cheerful, high-pitched giggles, I felt compelled to try to find it. The trail led me to a magnificent sight: a picturesque, emerald-green meadow. Delicate white flowers swayed in the breeze, and a group of fluffy sheep grazed, their woolly coats shimmering in the sunlight.

Two children played in the distance. They looked like they were about four and five years old, a boy and a girl. The girl had long, shiny black hair that cascaded down her back, and the boy's black locks fell in soft waves around his shoulders. I wondered who they were, as Corinth hadn't mentioned anyone living nearby. The girl tittered uncontrollably as she tossed her hair back. The boy chased her, his laughter ringing across the valley. They seemed to be siblings. I could feel their bond even from over here.

I smiled—until I thought about Peter. My stomach dropped.

I adjusted the straps on my backpack and tried to focus on what was in front of me. A small stone cottage stood on the other side of the hill. One of the children—the young boy—turned and saw me—a stranger. He froze in his tracks. The little girl was oblivious to his sudden stop and crashed into him with full force, sending the boy sprawling to the ground. As he sat up, he clutched his knee in pain, tears streaming down his cheeks.

Crap.

Feeling responsible, I quickly climbed the rock wall that separated the field from the path and ran toward the children. The girl finally saw me and stared. The boy was still sobbing.

"Hey there!" I greeted them with a friendly wave. "I'm Zo." I pointed at the boy's knee and asked, "Would you like a Band-Aid?" His leg was scraped and had some dirt in the wound, but it didn't seem too serious.

The child nodded, rubbing his nose, not saying anything. I gave the girl a friendly grin. Her brown eyes were stunning, almost golden. She had a warm olive complexion, exactly like the boy's.

"Do y'all live around here?" I took off my backpack, rummaging through it.

They glanced at each other, and the young girl nodded shyly.

The small white kit was at the bottom of my bag. I extracted a pre-packaged antibacterial wipe and said, "Do you like *Pokémon*?" Inching closer to the boy, I rolled up his pant leg. Luckily, he didn't pull away or scream, indicating that he trusted me enough to help him. "I have these cool Band-Aids that look like *Pikachu*."

The boy looked curious, his eyebrows raised, but he remained silent as I pulled out the supplies.

"What's your name?" I asked.

"Jack. My little brother," the girl replied in an all-knowing tone. "And I'm Vienna," she added with a sweet smile.

Jack was less enthusiastic about greeting me. "We aren't supposed to talk to strangers," he said, glaring at his sister.

"Technically, I'm your neighbor," I said, cleaning Jack's wound and applying the bright yellow dressing. "I'm staying with my brother, Corinth, for the summer."

"Then you know Dada," Jack said, tilting his head to the side. His eyes were darker than Vienna's, but they were just as arresting.

"Who is your dada?" I asked slowly, thinking. It knew it wasn't Alastair or Cor.

"*Dada! Dada!*" Vienna squealed, taking off in the direction of the path once again.

I shifted my gaze to watch her run to a man standing atop the hill beyond the rock barrier. There was an uncanny air about him. His towering presence, eerie calm, and unwavering strictness gave off an unsettling vibe.

Jack leaped to his feet and took off after his sister.

I slung my backpack over my shoulder and stood up to study the stranger more intensely. First, he was tall, with thick black hair and an equally impressive beard. He was clad in a plaid flannel shirt paired with dark-wash blue jeans, his expression stoic and unreadable. The severe expression he directed my way sent shivers down my spine, triggering a memory.

He'd been on guard outside my bedroom door during my stay at the cottage after I had sustained an injury in the demon realm.

This was Vinson, the grumpy guy Cor had warned us about.

This guy has kids?

Vinson picked up both children and held them close to his chest.

They buried their faces in his scraggly beard. He laughed, whispering something to Jack, then gently caressed his knee where he'd scraped himself.

Okay, maybe Vinson wasn't so grumpy. Seeing such a burly, intimidating man being so gentle and compassionate surprised me. I would never have guessed that he had a soft side.

Vinson caught my eye as I waved in greeting. He didn't reciprocate the gesture or smile back. He just glowered before turning around and walking in the opposite direction, carrying his children.

"You're welcome," I muttered.

A small part of me wanted to follow Vinson, but then I remembered Cor's warning. So, I shrugged off the thought and continued toward the guest house. Going off on a side quest wasn't a good idea, anyway.

I knocked on the guest cottage's door. Leo, my half brother, opened it. He wore a light blue sweater with black slacks, looking more relaxed than I'd ever seen him. It was nice that Leo had stopped hiding his true form. A thin ring of violet circled his irises, which pulled me in like a magnet. Electricity crackled around the angel, sending tingles through me when I accidentally brushed against his shoulder. With a shudder, I stepped past him into the den.

Leo looked nothing like the other angels, all with golden, bronzed skin like Nakir or black skin like Tamiel and Samyaza. If anyone resembled a vampire, it was Leo, with his raven hair and a pale complexion.

"You look way better than when I last saw you—restored to full health," I said.

"It's great to see you, too, Zo," he said warmly in his British lilt.

The living room was furnished with reclaimed and distressed furniture, all in natural, earthy tones. The pastel and green decor palette highlighted the original white oak beams of the ceiling, creating a pleasant atmosphere.

"Is everything okay?" Leo turned back to me, his forehead creased in concern. "Because I didn't get an alert of trouble." He lifted his wrist to show me his smartwatch.

Keeping tabs.

"No, no," I reassured him quickly. "Everything's okay. It's just that I haven't seen you in a while and wanted to know how you are doing."

"I truly appreciate your concern." Leo leaned back against the chocolate-colored leather sofa, slipping his hands into his pants pockets. Nodding, he said, "Rest assured, I have fully recovered from my previous ailments."

Prim and proper to a T, I thought—so British and angelic at the same time.

"I'm glad to hear it."

I wandered over to the couch and sat, glancing around, hoping to catch a glimpse of one of the other angels or perhaps Nakir. Some of me hoped he was staying with them, but I didn't see any signs of it.

"Something's bothering you," Leo said as he joined me on the sofa. "What can I do to help put your mind at ease?"

The angel's penetrating gaze unsettled me. Even though I knew the truth about the supernatural world, the concept of a higher power was still hard to fathom. How in the world could he read me so well?

Leo gave me a minute to gather my thoughts.

"Can you shed some light on archangels?" I finally asked.

Leo seemed to ponder this. "Given that I am one, I suppose so. What are you curious about in particular?"

"I'm aware that, you know, Nakir, as well as you and Cor, are archangels," I murmured, "but I was just wondering what distinguishes other angels from archangels. How does that work?" The moment I said it, I felt silly. It was a stupid question.

"What I find so interesting is that you mentioned Nakir first." Leo's voice was pointed and curious. "This leads me to believe you're fishing for information about him—not all angels."

I couldn't fathom how he knew, but he did. "Stop delving into my thoughts!" I exclaimed.

Those penetrating eyes seemed to see right through me. I'd forgotten how wise he was.

"I promise I am not reading your mind, but I *can* read everything else," he said without further explanation.

"What is that supposed to mean?" I asked.

"Nonverbal communication speaks louder than

words." Leo shrugged like it wasn't a big deal. "Body language. Intonation. Posture. Eye contact, and you're fidgeting."

"Oh, uh," I glanced down at my intertwined fingers. "Your perception is annoying. I only mentioned Nakir because I saw him in the demon realm." I tried to sound nonchalant.

Add lying to the list of things I was *not* good at.

"Ah," he said, a half smile forming on his lips. "Nakir came to see you recently."

"Well, I guess subterfuge isn't my forte." I picked at a fingernail.

"Nakir can't be trusted. What did he tell you, Zo? You realize the archangel almost killed Cor. He left Alastair a wreck. We must know what his motives are. I need to speak with him as soon as possible. Where is he?"

"I—I don't know," I said quickly. "And I *know* what he did to Alastair and my brother, but he saved my life." My gaze met Leo's. "I'm not sure what else Nakir wanted. I left to come here before I could find out."

Leo appeared to consider that information carefully before continuing. "If you see Nakir again, please let me know, alright? It's crucial. Certain elements are at play here that you may not fully grasp and are too risky—"

"Then why don't you fill me in?" I asked, agitated. "Treat me like an adult, Leo."

"You're *not* an adult. Trust that we will handle all things divine. *You* handle growing up and going to school. Mortal things."

"Do you also handle condescending?" I snapped. "Throughout Scripture, from Genesis to Revelation, God has given humans responsibility. The first human God ever created was charged with working and caring for the Garden of Eden. In that respect, mortals are responsible for the divine too."

"Laying it on thick, aren't we?" Leo sat back, cocking his head, smiling as if he had a secret he wasn't going to share. "You really are like your brother: brilliant and verbose."

"Thank you," I said, pride washing over me at his praise. "Well, you still haven't answered the question about the difference between archangels and angels."

"Heaven is like a court where angels have different ranks and skills, similar to siblings in a family. We communicate through linked bonds. Due to my lower rank and unique birth, I don't have a specific assignment. Archangels defend against rebel angels led by Lucifer and the higher-ranking demons. Cor is a Nephilim whose role is to bind our worlds together, humanity and angels alike. Wielding the Lance comes with a whole other level of responsibility. In some respects, Corinth is more influential than any of us."

"That sounds … taxing," I whispered, awed and overcome. I imagined sitting next to Nakir at the party and drinking. "Wait, does that mean my brother is more powerful than archangels?" It was hard to believe that Corinth, whom I used to kick and call stupid, could be superior to anyone. "I can't relate to Cor the way I used to—he's not who I remembered growing up with. But then I feel bad, because he's trying his best …"

"I never said Corinth was more powerful. He's more *influential*. Influence does not require position. The key to successful leadership is influence, *not* authority. Your brother has had much growing up to do in a short time— just like you." Leo stood, letting his hands slip out of his pockets as he laced his fingers. "Your brother has been trying to protect you from *our* problems, but at the same time, he loves you deeply and wants you to be a part of it all."

I thought about that for a while and took it in.

Maybe I hadn't given Cor enough credit for keeping our family and planet safe.

"So … do you have more information on Ephrem or the *other* Shade's whereabouts? The one that tried to attack Cruz?"

"I understand how important this is to you," Leo began, "but as far as we know, Ephrem is still trapped in hell. We are doing everything we can, but the information about it remains elusive. Ikari, Tamiel, and Samyaza are scouring the planet for clues that could lead us to it. Rest assured, I will inform you of any developments as soon as they come to light. You have my word on that."

I appreciated Leo's honesty. It surpassed the level of transparency I'd been shown for a long time.

"Things are improving with Cor … but a small part of me still harbors resentment for him leaving after Pete's passing. Am I wrong to feel this way? Is it selfish? The highlight of my childhood was trying to make my brothers laugh so hard food came out of their noses."

Leo shook his head gently. "Wanting to spend more time with your loved ones is never selfish. Families are like branches on a tree. They grow in different directions, yet their roots remain as one. Should you ever need to talk, I'm here for you."

I nodded, unable to speak.

After a beat of silence, I said, "Why aren't you searching for the demon with everyone else? Wait. Are you on babysitting duty?"

Leo met my unwavering gaze.

"Cor asked you to keep an eye on us, didn't he?" I pressed.

"One of us has to be here at all times." He crouched before me, placing his hand over mine, which I had fisted in my lap. "We're called guardians for a reason."

"Is there ... anything I can do to help? I'm good at research and know my way around a library."

"Yes." Leo immediately nodded. "You can train with Cruz. Learn to defend yourself. This needs to be your top priority."

A sinking feeling hit me. "That's what I was afraid you were going to say."

Leo regarded me with those stupidly vibrant lilac irises again. "I could lie and tell you everything is fine."

"No." I shook my head. "I wanted to be treated like an adult."

"Good," he said, nodding in approval. "Sitting around doing nothing can make you doubt yourself. So, if you want to overcome your fears—go out and do something about it."

22

ALASTAIR

The dimly lit dojo smelled of sweat. Cruz lay on a bamboo mat, his forehead damp as he struggled to catch his breath. The kid could not master the rising handspring, which would transition him from prone to landing on his feet. Cruz possessed a remarkable ability to work and an unwavering focus that would help him make significant strides quickly. Skill, hard work, and determination were a huge asset. But, despite these considerable strengths, Cruz's greatest weakness was his fiery temper. It was almost crippling. He had too much fight in him and couldn't seem to control his emotions or body.

Alastair carefully stroked his chin, his eyes narrowing in thought. "Well, Saldivar, I think it's time to take a break. You've been at this all day and hit a wall. Let's call it quits for now."

The sky outside had turned a menacing shade of grayish-green. Raindrops began tapping against the tin roof. The sound grew louder, and Alastair's skin prickled. He felt the storm brewing in his bones and knew it would be nasty.

"I am *not* calling it quits until I get this right," Cruz hissed between his teeth, angry. Saldivar's face was mottled red from exertion. His hair stuck up on both sides of his head, giving the impression of horns. Despite completing a five-kilometer run this morning and spending the entire day on the mats, his pupil still had some gas left in the tank. It was time to test that dark, burning energy and see how far Alastair could push him.

"Place your palms flat on the ground next to your ears, as if you're about to lift up and do a backbend. Point your fingers toward your shoulders. Roll your body back, resting your weight solely on your hands. Then kick up high, but make sure your legs are straight up, not at an angle—like doing a backward push-up—and land in a squatting position. Got it?"

Cruz released an exasperated sigh and grumbled, "Yes, Sensei."

Alastair stood tall, adopting a boxer's stance with fists poised for action. "Focus, take a deep breath and trust your instincts. When you're back on your feet, confront your opponent head-on and go for the point."

On the mat, Saldivar lay still. He took in a long breath and shut his eyes, as if in deep concentration. With a sudden and powerful motion, he lifted his hands high over his head, launched himself into the air, and smoothly executed a flip—landing with incredible grace and agility. However, Cruz's momentum kept going, making him stumble and lunge forward as he threw a wild punch.

Alastair swiftly intercepted Cruz's oncoming fist and then he threw Cruz over his hip, causing the kid to land on the ground with a thud. A jolt of pain went through Alastair, and he struggled to maintain his balance. Despite making progress daily, the strain of Alastair pushing himself to the limit was evident. After steadying himself, he panted and remarked, "Sloppy."

Was he talking more about himself or Cruz?

"*I did it,*" Cruz gasped, his voice a mixture of exhaustion and pride. Still, a wounded expression came over his face as he massaged the back of his head.

"Well done, Saldivar. Unfortunately, you did not complete your mission. You failed to get the point by hitting me. For that, give me fifty push-ups."

As Alastair hobbled toward the open doors to retrieve his cane, Saldivar cursed furiously in Spanish.

Alastair responded in Spanish. "Make it seventy-five."

23

CRUZ

Cruz had just completed his push-ups and was stretching his aching muscles when Zoey rushed into the gym, drenched from head to toe. The rain pounded the roof so hard that he could hardly hear anything besides his labored breathing.

He had achieved a kick-up. It was a small but meaningful accomplishment. Alastair's look of pride afterward was what mattered most. Cruz, leaning back on his hands, his legs stretched before him, gazed wordlessly at Zoey. He was too exhausted to converse. Fatigue permeated his entire being.

A sizable puddle was already forming at Zoey's feet, a testament to the storm's severity. She threw back her hood, removed her backpack, and plucked the headphones from her ears.

"Hey," she greeted him with a nod. "Is there a towel around here?"

Cruz nodded to the back corner of the room. "Over

there. But take off your shoes before coming onto the mats, like I've been told repeatedly by Sensei Alastair."

"Sensei?" Zoey smiled as she slipped out of her Converse, grabbed a towel, and came to plop down next to Cruz. Her socks left a wet trail behind her.

"So ... serious," she joked, slapping a wet hand on his shoulder.

"Your hands are *freezing*," Cruz muttered. "And yeah, Alastair has me calling him Sensei when we're training. I've never done martial arts before, but I've been told that's the custom. He's going to get me a karate gi and everything."

"That's cool." She gave him a once-over as she tried to towel-dry her hair. "How's training going?"

Cruz grunted, hoping to convey how tired he was. He inched closer to her. It was chilly outside, and she was shivering slightly.

Zoey hugged her knees to her chest, gazing out the open doors. She seemed to enjoy the steady drumming of the rain. "It's so peaceful here."

"Doth my ears protest?" he asked, leaning into her shoulder. "Are you actually enjoying yourself?"

"Maybe a little." They listened to the distant thunder in peace awhile before Zoey said, "I talked to Leo. He admitted that they're keeping a close watch on us. When I asked about Ephrem, he said there were no updates. I'm kind of skeptical about that, though. What if the demon got free, and they're lying to us?"

Cruz turned his head sharply so he could see her face. She had a slight crease above her nose. He pictured Zoey's small form imprisoned in that demon realm, and a surge of heat spread through his body. Ephrem was an A-hole. "I hope that guy is rotting down there. The last thing we need is that jerk on the loose."

"I know." Zoey rubbed her chin against her knees.

Cruz felt antsy and uneasy just sitting around, waiting for the next attack. He knew he needed to be proactive. But besides working out, how was he supposed to do that? Zoey was actively seeking information, so Cruz made a mental note to follow her example.

"I need to call my mom," he finally said. "She's alone."

"Trust me," Zoey replied, "your mom is *not* alone. Didn't you tell me she's a social butterfly now? She's out having the time of her life—I mean, the *safe* time of her life. Cor meant what he said. He'll protect her."

"Thanks for saying so," Cruz murmured, feeling slightly better.

Thunder rumbled outside, and they sat silently again, listening to the storm rage on.

"What's driving you so hard?" Zoey whispered.

Cruz took a moment to gather his thoughts. "Everything feels so chaotic. I guess working out is me trying to gain some form of control. When my mother was dying, I had *no* control whatsoever ... it *sucked*."

Zoey smoothed down her hair and dropped the towel. She paused, then said, "Can you show me how to do a push-up?"

"You—you want to do a *push-up*?" Cruz cocked his head to the side. "I thought you *hated* working out?"

"I guess I want to take back control, too," she said resolutely. "That and Leo gave me a pretty convincing speech."

Cruz flipped onto his stomach, his muscles stiff and sore. "Place your hands wider than your shoulders. Keep your arms and legs straight, like getting into a plank position, then lower your body until your chest almost touches the ground. Pause for a moment, then push yourself back up. Repeat this process until your arms fall off … like mine."

"That sounds … awful," Zoey muttered, mirroring Cruz. She got into a plank, attempted to push herself down, and groaned loudly. "Yup. It's official. I hate exercise."

Cruz snorted his agreement.

Zoey's body started shaking within seconds, and her head and arms drooped down as she tried to raise herself back up. She gasped, "This—hurts."

"Welcome to my world," Cruz said with a sigh. "Make sure to keep your butt down and your back straight."

Zoey's arms buckled, and she fell flat on her face. "I only fell because I'm soaked, and the mat is slippery."

"Sure," Cruz said, drawing out the word and flashing her a big grin. "Okay, maybe try inclined push-ups until you can graduate to a full push-up." He shot to his feet, reinvigorated. He headed to the opposite side of the dojo, where the workout equipment was lined up. Cruz grabbed a couple of pallets, returned, and stacked them together. "You want to stay on your knees and then use the pallets to push off of while keeping your abs tight. Breathe through each rep."

"I think I can do that." Zoey exhaled as she took Cruz's place and splayed her palms on the makeshift bench.

"Try doing ten reps," Cruz suggested.

To Cruz's surprise, Zoey made another attempt at a push-up and managed to do one with relative ease using the incline.

"You're stronger than you look," Cruz told her, meaning it.

"Okay, ten. I can do that," she said, sounding more

confident. Repeating the process, she exhaled through her nose and counted as she did each one. When she completed the tenth rep, she collapsed, gasping.

"Good job! Just remember to exhale through your mouth," Cruz advised. "Breathe through the pain."

"What about running?" Zoey said slowly as she tried to recover. "Can you teach me how to run a 5K?"

"Running?" Cruz asked, flabbergasted. "You want to run, too? Who are you, and what have you done with Zo?"

"Very funny," she said.

Cruz was thrilled beyond words. Having a workout partner was always beneficial, but having Zoey as his workout partner was the cherry on top. They could keep each other motivated and accountable.

"I'd say let's start right now, but my legs no longer work," Cruz mumbled. "I've been trying to do this backward handspring all day. I finally did it, but now I can't move."

"That sounds way too ... bendy," Zoey teased.

Cruz let out a small squeak as she got to her feet and stuck her hand out. "How about tomorrow morning?"

He took her hand, but the floor was slick, and his legs were Jell-O. He lost his footing, toppling backward and taking her with him. Air left his lungs as she landed heavily on his chest, her wet hair smacking him in the face.

Cruz let out a throaty "*oomph*" as Zoey planted her hands on either side of his head. Warm breath tickled his cheek. He felt a tingling sensation, as if there was an electric charge under his skin where her body touched his.

Her eyes looked like tiny sunbursts. He cleared his throat.

"This is why I don't workout," Zoey gasped

awkwardly. She flipped off him and landed on her back with a *thud*, and they laughed until they made themselves sick.

24

ZOEY

Biscuit sat on the windowsill, flicking his tail while I bent down to tie my shoelaces. There was a twinge of resentment in those piercing green eyes, as if he was thinking, *Why on earth are we up so early?*

I glanced at my watch and realized it was the crack of dawn. The biting cold outside had seeped into my core, despite being bundled up. All I could think about was retreating back under the warm covers.

"Why am I doing this again?" I asked Biscuit.

Because your life depends on it, came the persistent reply.

Ugh.

Treat it like schoolwork.

Cruz emerged from the bathroom with a spring in his step, exuding an aroma of mint and deodorant. He was already in his athletic gear, ready to run, with—and this can't be overstated—*way* too much enthusiasm.

I frowned. "Why are you so ... peppy?"

His dark brown eyes studied me for a moment before he grinned. "I guess I'm glad for the company."

"You need to take that attitude down a notch," I muttered, yawning.

Cruz only had three sets of sweats that he rotated between. It was evident he needed to do laundry soon. The corner of our room, where he had been thoughtlessly tossing his clothes, was starting to emit an unpleasant odor.

"Are you ready?" he asked.

I zipped up my hoodie and put on a baseball cap. *"No."*

A gust of frigid air slapped me as we stepped outside. *Why do people do this?* The darkness was almost absolute, with only a half-moon casting an eerie glow, creating long shadows that seemed to taunt me. Irritation bubbled up. Being awake felt like a cruel joke. I rubbed my hands together, hoping to generate some warmth, but to no avail.

The path was paved and decorated with small solar lights, a little trail of sparkling stars leading into the distance.

"Are we not going to eat first?" I asked.

"Unless you want to throw it up, better not. Take this." Cruz handed me a banana. "It has potassium, which prevents lactic acid buildup. I also like a protein bar beforehand, but since we don't have any …"

"Banana it is." I took it, grateful for anything, and ate as we walked.

It was too early for small talk, and thankfully, we both stayed silent until we reached the dojo. Cruz pushed open the doors and turned on the lights. He bent down to take off his shoes, neatly setting them aside before striding purposefully to the center of the room.

"We'll start with some stretching, then we can go for a short run to gauge your pace and endurance. I suggest we alternate between running and walking to help increase your stamina." He flopped onto one of the mats, stretching his legs. His fingertips brushed against his toes as he reached forward, taking a deep breath.

I settled a few feet away from him. My muscles were tight, stubbornly resisting any attempt at slackening. The backs of my knees throbbed, and every inch of my body felt sore and tender. I *hated* this, and I hadn't even started.

"Where's Alastair?" I was surprised that he wasn't here to greet us. I expected him to have us up and at '*em*.

"Oh, trust me, if I'm not here at a set time, he tortures me with push-ups. Anytime I mess up, push-ups. Breathe wrong, push-ups. If I don't call him Sensei, push-ups. He's been meeting me after I finish my runs, though. Since his injury, I think he struggles to get going in the morning …" Cruz's voice trailed off. "Maybe he's pushing himself too hard. The pain is so evident on his face."

I felt sad as I thought about Alastair using a cane. He'd saved our lives, and rehabbing his injuries seemed to be his life now. It wasn't fair—but at least he was alive.

After stretching a bit longer, I put my shoes back on, and Cruz did the same.

"So, if we take this path, we'll end up back at the cottage. From there, we can head toward town. I've been running this route for a while—it's nearly three miles. I haven't ventured beyond the road yet. Here's the plan: we'll run for two minutes and then take a three-minute break, and we'll keep repeating this pattern until we reach the one-mile mark. Do you think you can manage?"

I nodded as a sudden cold breeze made me shiver. I pulled my hoodie over my cap, hoping to stay warm. "Won't the angels track us down if we go too far?"

I hoped he'd say yes, so we could head back inside.

Cruz lifted his sleeve, showing me his smartwatch. "They *are* tracking us. As long as we have these on, I don't think they're too worried about *where* we go—angels can portal to us instantly if they see we're in danger. Our watches are our lifelines. They keep track of our activity, pulse, time, and location." Cruz deftly manipulated the digital display and showed me the options.

"Let's just get this over with," I grumbled.

As Cruz tapped the timer on his display, a wisp of white breath floated from his lips. With that, he began to jog lightly. I trailed behind, already lamenting my spontaneous choice to run. My muscles felt rigid and out of sync.

After about thirty seconds, he noticed me struggling and said, "Keep your arms loose and relaxed, and breathe through your mouth. Get into a rhythm and focus on that. You have to be comfortable with the uncomfortable."

"*Never*," I gasped. *Rhythm?* If by rhythm, he meant me making weird sounds through my nostrils like a buzzsaw ... sure, I'd focus on that.

I slogged behind Cruz. My breaths grew increasingly shorter and louder. Despite moving forward, our pace was so sluggish that I might as well have been walking. Before long, every breath felt like an inferno in my lungs.

"How ... much ... longer?" I gasped.

"Forty-five more seconds," Cruz encouraged.

"Seriously?"

"Good job, Zo," Cruz said. "You've got this."

His arms hung limply at his sides while mine felt increasingly tense.

"I ... hate ... you and ... I'm ... dying." I clenched my fists and hunched over.

Cruz whirled around, sprinting backward, much to my frustration.

My chest was heaving, and I struggled to catch my breath. I felt like an astronaut stranded on Mars without a helmet. But even though I was tempted to throw in the towel, I was determined not to give up. I was beyond annoyed.

"Hang in there—not much longer." I barely heard him add, "Easy does it."

Cruz's voice seemed to echo from a distance. As the timer buzzed, he started walking, unfazed. "Nice work!" he cheered, not even out of breath.

Irritated, I slowed beside him. "Please ... tell me we've gone at least one mile."

Cruz gave me a sly, amused look as he allowed me to catch my breath. "Close," he said with a grin. "So, we'll take a three-minute walk and start running again. Sound good to you?"

I nodded, but my confidence wavered.

Forty-five minutes later, I was completely drained.

My lungs were on fire, and my legs had turned to lead.

The banana I had eaten earlier churned in my stomach.

Despite this, we had only managed to go three miles. All I could see in front of me were Cruz's bright, fancy running shoes, while my off-brand sneakers gave me blisters.

I took a moment to stop and admire our surroundings. Wow, it was stunning. The biting cold of the early morning had dissipated, giving way to a milder temperature. The sun had crept over the forested hills, casting its warm glow across the landscape. A profound and vibrant green, a glimmering gold, and a poppy pink danced across the sky. It was as if we'd stepped into a painting.

"Whoa." Cruz returned to me, putting a warm yet tentative hand on my back for a second as he gazed across the valley. "That sky sure is ... something else."

"Seeing that sunrise might be worth some of this pain ... *some* ..." The stitch in my side was unforgiving.

My smile disappeared instantly when Cruz asked, "Do you want to keep going or turn around?"

"Are you kidding me?" I felt my mouth go dry as if filled with cotton. "*Turn around.*"

25

ALASTAIR

When Alastair arrived at the dojo, he was pleasantly surprised to find Zoey sparring with Cruz. *Sparring?* He also learned that she'd gone for a run, and that after, Cruz showed her the katas and breakfalls he had been doing. This news had been most welcome, considering Alastair thought he would have to try something much more drastic to get her to work out. Idly, he wondered what had convinced her otherwise. It didn't matter. All that mattered was that Zoey was here now—even if she looked exhausted already.

Could she handle the intensity of the workouts to come?

Not everyone possessed the willpower to endure lengthy training sessions. Alastair had seen many people quit due to a lack of mental fortitude. Although, almost dying at the hands of a deranged demon was a good inspiration, he supposed.

After a brief lunch, they returned to the mats to find

Corinth waiting for them. He was wearing relaxed-fitting workout gear and was barefoot.

Time for Magic Class.

Good, Alastair thought, *a much-needed break.* He was making a speedier recovery thanks to Alastair's consistent daily movement, although his body felt the effects.

After two hours, it became clear that Corinth could not effectively demonstrate how to channel angelic grace through their amulets.

They stood in the center of the dojo, with smooth mats underfoot that provided a soft, stable surface. With a hopeful expression, Corinth turned to Zoey, who stood opposite him. "Do you sense anything at all? Perhaps the faintest glimmer of energy?"

Zoey wound her fingers around the red gem on her ring and shook her head. "Nothing," she muttered, unhappy with her lack of progress. "I expected this to be much easier—and way more fun."

"What about you, Cruz?" Corinth asked, turning to him.

Cruz held the shield close to his chest, his eyes tightly shut. With a furrowed brow, he concentrated intently. After a moment, he opened his eyes and shook his head. "Nope."

Corinth wiped his mouth. "It appears to activate only during the direst of circumstances—"

"When demons or Shades are around," Cruz piped up, sounding tired and bored.

Alastair considered ending their evening's session, as they had already accomplished a lot. Additionally, he knew that both of them had to make calls home, *and* finish their homework, on top of everything else they had been doing.

Corinth asked with a tinge of frustration, "Do you have any suggestions, Al?"

Alastair sat in deep meditation just outside the dojo's entrance, legs crossed. "Tell me, and I forget. Teach me, and I may remember. *Involve* me, and I *learn.*"

Corinth raised a hand as if he had come to an epiphany. "You're brilliant, Al." He turned back to Zoey and Cruz. "The moment you used the shield, it turned into a dagger, like mine—that feeling. What was it like when it happened?" he asked, glancing between Cruz and Zoey.

Zoey was the first to speak up. "Like a burst of static, but much stronger."

"Yeah, what she said." Cruz nodded. "I felt it in my stomach, even my muscles."

"Maybe you just need a little boost." Corinth grinned back at them.

"Like a car battery?" Cruz asked slowly. "Cool."

"Sort of." Corinth held out his hand, and suddenly, a brilliant flash of blinding light filled the air. A magnificent holy blade materialized in his grip as the light faded. Its razor-sharp edge emanated blue sparks that cracked across the hilt, causing everyone to jump back in awe.

Damn, how Alastair missed that sensation. He slowly returned to his feet and entered the dojo, using his cane. The energy in the small space was spine-tingling, and the hairs on his neck rose. It was probably wise that Alastair no longer yielded that sort of power. His heart was racing.

"Can you feel that?" Corinth asked, glancing between Cruz and Zoey. "It's called angel grace."

"How can you *not* feel it?" Cruz asked, his mouth hanging open.

"Theoretically, if you can harness it, you transfer it into

you—and then turn the energy into your desired weapon of choice. You tap into it when the charge intensifies. Once you've got the grace, focus on your shield, Cruz. And Zoey, focus on your ring."

"But how do we *tap* into the energy if we don't possess it in the first place?" Zoey asked, disgruntled.

Alastair knew Zoey was used to catching on quickly when learning new skills. He could see that all of this was irritating her.

"Exactly where the boost comes into play." Corinth swept into the center of the room like Archimedes. "Step back," he said, as he placed the blade in his open palm.

Alastair knew that the light show Corinth put on was nothing short of explosive. So he shuffled closer, leaving his cane behind to grab hold of Zoey and Cruz. He forced them to step back right as blue flames burst from Corinth's body, emitting a surge of energy that engulfed him.

"*Holy hell,*" he heard Cruz exclaim as they all briefly threw hands over the eyes.

Alastair couldn't tear his gaze away from the scene before him. The room was filled with a mesmerizing, fragmented light that danced and flickered. Everyone stood in awe as wings of shimmering gold erupted from Corinth's back, showering the air with sparkling silver light.

"Don't worry—I won't hurt you. I promise." Corinth motioned for Zoey and Cruz to approach. "Place your hands on the hilt with me."

Zoey exchanged a hesitant glance with Cruz, before cautiously stepping forward. She looked slightly frightened, but also entranced.

Cruz, on the other hand, rushed headlong toward the blade, beating her to it.

Before he could react, an all-encompassing peace and healing overtook Alastair—so significant that the pain in his thigh and ankle vanished. He was accustomed to the constant ache, and being free of it felt extraordinary and strange. Sweet relief washed over him. He looked at Corinth, who was grimacing.

He'd taken on the pain for Alastair.

Dammit, Corinth.

As they passed through the crackling energy barrier, Zoey and Cruz emerged on the other side and gazed at the heavenly sight before them. It left them in a dreamlike stupor; they closed their eyes. When they reached out to touch the blade's hilt, sparks erupted from their fingertips.

"Now, think about your relic and what you want them to do," Corinth directed. "You must have the right intention—strong, stable, and immediate moral beliefs. It won't work if you only want to show off. Cruz, I'm talking to you, buddy."

"I'm trying," Cruz grumbled, clasping the shield between his fingers. "I *want* to do the right thing," he whispered.

Suddenly, the charm in his grasp transformed into a full-sized, pure gold shield—heavy, sturdy, radiant. He almost toppled over from the abrupt weight. Cruz blinked in disbelief. His right arm was slung through a leather buckle at the back, holding the handle for support. He stood, unsure what to do next.

Alastair's mouth dropped open.

The shield looked like it had been made only for Saldivar.

But then, Cruz's concentration must have slipped. The armor evaporated into a ball of flames and shrank back down to the original charm again. Simultaneously, Zoey's lips moved. The ring she held underwent a breathtaking transformation. It turned into a magnificent gleaming bow, with a ruby-colored arrow nocked and ready for release. Her eyes widened, so taken aback that she dropped the bow.

The arrow clattered to the mats at her bare feet. "*Whoa*," she whispered, as the celestial weapon vanished in flames, leaving behind her ruby ring.

Corinth lifted his head as he slowly let the power fade. His holy blade and wings disappeared in an ethereal light. Sparks shot around his back like fireworks, raining down and evaporating.

A small part of Alastair wished Taylor wouldn't let the energy go.

It was a selfish moment, but he couldn't help but revel in the freedom from pain—his first relief in months. A gentle breeze blew in behind him, ruffling his hair as the pressure in the room returned to normal.

Alastair, pulse racing and his body leaning heavily on his cane, felt the familiar throbbing return to his limbs. "On that remarkable note, let's call it a day," he declared, his voice tinged with exhaustion and pain. He began to limp toward the open doors, but then turned back. "Cor— whatever that was … it was truly … divine. Thank you for that moment of peace. Zoey and Cruz, we'll reconvene in the morning. Make sure to get some rest and ice those muscles."

With that, he left the room, leaving the others to their thoughts and the remnants of their magic.

In the kitchen, Alastair stood by the stove, listening to the soft hiss of boiling water. He gently stirred the noodles, mesmerized by the hypnotic dance of rising steam. His thoughts drifted to the remarkable skill displayed by Cruz and Zoey—their extraordinary capability to control angel grace, a power that could manipulate matter. He knew how harnessing such a supernatural power felt. If Alastair possessed it now, he would be completely injury-free.

He shook his head, trying to banish those thoughts from his head. *Better adjust*, he chided himself. *That's all there is to it.*

It had been far too long since Alastair had indulged in the pleasure of cooking.

Biscuit was at his side, looking up at him with pleading eyes, hoping for a scrap. Alastair tore a small piece of French bread and dropped it on the floor. Biscuit purred before snatching it and running away.

"Spoiled cat!" he yelled after it.

Sitting at the kitchen table, Cruz had duct-taped two bags of ice to each of his hips, while Zoey had an icepack on her elbow and another on her calf. They were whispering to each other, their faces full of excitement as they recounted the unforgettable events of their lesson.

Alastair was glad to see their cheerful faces. However, the calmness on the demon front made him anxious. He suspected they were scheming something sinister, or had already set something in motion.

Another troubling thought: Corinth had yet to locate the Shade that had attacked Cruz.

Alastair's mind wandered to the demon Nakir had warned them about. Despite Ikari and Tamiel's week-long search, there was no news of its whereabouts. Alastair hoped the lack of news was good, but the uncertainty made him uneasy. Corinth had been in and out, searching for that one-eyed Shade. Maybe it was Alastair's lack of action that set his nerves on edge.

Zoey was at Alastair's side, disregarding her aching muscles to look down into the boiling pot. "Is it ready? I'm dying."

Alastair handed her the spoon he'd been stirring with. "Try it."

Zoey dipped the utensil into the marinara, blew on it delicately, and took a small sip.

A look of pure pleasure spread across her face. "That is the best pasta sauce I've ever had in my entire life. Corinth ain't got nothin' on you, Mr. Magician," she said in her Texas drawl.

"I think you're just hungry." Alastair chuckled at the compliment. "But I'll take it. Food's almost done. I made meatballs and garlic bread."

Cruz rubbed his stomach, sitting back. "I *love, love, love* garlic bread."

"Me too," Zoey agreed as she returned to her seat beside Cruz. "Where did you learn to cook, Alastair?"

"All over—but my favorite place was at *Le Cordon Bleu*," Alastair told her. "I didn't stay long, though."

Watching Alastair pull the meatballs from the oven, Cruz licked his lips. "How long ago was that?"

"1948." Alastair placed the hot trays on the table. "I cooked with Julia Child when she was there—taught her a thing or two, I'm proud to say."

"*1948*? Julia Child?" Cruz looked stupidly at him. "That was—" he did the math on his fingers. "Like forty-five years ago. You're only twenty-eight, right? I keep forgetting you used to be a vampire."

Alastair ignored the vampire remark. He shook his head, flabbergasted that Saldivar hadn't heard of the famous chef. "That hurts my soul. *Un bon repas commence par la faim.* I can't believe you don't know who Julia Child is."

"Wasn't she one of the first-ever TV cooks?" Zoey asked. "And what does that thing you said in French mean? It sounds"—she cleared her throat—"beautiful."

Alastair served up the noodles and sauce, one plate at a time. "Julia used to say that you don't have to create fancy or complicated dishes to make good food—just fresh ingredients. Those words always stuck with me."

Zoey headed straight for the spaghetti. Cruz skewered three meatballs, placed them on his pasta, then seized some garlic bread. He devoured one immediately, before using the others to sop up the sauce on his plate.

"Oh—my—gosh, this bread … is phenomenal!" Cruz exclaimed, dunking another piece in the sauce.

Alastair's face lit up with a smile. "I use fresh dough."

Cruz barely glanced up from his dish. "Why haven't you been cooking *every* day?" he asked, wiping a generous amount of sauce off his chin with the back of his hand.

Alastair couldn't hide the regret in his voice. "Cooking is my sanctuary and brings me immense joy, but maintaining a marriage, doing rehab, and training the both of you … well, it doesn't leave me with extra time left over."

"I guess I'll need to become skilled faster, Sensei," Cruz said as he stuffed another piece of bread into his mouth.

26

LEO

Leo had stayed by his mother's side, a wicked archangel, for centuries—all to keep his little brother, Corinth, safe. In the past, distinguishing between good and evil had seemed much more straightforward.

That's why he knew something was highly off-putting about the Shade standing before him.

Ari was not entirely a *Shade,* but a half of one ... or half of ... something. It was as if Ari hadn't completely lost all his humanity. Gold veins traced lines up and down his arms and the sides of his neck. Other Shades he'd seen had silver lines. *Strange.* Of course, Ari still had that shiny, onyx-colored skin, and bald head like the rest.

Leo stood at full height, much taller than Ari, his arms crossed. He glowered at the Shade, formerly known as Peter Taylor. Demons and Shades were immoral, wicked, vile creatures that couldn't be trusted.

But he was forced to trust this one now.

The desert was dotted with towering saguaros, prickly cacti, and red rock cliffs. There were no traces of human settlements for miles around. This could be a trap. This *was* a trap.

"You wanted to meet alone in the *Sonoran Desert* for a reason," Leo said. "I don't mind the heat, but make this quick, Pete."

"Call me Ari." The Shade's voice was a low hiss. "I used to like deserts—minimal population. Striking colors. Solitude. Hiking. It takes a special person to survive and thrive in such a place. Nature picks everything clean here."

"Okay, *Ari*. You asked for this meeting." Leo spread his arms wide, glancing around at the dry landscape. "Stop stalling."

"I know where the demon is, the one who escaped." A slow, cruel smile spread across the Shade's face.

Leo perked up at hearing that. "Where is it?"

"It?" Ari laughed derisively. "You act like *he* doesn't resemble a human in every possible way. We all sin, Leo. Lucifer was once a beautiful angel, you know." He inclined his head, gesturing with his chin toward the area behind Leo. "Oh, and *it* is right behind you."

The hairs on Leo's neck stood on end, warning him of the danger a moment too late.

He spun around.

A demon stood about thirty yards behind Leo at the cliff's edge. The earth was charred under his feet, forming a large crater. Although it looked like a man in his early twenties, Leo knew it was anything but. The greater demon had dark, wavy blonde hair, freckles, blue eyes, and light skin. Precisely what the kid next door might look like— pleasant, respectable, and likable. Except for the blood-red suit and wing-tipped shoes it wore, and the sword with a lion's head handle in its grip.

Leo sucked in a sharp breath.

He knew this weapon was meant only for the strongest angels—an original archangel. The last time he'd seen something this powerful was the Holy Lance.

Calling forth lightning, power surged through Leo's body as he harnessed his grace. He raised his arm to unleash a devastating blast that would obliterate the creature before him.

But a sudden, sharp pain pierced his back. Leo faltered, losing his balance. In ridiculous slowness, he turned around to see Ari holding something sharp and pointy in his hands.

The smile on Ari's face vanished.

Leo's legs buckled, and he dropped to the dusty earth. The energy that had previously surged through him dissolved, leaving only a faint crackling across his skin.

Ari crouched down before him, resting an elbow on one knee, relishing the moment. His fingers were curled around something—a horn. Its surface was sleek and black, a conspicuous gold crack running down the center. A tiny droplet of Leo's blood was still on the pointed end. *Impossible.*

"You stabbed me ..." Leo said incredulously.

"Duh." Ari's voice sounded muffled and far away. He lifted the ancient object to show him. "A gift from my new best friend, Rimmon, over there." He clicked his tongue. "You sure don't learn your lesson. *Never* turn your back on a Shade."

Corinth's brother sure could be an ass.

Rimmon closed in on Leo. The tips of its jet-black shoes were dusted with crimson as it loomed over him. An immense cold emanated from its body as it pointed the tip of the sword at Leo's jugular.

"This horn, from Lucifer, kills angels. Pierces tough angel skin like nothing else." Ari laughed maliciously. He turned to look up at Rimmon. "Another one bites the dust, huh?"

27

NAKIR

Upon returning to Texas after visiting Gabriel Stanton, Nakir was surprised to find that Zoey Taylor was nowhere to be found. Although her family members were still at their home, she was absent from school and from her house. He suspected that Corinth and the other angels had taken her to Scotland. Nakir had accessed Alastair's memories to get the safe house's location.

After ensuring Zoey was well-protected, Nakir made it a top priority to recover his armor and sword. These weapons were far too dangerous to be entrusted to anyone else. He would not have lost them in the first place, had he not used all his energy saving Alastair Iszler.

Despite the challenge of adjusting to his weakened powers on Earth, Nakir's sword, *Stronghold*, remained a beacon of power. Forged from the sun's rays and blessed with grace, this blade was revered by all supernatural beings, angels and demons alike, for its unmatched strength. It could cleave through anything, and its pommel was a testament to its majesty, sculpted in the likeness of a white lion's head.

Nakir had been gifted this sword with a single purpose: to eradicate evil.

He lay in a lounge chair by a pool, on the rooftop of a towering apartment building in downtown Fort Worth, Texas. It was late, so the pool was closed to visitors. Nakir had fried the security cameras the moment he'd popped in. The chatter of the city below was background noise—the sounds of people bustling about, cars whizzing by, the occasional blaring of a horn. He appeared only to be napping, but his mind was far from resting.

The melding of minds was a perilous and intricate experience. It was a window into the past, present, and future, through the eyes of demons. Nakir's *Sight* was a treasure trove of knowledge and insight, a gift he shared with Alastair and the world around him. Yet, he had refrained from attempting this, fully aware of the grave dangers it posed. To delve into a greater demon's mind was to open his own mind to that evil. He had to tread with utmost caution.

With a deliberate effort, Nakir blocked out all surrounding noise and honed in on his controlled, rhythmic breath.

Gradually, everything else dissipated, plunging him into a profound and encompassing tranquility. The darkness behind his closed eyelids transformed into a breathtaking golden twilight. When he entered his Halo, he experienced a profound change—one that transcended the limits of existence. Each twinkling point in that shimmering expanse held a different memory, mood, or awareness. The overwhelming deluge of information flooded Nakir's senses. He caught a minuscule yet distinct red speck; it flickered into existence as he gazed into his mind's horizon. Unlike the golden glimmer, this red point lay beyond the scope of his Halo. Nakir pushed past his crushing sense of peril to pursue it. He knew he shouldn't, but he had to—so he focused on the variance ahead.

The crimson point came into sharp focus, twinkling innocently before him.

There was nothing innocent about it.

This was the access point—to the greater demon's mind.

He reached out and touched the point. A fierce blast of cold struck him with such intensity that it felt like a physical blow.

Everything around Nakir dissolved. His vision's disappearance left him disoriented, as he was yanked out of his physical realm and into another dimension.

An ear-piercing screech came from every direction, so loud that it felt like it could rupture eardrums.

Peekaboo, I see you. A harsh, vibrating voice abruptly entered his head. *Thank you for Stronghold.*

And then, in the blink of an eye, Nakir was falling.

His surroundings transformed into a dizzying array of colors—shades of blue, gold, and white swirled around him in a kaleidoscopic jumble—tumbling out of the sky and plunging back toward Earth.

Somehow, he'd been transported thousands of feet above the planet, and did not have wings to stop his descent.

The smell of burnt flesh and sulfur struck as the malevolence circled him like a vulture, waiting to pick his carcass clean.

It took only seconds, but it felt more like a century for

him to make brutal contact with the ground. The impact was so severe that his vision faded to deep, dark black. His fingers closed around something brittle and crumbly, and he moaned. The stench of charred earth was pungent.

Nakir fought through the haze, steadily reorienting to the world.

He was lying on his back, a cloud of ash and dust rising into the sky like a tornado.

Was he still on fire?

But as he blinked away the ash stinging his eyes, he realized the inferno had died down—leaving him battered and bruised, but miraculously alive. His hands were caked with filth and charcoal, leaving dark, smudgy streaks on his tattered clothes.

Nakir swayed to his feet, surveying his surroundings. Cacti, sand, mountains—desert as far as the eye could see. It was sweltering.

Detecting a presence nearby, Nakir spun around.

A towering figure stood precariously close to a cliff's edge.

Nakir blinked in confusion, recognizing them.

Leo, Corinth's half brother, turned his attention to Nakir, a mixture of surprise and uncertainty in his eyes. *Nakir?* a voice exploded into his head. *Did you fall out of the sky?*

They'd dueled back when Leo had thought Nakir was going to kill Corinth—which, at the time, he had been trying to do.

Leo brushed off the dust and debris from his clothes, coughing. "I had a plan, and you ruined it. Also, did you know a fallen angel now possesses your sword?"

28

LEO

Leo was astonished to see Nakir drop out of the sky and hit the ground. It was an abrupt and … what looked like a horrifying landing.

Leo *had* had a plan: being stabbed by Lucifer's horn was *supposed* to be staged. Except, the impulsive Shade, Ari, had actually stabbed him. The act was meant to impress Rimmon, and integrate Ari into their legion.

It had worked. Barely. Leo's fingers grazed the entrance wound at his back. He wouldn't be able to heal it on his own. Thankfully, he'd live.

"You saw my sword?" Nakir's piercing gaze was fixed on Leo, who felt was being evaluated as a potential enemy. A tense undercurrent also suggested that Nakir was ready to obliterate anyone who got in his way.

"Where is it?" Nakir growled, stepping closer. "Which demon has it?"

"Rimmon. And you're too late. They're gone. You scared them off with that insane entrance. Did you know you're supposed to have *wings* to fly?" Leo grimaced. "Also, you're lucky it worked out—Rimmon thought I was dead. The plan had been to kill the demon when it had its guard down, as soon as it got close to me. They were about to check to make sure, but then you came screeching out of the sky."

"*By the stars*, out of all the demons, it had to be Rimmon," Nakir snarled. "And they? Who was with Rimmon? This is not good *at all*." He rubbed his mouth and moved to sit on a rock a few feet away.

"Um, a contact I have been working with."

"Rimmon was one of the original fallen who sided with Lucifer. He's *extremely* powerful. Please, tell me you know where he was headed?"

"I'm working on it." Leo shook his head in frustration. "Look, while you're here, do you mind?" He lifted his shirt and turned around, showing Nakir the still-bleeding laceration.

Nakir raised his eyes to the sky, looking solemn. For a moment, Leo thought the angel would deny him aid. But then he strode over to Leo and placed a hand on his back on the left side. A healing warmth flowed through Leo.

Nakir hissed as if in pain. "How in the world did you get this wound?"

Leo went quiet for a second before he said, "Lucifer's horn."

"That's a nasty weapon." Nakir sucked in a sharp breath. "No wonder this hurts so much to heal."

"Try being stabbed with it." Leo pulled his shirt back down and turned back to Nakir. "Thanks."

Nakir nodded. "Your contact … is it a demon? You realize you can't trust any demonic entity, right?"

"It's not a demon. It's a Shade, and this one is different—it's Corinth's brother, Peter Taylor."

"Was Corinth's brother the one who *stabbed* you?" Nakir remained composed, but Leo could easily detect the underlying contempt in his voice.

Leo went silent. *Yes.*

"How do you suggest we get my sword back, then?" Nakir finally snapped.

Leo raised his eyebrows when he heard the word *we*. He knew the two of them weren't strong enough to retrieve the sword alone.

"We'll need assistance, and a lot of it," he told the archangel. "I guess you're coming with me to Scotland."

Nakir paused. "I won't work with the Nephilim, but I'll hear him out."

29

ZOEY

I kept pushing myself to exercise earlier each day, determined to improve my stamina. Despite the strain on my muscles, I could almost manage one push-up without using an incline for support. My goal was to beat Cruz.

Yeah, right. Not at this rate. He could do a fricking reverse handspring—now *that* was significant progress. Meanwhile, I was wading in the kiddie pool of katas, which were the *bane* of my existence. I hated them. The movements were too complex. Despite being told perfection wasn't the point, I couldn't help feeling troubled by my lack of improvement.

My brain was better suited to studying than athleticism.

Back in the dojo, sweat dripped down my forehead as I unleashed a palm strike, making solid contact with the wooden dummy's arm. My hands ached from the impact.

Keeping my forearms vertical and my elbows close to my body, as I had been taught, I tried to go through the straight punch, tiger claw, backhand, thumb, and elbow strikes. Why couldn't I get the hang of combining them all? I needed to stop overthinking it and just let my instincts take over.

Taking a moment to wipe my brow, I heard a voice from behind. "Need a sparring partner?"

I spun around to catch Cruz slipping out of his shoes.

"You're making progress," he commented. He walked to the corner of the room, where an array of gym equipment was set up. He picked up a pair of boxing gloves and strike pads.

"It doesn't feel like it," I muttered, still winded.

Cruz confidently returned to where I was standing and handed over the gloves. I hesitated to take them, not eager to show him how unskilled I was at this. Did I want him to see how clumsy I could be? Then again, I reasoned, he'd already witnessed my embarrassing attempts at running. Maybe looking awkward now wouldn't make much difference.

"Oh, come on," Cruz added with a wink. "It'll be fun."

"I *highly* doubt that," I grumbled, putting the gloves on anyway.

He was all set with the strike pads, anticipating my first punch. A stray strand of hair obscured his vision, and he struggled to brush it away from his forehead with the pads on. After a frustrated sigh, he shook his head, ready to begin our training session.

In a moment of impulse, and without considering the consequences, I rose on my tiptoes to tenderly brush the hair behind his ear. As I leaned in, I caught a hint of the fresh soap on his skin.

Suddenly, his face and mine turned crimson.

Awkward, table for one.

Cruz cleared his throat. "So ... how about we try palm strikes first?"

"Okay." I slipped on the gloves and raised my arm, testing the movement to distract myself from the flurries in my stomach.

Cruz held the pads up, and I assumed a fighting stance, concentrating on centering my weight and aligning my hips and shoulders. Rotating my body, I slammed my palm into the pad with all the force I could muster, which wasn't much.

Laughable, Zo.

"Good job, but can I make a suggestion?"

"Go ahead," I grumbled. "Mansplain."

"Technically, I'm regurgitating what Sensei taught me, so he's the one mansplaining." Cruz flashed me a grin and held his hands up as if in surrender. "Stance is the foundation of karate. Without a proper stance, no strike will be effective. Sensei's been drilling that into my head. Wiggle your toes and grip the floor with your feet as hard as you can, like you're sinking into the ground, and swing from your hips."

I followed Cruz's advice, shifting my weight onto my feet, steadying myself. I inhaled deeply and refocused my center.

"Your posture is off if I can make you lose your balance," Cruz remarked, pushing my shoulder with the pad.

Luckily, I stood firm and didn't waver.

"Great! Now, take a deep breath and exhale, engaging your core," he instructed.

After taking his advice, I followed Cruz's lead, since he had significantly more experienced than me and was pretty skilled at hitting things.

I repeated the motion, striking with increased speed and force, hoping to catch him off guard.

It worked. He stepped back, his mouth slightly agape. I beamed back at him with pride.

"Jeez," Cruz remarked, taking off the pad and shaking his hand. "Let's move on to elbow strikes."

I nodded, feeling the moisture dripping down my arms. "Your turn." I handed him the gloves, and he smiled as he took them.

After an hour of Cruz and I taking turns practicing front, side, round, and back kicks, I was utterly exhausted. Alastair was running late again. I wondered if his delay was related to his injury or another issue or maybe he was testing us.

"Have you seen Alastair?" I asked casually, trying to mask my concern.

Cruz glanced toward the open doors, scratching his head. "I'm sure as heck not going to go looking for him. I'm beat."

I chuckled, let myself fall onto my back, spread eagle on the mats. I tilted my head so that everything appeared upside down.

Black tactical boots filled my vision at the open doors. No cane accompanied those shoes.

I sat up quickly, expecting the worst. At the same time, Cruz jumped to his feet.

It wasn't Alastair or Corinth.

"*Nik?*" I blurted out. "What are you doing here?" My heart thundered in my chest. There could only be one reason: Ephrem.

He wore a black T-shirt and trousers, and his amber curls were piled high on his head. The archangel greeted us with a squinty-eyed look, his calculating gaze studying Cruz. There was noticeable annoyance in his demeanor—not directed at Cruz, but seemingly at me.

"Nik?" Cruz asked from beside me.

"Zoey, last time we spoke, you did not mention you were leaving Texas," Nakir said dryly.

I was taken aback by the parental tone in his voice. "And?" I shot back, crossing my arms and subtly flashing my watch at him. "It's not as if you angels don't have trackers on us anyway."

"*I* don't," Nakir told me.

Cruz caressed the shield at his chest. "So, you're *Nakir*?" He glanced between us. "The archangel who possessed Alastair?"

"Vessel," Nakir corrected Cruz, as his gaze returned to me. "I am here because we found the demon who escaped hell. His name is Rimmon, and I have enlisted the help of the other angels to send him back there."

I raised my shoulders as a thought came to me. "So, you're lurking around, hoping that he or Ephrem will show up for revenge or something?"

Nakir said, "I'm not lurking. I was invited."

I had to lick my lips to bring some moisture back into them. "How are you going to send this Rimmon demon back?"

"Ephrem is still in hell. And as far as sending Rimmon back, that's what we're working on," Nakir said evenly. "You two will be safe here among the other angels."

I was not reassured, but I nodded.

Cruz shook his head and said, "I want to help."

Nakir scrutinized Cruz as if he were an entity devoid

of intelligence. The archangel's intense stare appeared to unsettle Cruz, and despite his best efforts to remain composed, Cruz began to fidget.

"I commend you for your resolve, but it is not necessary. We are much better equipped to handle this task. As a mortal, you are vulnerable," Nakir murmured, not sugarcoating anything or gently breaking it to Cruz.

Uh oh.

"Who you calling vulnerable?" Cruz balled his hands into fists. "I've been training with Corinth, who is a Nephilim. *I can help.*"

Nakir snorted. "Nephilim are not as powerful as angels. He's half mortal." He regarded Cruz for a moment longer before returning his attention to me, clearly dismissive.

The heat came off Cruz in waves. "Have you even *met* Corinth?" he snapped. "The guy is a superhero."

I'd seen that hotheaded look from Cruz before. At the time, though, it had been directed at Ephrem.

"Here, I'll prove I'm ready." Cruz dove toward a rack of wooden swords behind him, seized one, and, without warning, lunged at Nakir.

It was the wrong move.

The room sizzled with an overwhelming surge of power. Lightning crackled across Nakir's skin. His grace cascaded down his arms, filling the dojo with a tangible, pulsating energy. The sensation reverberated through my chest. I stood in awe of his sheer power.

Nakir didn't have to lift a finger to prove his point. Cruz scuttled backward. He dropped the sword as a slow, arrogant smile spread across the angel's face.

Cruz stormed past Nakir and out of the dojo, forgetting his shoes.

"*Not—ready,*" Nakir thundered after him.

30

NAKIR

Zoey had pursued Nakir, desperate to uncover more information, but he had vanished, leaving her with more questions than answers. It wasn't a ploy, a game, or a mere coincidence. Nakir's presence was a necessity, a force that drew them together. A puzzle, perhaps. Fated, perhaps. Engineered. There was something between them, which was why Zoey's absence had unsettled him.

Nakir's weapons were gone, and he now relied on the help of outsiders. The air was thick with tension within the cramped living quarters of the cottage. Corinth stood with his arms tightly folded across his chest, his gaze piercing Nakir. The two unfamiliar angels before him, Tamiel and Samyaza, were giants who barely fit in the room. Samyaza had a battleax sheathed at his back, while Tamiel had a giant sword hanging off her hip. The pommel was bronze and infused with angels' grace. Although Tamiel's blade wasn't as mighty as *Stronghold's*, it showed promise.

Leo seemed lost in thought, gazing out the window with his chin propped on his hand. Neither Leo nor Nakir had revealed what had happened in the desert with the Shade.

By the stove, Alastair leaned on his cane, a strained expression on his face, his distress palpable—consequences of a shared bond. The poor soul seemed to be in constant torment. His weary eyes, burdened with dark circles, hinted at sleepless nights. Nakir sensed an underlying, tangible tension that defied clear understanding. It was as if Alastair's emotions loomed larger than Nakir's own, casting a disconcerting pall over him.

Corinth sat on the couch, his attention on Tamiel. "Any word from Ikari? He was supposed to report back hours ago, but there hasn't been any word from him. I'm starting to worry."

"I have not heard from Ikari either." Tamiel pursed her lips. "He was following up on a new lead."

Her voice betrayed her unease, Nakir noted.

Corinth squeezed his eyes shut, frustration evident on his face. After a moment, he let out a soft curse. "He's still not answering. Sam, Tami, can you track him down, STAT? This does not bode well. Y'all know we don't need to be investigating leads without back-up."

Samyaza acknowledged him briefly, his intense gaze fixed on Nakir. "We will leave straight away."

A low rumble shook the room as Samyaza and Tamiel entered their respective portals. The walls warped and bent, distorting the fabric of reality as they disappeared through them.

"You expect us to believe you're here to help, Nakir?" Corinth said. "You tried to kill me, almost killed Al and Larns—and then you just up and vanished, expecting us to clean up your mess. Now you're telling me this *fallen angel* has your sword and armor? I'm only listening because you said you and Leo know something about this escaped demon. What was his name again …?"

"Rimmon," Nakir said calmly. "And if I had intended to kill you, you wouldn't be standing here. Moreover, I saved Alastair Iszler from certain death by bringing him back. It was *you* who put a blade in him, *Nephilim*."

"Would you please stop using *Nephilim* like a swear word?" Corinth's gaze shifted briefly to Alastair before returning to Nakir. "God loves me. So should you."

Even with that biting wit, Corinth's guilt hung over him like a dark cloud. Nakir could see that the Nephilim's humanity burned brighter than the sun, and his raw emotions were fully displayed. It was clear that Corinth still felt immense guilt for his role in stabbing Alastair. Those feelings could be the Nephilim's undoing one day—they were too strong, too overwhelming.

Nakir furrowed his brows. "Interesting how humans use humor to deflect."

"Interesting how angels don't possess humor." Corinth stretched his arms out. "Can you recall Rimmon's appearance?"

He leaned his back against the wall, thinking. "I don't know about Rimmon's mortal form. But I can show you his demonic state." Nakir pictured Rimmon's appearance and projected this image through their Halos: crimson claws for hands and feet, two horns atop his head, a pointed tail, and razor-sharp teeth.

Leo took an unsettling step back. Corinth gripped his head and doubled over, grimacing.

"Holy mother of—what in the literal *hell* was that?" Corinth gulped.

Nakir understood that reaction. Fear and repulsion. "Do you not share images with the others?"

"No, and for good reason!" Corinth rubbed his head, his eyes pinched closed. "Don't ever do that again. *Blech*! That thing was hideous."

"What?" Alastair asked. "What did you see?"

"Have you ever seen the movie *Legend* with Tom Cruise?"

"I hate admitting this, but—" Alastair nodded. "Thanks to Larna."

"He looks like that villain, Darkness, with the horns and everything …" Corinth said.

"Yikes," Alastair replied.

"Yup," Corinth answered.

"Excuse me. I hate to interrupt this riveting conversation, but perhaps Leo could share what Rimmon's human appearance looks like," Nakir said. "He spoke with him."

"*What*?" Corinth asked, quickly turning to Leo. "You spoke with *Rimmon* and failed to tell us about it? Why did you not call on us for help? We could have taken the bastard down and been done with all this … please tell me you have an explanation."

Leo clasped his hands together before spinning around to face Corinth. "Rimmon appeared in his early twenties, with thick, wavy blonde hair, pale blue eyes, and fair skin. The most distinctive feature was his flashy attire, a blood-red suit with wing-tipped shoes—"

"For pity's sake, you did the whole spy routine again, didn't you, Leo?" Corinth interjected. "Mr. Lone-Wolf, as usual."

After a considerable stretch of silence, Nakir's gaze shifted to Leo. "Should I tell them what happened?"

Leo's eyes narrowed, and his body tensed. "I wish you wouldn't."

Corinth stood back up and locked eyes with Leo, who was taller than him. "Leo?" Corinth's eyes flashed with lightning. "Now."

"The Nephilim deserves to know about his brother," Nakir pressed.

A frown marred Corinth's face. He glanced back and forth between Nakir and Leo. "What about Jimmy?"

"Not Jimmy. Peter," Nakir corrected. "Peter Taylor."

"What about Peter?" Alastair asked, finally piping up.

Leo ran a hand through his hair. "I swore an oath to the one who saved my life that I wouldn't say anything. My word is sacred, Corinth." Leo's gaze flickered to Nakir. "But Nakir … he didn't promise anything to anyone. Therefore, he has my consent to tell you."

Nakir inclined his head. "Leo was grievously injured in the demon realm."

Corinth shook his head slowly. "I knew he was hurt … but just how bad—he kept that from me."

"Us," Alastair interjected, glancing between Corinth and Leo.

"He was on the verge of death," Nakir explained.

"You didn't think to tell me you were *dying*, Leo!" Corinth clenched his fists, his skin arching with grace. "What makes it worse is that you told *Nakir* over your own brother!"

Leo hesitated but stood firm and silent as Nakir spoke. "Leo ventured into a cavern of demons in search of a cure. At the brink of death, a Shade broke away from the others and healed Leo, removing the shard. It was Peter, Corinth. *Peter's actions saved Leo's life.*"

Corinth was speechless for a moment, his mouth hanging open. "You're family, Leo. You could have been gone. And on top of that, you kept from me that Pete is still out there? How long have you known?" His voice shook with anger, grief, betrayal. "You've never been good at communicating, have you?"

Leo sank onto the couch, his head drooping under the weight of everything he had grappled with.

Corinth turned to the window to gaze at the gray, foggy day. Nakir followed his line of sight. In the pasture, Nakir could see a boy and a girl playing. Sheep surrounded them.

When Corinth spoke again, he sounded wounded. "How long have you been letting me wallow in guilt and grief? Suspended in a state of loss, so … so profound, I …" Corinth shook his head, and his voice cracked. "I can't even look at my parents, Zo and Jimmy. You …" His voice trailed off as he broke down, his cheeks glistening.

Corinth's heart was breaking. Nakir felt it—everyone in the room did.

"This is exactly why I didn't tell you." Leo gripped his knees, his knuckles turning white. "Pete is no longer your brother. He's taken on a new identity now: Ari, a Shade. Demons created him. There *is* no saving him. Peter, or Ari, asked me to keep this from you because he believes it's for the best. I do, too. Ari … he wants your family to move forward. He knows he's a lost soul."

"Lost soul!" Corinth spun around, his chest heaving. His voice rose to near-hysteria. "WE'RE ALL LOST!" Thunder reverberated throughout the room, the vibrations shaking Nakir's core. The windows rattled with such ferocity that he feared they might shatter.

Alastair threw his hands over his ears, shuddering.

Maybe the Nephilim had more power than Nakir had first thought. Nakir was only half-surprised by Corinth's fury. All humans' emotions were too delicate and complex.

"*Move forward*? He's my brother, Leo! I wouldn't move on from him, as I would never move on from you," Corinth bellowed.

Leo didn't say anything to that. No one did.

"Where is Pete?" Corinth demanded, his voice a whispered threat, his skin popping.

"Working alongside us, Ari aims to bring Rimmon to his knees," explained Nakir. "He is in a prime position to gather intel from the inside. That way, we can take action and track down—"

"You mean Peter. *Pete* Taylor," Corinth snarled, his voice trembling. "He's not just some random person, Nakir. He's my friend, my brother. I can't fathom the thought that both of you would put him in harm's way. It's like a living nightmare, a haunting echo of what happened to Al—like déjà vu. You call yourselves angels, but where is your compassion and decency? I will find Pete and do everything I can to heal him, to help him become whole again." Corinth ran a hand down his face, his frustration profound. "I know you think I'm emotional and reckless—half-human. But Jesus experienced more emotion than most people. He went from birth to death, experiencing pain, heartache, and love. Sometimes, I think you celestial beings forget that part."

"Trust me," Nakir said gently, his voice a soothing balm amid Corinth's storm. "We experience pain." A long silence settled around the room before he continued, his words carefully chosen. "I understand your concern, but the situation is multifaceted. Even if we knew Ari's whereabouts, we wouldn't disclose them to you, Corinth. An attempt to extract the Shade could endanger his life by exposing him to Rimmon."

"Not if I obliterate Rimmon from this planet," Corinth growled, his voice filled with a fierce determination. "And Shade? Really?"

"Reveal the whereabouts of his *brother*," Alastair said firmly, siding with Corinth.

Leo raised his head, then, with a pained expression, he said, "I support you, Corinth. I do. But this war is a labyrinth of complexities, and you're too young to navigate it. I have been around for millennia, and I'm your eldest brother. This situation must be handled strategically. We must discuss—"

With a sudden burst of anger, Corinth raised his clenched fist into the air and let out a loud shout that echoed through the room.

"Don't do—" Leo began.

The sudden appearance of a portal, conjured by the Nephilim, vibrated in the cramped space.

Corinth lunged forward and vanished into the swirling vortex.

"Anything stupid," Leo finished, his voice mingling with the echoing thunder.

31

ALASTAIR

Dread dragged at Alastair's bones. Maybe Nakir's presence was causing him more pain—or perhaps Alastair had just been doing too much lately. His ankle was aching more than usual. The archangel expected him to accept the situation he had been dealt. Alastair was still pissed. He gazed at Nakir. The archangel's silence spoke volumes. Nakir didn't feel guilty about what had just occurred with Corinth.

Now, the two of them were alone in the cabin. The other angels were occupied with locating Ikari, who had yet to report back, which was highly troubling.

Nakir was concerned about the danger they were facing. They all were. He thought Corinth's attempts to find his brother, Peter, only added to the peril. Nakir had warned them to keep an eye out, especially since Rimmon now wielded *Stronghold*. Nakir claimed this weapon could strike down even the strongest archangels—which was alarming in and of itself.

"Out with it," Nakir said to Alastair, as he sat on the

couch. The angel wore all black, including his boots. It was good they could manipulate Earth's matter. They didn't have to go to the store to buy clothes; they just fashioned them out of molecules.

"Since your armor is gone, and Rimmon took your sword"—Alastair's tone betrayed his disapproval—"then what's the level of danger we're looking at for these kids?"

"The highest," Nakir answered, frowning.

"That's heartening."

"Would you like me to assist with your pain?" Nakir asked, glancing at Alastair's leg. "Your injuries were partly my fault."

"*Partly?*" Alastair's emotions were running high, and he shook his head, annoyed. "And I'm not in pain. I'm fine."

Without taking no for an answer, Nakir strode over to Alastair. He rubbed his hands, causing sparks to shoot off them. The pressure in the room was unbearable, as Alastair gazed at the angel's jade-green eyes.

Alastair was not in the mood to be patronized. "*I said I'm fine,*" he snarled.

Nakir lowered his hands and nodded, his grace dissolving. "Just know that if you have a change of heart …" His voice trailed off. "I will be here."

"So, you're staying, then?" Alastair asked, lifting an eyebrow.

"I have to be near in case we receive word from the Shade," Nakir explained. "And as the only one who can contact Ari, Leo's presence is indispensable."

"Pete is more than just a Shade. He's willing to risk his safety, and from the sound of it, he's keeping his distance from Cor to prevent him harm—which leads me to believe the *Shade* is worth saving."

Nakir tilted his head as if contemplating Alastair's words. "Perhaps." After a moment, he conceded. "It seems highly likely that there is a great deal more to the Taylors than first meets the eye."

"Indisputably," Alastair concurred. "Look, my wife is back, and I'm eager to see her. But let me know if you get any more information on Peter or Rimmon."

Alastair made his way into the kitchen. He found Larna standing before the open refrigerator, rummaging for something. He limped up behind her without using his cane. He wrapped his arms around her waist and sighed heavily as she sank into his embrace.

Although Larna was short and he was tall, they fit together perfectly. Every time he saw her, he felt an inexplicable attraction. Alastair always missed the sweet aroma of her vanilla-scented hair, the light fragrance of fabric softener on her pale blue sweater, and her calm demeanor. They stayed glued together for some time, cherishing each other's company, not wanting to let go of the moment before jumping back into the chaos of their lives.

"Hello, my love," she finally said in a husky voice. "You can walk unaided now—which is a massive improvement."

"I can do more than that." Alastair nudged the side of her cheek with his nose and lightly nipped at her neck. She shivered against him and turned around in his embrace, her hands resting against his chest. She locked her gaze onto his. Her hazel eyes were wide and dilated, a clear message of desire as she leaned into him. Alastair responded with a playful smirk. "How are our affairs?"

"We have an empty shop in London that requires lots of work. That includes painting, installing new kitchen equipment, and repairing the electrical wiring. We also need to hire contractors and gather the necessary permits to open. Unfortunately, I have been on a three-day shift at the hospital and can't keep up with this pace."

"I think we should hold off on the bakery," Alastair suggested, trying not to let regret color his voice. "I'm not happy about being pulled back into this mess with angels and demons, but at the same time, I can't leave these kids to fend for themselves. And the thought of you being in danger is … agonizing …"

Larna waited for a second before answering. "When are we *not* in danger?" She sighed. "This is your dream, love. I'm giving you the rest of this summer to train these kids. After that, we'll face our challenges without demons, angels, *or* Gabriel Stanton. We're done with all of it, okay?"

"You just *had* to include *his* name, didn't you?" Alastair grumbled.

Larna's playful shove made Alastair chuckle. She took his hand and gestured toward the makeshift clinic where they had spent most of their time lately. "Shall we head over there, darling, and work on your physio?" she asked, a soft grin on her face.

"I'd rather work on something else …" Alastair said throatily.

Larna's eyebrows raised. She smiled widely at him, her cheeks turning a rosy pink.

Alastair adored it when she blushed.

"Me too," she purred not-so-sweetly.

32

ZOEY

Lying on my stomach on the bed, alone in my room, I had just finished my homework.

Corinth barged in, upset and stressed, his eyes red-rimmed.

I sat up quickly and pulled the headphones out of my ears. "What's going on?" My mind raced. Had something terrible happened to Jimmy or our parents?

As Corinth started to shut the door, Biscuit came bounding in. He jumped onto the bed and snuggled beside me. I ran my hand along my cat's back.

"I promised you I wouldn't keep any more secrets about our family." My brother paced at the foot of my bed. The blade secured to his thigh emitted an unnerving hum. "Hold on. I need to collect my thoughts first." He pinched the bridge of his nose. "I'm still furious."

"Cor, you're scaring me," I said, slowly standing, refusing to blink or look away from him. "What is it?"

Corinth rubbed his tired eyes and hesitated. "Pete is alive."

I froze, my nerves on fire.

Out of all the things I'd expected him to say, this was not it. *Could it be true?* Gradually, as what he'd just told me sank in, my legs gave out. I collapsed back onto the bed, trembling. "Pete … is … *alive?*" I whispered. "Please don't lie to me, Cor. I can't handle it."

Corinth strode over and sat beside me, gently touching my shoulder. "I'm not lying, Zo. Pete's supposedly been helping Nakir and Leo. They kept it from me, and I'm furious at them for their deception. I could have helped Pete—if only they'd told me. I could have …" Corinth's voice broke, and he buried his head in his hands.

I wrapped my arms around him. He leaned into me, seeking solace.

My throat constricted. "But I saw Pete die."

"Shades can revive themselves. Ephrem demonstrated that to us in the demon realm, remember?"

I shuddered at the memory. "But why hasn't Pete come back to us?" I murmured. "Mom, Dad, and Jimmy deserve to know the truth. Shouldn't we tell them?" I thought about that more. "We have to go home."

Corinth placed his hand over mine, his eyes softening. "I already did. I told them."

I still felt winded and shaky. "How did they react?"

"A lot like you did. But now they have hope," he whispered.

"Hope?" I said bitterly, shaking my head. "Pete disappeared. Have you spoken with him?" My mind was muddled but also racing with different scenarios and ideas—possibilities. Pete had told me he loved me after he'd been turned into a Shade. "Pete saved my life," I murmured. "If he escaped after Ephrem was killed, why would Leo and

Nakir not be honest about it? Why all the mystery?" Nakir and Leo had told me nothing. Now, I was mad at them, too.

A hesitant knock sounded on the bedroom door, making me jump.

Corinth sprang up to open it.

It was Cruz, dressed in gray sweats. A basket of freshly laundered clothes was tucked beneath his arm, and his damp curls went every which direction. "The door was closed, so I thought I'd better knock first," he said softly, studying Corinth's mottled cheeks and red eyes. "Uh, this looks like a bad time. I'll come back later …"

Cruz turned to leave, but Corinth stepped aside and said, "Come in, Cruz."

Cruz, looking uncomfortable, came in, placed the hamper on his bed, and faced us. "You found the one-eyed Shade, didn't you?" His gaze shifted from me to Corinth and finally landed on Biscuit, whom I had pulled onto my lap without realizing.

"No." Corinth placed a hand on the hilt of his blade. "Not yet. That's not what this is about." He met my gaze, and I nodded, giving him the go-ahead to speak freely. "Peter is … alive, in a way. He's still a Shade but not dead, as we initially believed. Nakir has informed me that the escaped demon has resurfaced. The demon has taken on human form—a man named Rimmon. As far as we know, he appears to be in his early twenties, with wavy hair and blue eyes. So, it goes without saying if you see anyone who fits that description—"

"Run." Cruz flopped onto his bed and clasped his hands around the medallion at his throat, clearly shell-shocked. "Seriously? Where is Peter then?" He glanced at me, his brow creased.

"Yeah," I breathed. "Where is he, Cor?"

"I don't know," Corinth admitted. "But I'm going to find him. In the meantime, promise me you'll both stay within the vicinity of the cottage and hit the panic button on your watches if you encounter any trouble," he pleaded. "I'm serious, you two. No trying to be heroes."

We nodded in unison, acknowledging the gravity of the situation.

Corinth looked at us, his eyes filled with concern and determination. "I won't let anything happen to you two."

"No gallantry outta me," Cruz said earnestly.

Corinth shot Cruz a sideways look. "Oh please, you're the *first* one I'm worried would charge off into the fray."

"No, sir. I hate demons. There will be no fraying from me." Cruz lifted two fingers. "Scouts honor."

Corinth gave him a curt nod and then moved to the door. "I'm going to be gone for a little while. I need to find Pete—and Ikari is still MIA. I'll return as soon as possible. While I'm gone, listen to Al."

I picked at a fingernail and whispered, "Cor, please be careful and find our brother."

Corinth gave me a thin-lipped smile. "I'll do everything in my power."

33

GABRIEL

Gabriel Stanton stood in the boardroom, captivated by the sight of the iridescent metal helmet resting on the table. A sense of wonder and excitement washed over him as he contemplated the potential significance of its acquisition. This piece of Nakir's angelic armor seemed to exude a radiant, pulsating energy—an enchanting blend of magic, power, and celestial essence. Gabriel pondered whether this extraordinary artifact could hold the key to eternal life. Or, at the very least, it might serve as a highly coveted bargaining tool. The weight of its potential significance hung in the air, adding to the intrigue.

Score one for team Stanton.

But Gabriel found himself in a bind—he needed to keep this helmet away from the archangel. Outside, a team of colleagues and his security personnel were waiting for orders or to protect him in case Nakir showed up to reclaim his armor. Heeding Gabriel's instructions, nobody was to lay a finger on it; touching or handling it could be potentially hazardous.

Before this, the conference room had been a whirlwind of chaos and people, so Gabriel had arranged a private meeting with his top angelic expert to discuss the artifact.

Sitting across from him was a middle-aged man with thinning hair and thick glasses. The scientist kept sniffling and rubbing his nose, making it hard for Gabriel to concentrate. The human race was doomed.

Still entranced by the energy emanating from the helmet, Gabriel said, "So, how did you come across it again?"

The scientist pushed his bifocals up the bridge of his nose. "Solar flares occur when stored magnetic energy in the Sun's atmosphere accelerates charged particles in the surrounding plasma. This results in the emission of radiation across the electromagnetic spectrum—"

"Blah, blah, blah," Gabriel snapped. "Get to the point."

Mr. Scientist inhaled indignantly. "We have conducted interviews with other angels and analyzed ancient texts and scrolls, and have determined that the angelic substance is made up of solar flares from the sun." He formed a circle with his hands. "It's a highly concentrated outburst of radiation. I used one of your satellites as a detector to locate it. It was discovered in the dunes of Huacachina, Peru."

"Genius," Gabriel all but purred. The scientist beamed at the compliment. Gabriel added, "Wait. Is this thing going to give me radiation poisoning?"

"We did numerous tests to rule that out. Incredibly, it is not radioactive, but gives off the same heat signature."

"So, can I touch it without my face melting off?" he asked slowly.

The scientist nodded slightly, unsure if that was a joke or not. It wasn't.

"So, what are you still doing here?" Gabriel flicked his hand. "Go find the rest of the gear. I want that sword."

The scientist scurried out, leaving Gabriel alone at the table.

Should he touch it?

Yes, a voice answered in his head.

Did the relic hold the secret to immortality? He imagined how he would feel if he wore the armor. Would he be unstoppable? Although he was never one to act rashly, the temptation to pick it up and try it on was too much for him.

Gabriel stood, causing his leather chair to squeak. He pulled on a pair of white gloves, eyes fixed on the object in the center of the table. There was an inexplicable pull.

With a sudden, swift motion, he snatched up the armor, feeling its weight and texture in his bare hands.

He didn't die.

He didn't burst into flames.

His face didn't melt off.

As Gabriel examined it more closely, he noticed that the helmet was surprisingly lightweight despite being crafted from highly durable metal. Its sleek design hinted at the advanced technology within. He gently placed the object on his head with great care. A strange sensation passed through him, making his blood buzz with an unusual energy. He felt heady and dizzy, almost like he had just unleashed a hidden strength inside himself.

Bloody hell.

Gabriel would clearly need a complete suit of armor to harness this ability. The immense power that surged through his body quickly dissipated, overwhelming his mortal form. He collapsed. The helmet slipped off his head and bounced away.

Gabriel struggled to get back up, resting his weight on the table and panting heavily. Immortality seemed so far-fetched these days. He was aging every second, and his bones and joints ached. Realizing that he had gone from being godlike to a mere bag of flesh and bones was dreadful. Every day that passed, brought him closer to his inevitable decay.

Damn, how he despised Corinth Taylor for taking his life away from him.

Overwhelmed with frustration, he shoved a pile of papers off the table, letting out a roar. Still, his security team did not rush in. Gabriel's chest heaved as heat rose to his face. He had tried to accept change, but change hadn't accepted him. Gabriel turned around, angry—right into the tip of a sword pointed at his neck.

He swallowed, feeling acutely aware of his humanity, with all its flaws and vulnerabilities.

"Hello, Gabriel Stanton."

The young man before Gabriel wore an oxblood suit, shiny onyx-colored shoes, and no socks. The sword he held to his throat had a pearlescent lion's head, and under his arm, he possessed the helmet Gabriel had just dropped.

Great. He'd just found the damn thing.

"You're not Nakir," Gabriel said absentmindedly. "And no angel is *this* flashy—so you must be a … demon."

The demon shrugged. "Guilty."

"Commendable choice in suits. I love that color. Blood red is a bit on the nose, though, don't you think?" Gabriel's gaze traveled up and down the demon. Its eyes were as sharp as the sword it held to Gabriel's throat.

"My name is Rimmon."

"I assume you're not here to kill me, Rimmon," Gabriel drawled.

The demon cocked its head to the side. "I still haven't decided yet."

Gabriel arched an eyebrow. "Well then, what do we do now?"

"I've got a proposition for you," the demon finally said, refusing to drop the sword from Gabriel's throat.

Gabriel replied warily, "You have my undivided attention."

"I'm trying to access my kingdom, but the only way to get there is through one of the gates Ephrem created. Unfortunately, Corinth Taylor damaged it, and his Holy Lance's energy keeps interfering with my entry. Grant me access to the remote, and in return for your help, I'm willing to offer you this sword ... and, if you're a really good boy, the helmet too."

Gabriel raised his finger slowly and cautiously, trying not to provoke Rimmon. "Firstly, Corinth Taylor is *not* my friend. Secondly, I thought the demon realm was destroyed. And lastly, aren't you creatures usually averse to handling holy artifacts?" His gaze flicked down at the sword, still dangerously close to his jugular.

"Let's just say that I'm renovating." Rimmon gave a diabolical-sounding laugh. "I'm pleased to hear that we agree on the half-angel, Corinth Taylor, not being a friend. He does get under the skin—like a tick, doesn't he? How would you like it if I permit you to thrust this blade into the Nephilim's heart?"

"Corinth Taylor isn't one to trifle with." Gabriel lifted a shoulder in a half-hearted shrug. "These days, I don't like to get my hands dirty."

The demon laughed again. This time, it sounded annoyed, and the sword tip grazed Gabriel's neck. He flinched. *Too far.*

"Regarding this holy artifact, Stanton, that's the six-billion-dollar question I won't answer."

Gabriel pondered that revelation. It was fascinating information that he'd file away for later use. "Are you planning to bring Ephrem back?"

Rimmon shrugged. "Among other things."

He was not fond of that idea, mainly because Ephrem had expressed his extreme desire to kill Gabriel.

"I think we might have a problem there, Rimmon," Gabriel said through gritted teeth. "Ephrem holds a grudge against me, and I can't be of much assistance if I'm dead."

Rimmon whispered, "I understand your concern. But rest assured, Ephrem won't be a problem for you anymore. However, I need him. I also need your assistance. Do we have an agreement?"

Gabriel smirked back at the demon. "Indeed we do."

"Excellent," Rimmon cooed. "I have a few angels to handle before I can hand over the sword, and I need you to help me eliminate them."

34

CRUZ

Zoey's determination to stay on top of her fitness game was unwavering—even six weeks after discovering that her brother, Peter, had risen from the dead. This revelation only fueled her commitment to intensify her workouts and training regimen. Her hard work had paid off; she'd started to outpace Cruz during sprints. There was a remarkable transformation in Zoey's physique. Her muscles were becoming more defined, her body leaner and toned. He was genuinely impressed with her progress.

Even though the cottage felt safe, there was a noticeable strain in the air. The angels were concerned about Ikari's prolonged absence. Things were also tense with Leo because Corinth was looking for Peter. Of course, the one-eyed Shade was still out there. Nakir had been mysteriously absent most of the time, but Cruz couldn't shake the feeling that the angel had been secretly watching them. After that unexpected display in the dojo, Cruz grappled with conflicting emotions about Nakir.

Cruz only tried to demonstrate his skills when he pursued the angel with the sword, but his frustration clouded his judgment. He realized he should probably establish better terms with Nakir. He felt secure in his bubble, knowing that angels (*not* Nakir) were looking out for them. His mother was doing well. She was vacationing with friends, exploring, and camping, which brought him immense joy—she was experiencing life in a new light. He supposed they both were. Martial arts challenged him in the same way his fighting used to. This place was beginning to feel like a second home, and he was even—dare Cruz admit it—happy.

It was another chilly, wet day, the rain pouring down relentlessly. Undeterred by the weather, Zoey and Cruz sprinted toward the dojo.

"That was close!" Cruz shouted as he struggled to stop, his breath visible in the cold air. His feet slipped, but he avoided falling onto his rear as they entered. "You're improving so fast."

"It helps when you work out every—" Zoey said, but stopped midsentence when something across the way caught her attention. She faltered, her mouth hanging open.

Cruz followed her line of sight to see what she was staring at. Their evolving relationship added a new layer of understanding and connection.

Oh, jeez. Nakir—shirtless. In the dojo. *Ugh.*

Two vertical scars on the archangel's shoulder blades looked like angry welts—or, perhaps, burns. Cruz couldn't tell which. Nakir effortlessly wielded a heavy-looking sword, moving smoothly from one precise motion to another. Each strike was accompanied by a loud thunderclap from outside, making the sight all the more riveting.

Cruz had to admit the archangel was a machine. He low-key wished he could move like that.

Zoey caught Cruz's annoyed glower and shrugged. She seemed as uncomfortable at Nakir's lack of clothing as he was.

"Oh, for heaven's sake!" Cruz finally cried, annoyed. "Put a shirt on, Nik."

Nakir halted. The sword disappeared in a flash of cobalt, returning to its original spot on the training racks at the back of the room.

Zoey marched forward with her arms folded across her chest. "Have you heard from Cor? Pete?"

Nakir shot Zoey an exasperated glance. He strode over to a corner table and picked up the gray sweatshirt he'd draped over it. "I will never understand humans and their embarrassment about disrobing."

"Because some of us don't have angel physiques," Cruz whispered out of the side of his mouth.

Nakir rolled his eyes. "I thought I had more time to train before you finished your run."

"*Train?*" Cruz scoffed, swiping at the water running off his forehead and into his eyes. The stupid angel was all hard-packed muscle. "I didn't think angels had to work out. Aren't you all supposed to be immortal? All-powerful or whatever?"

Nakir made a dismissive gesture. "Or whatever," he said as he approached the table, picked up two clean towels, and returned to stand before them. "You two should dry off. You're drenched and, by the looks of it, half-hypothermic."

When he offered a towel to Zoey, she refused it with a shake of her head—even though she had a slightly bluish tinge to her lips, Cruz noted. She kept her arms tightly crossed, trying to retain body warmth.

"Tell me where Peter is," she insisted. "And where is Corinth? No one is talking to us. I'm tired of being left in the dark. I've done everything y'all have asked of me. I'm done waiting."

Zoey had been relentlessly attempting to extract information from Nakir for weeks, but the angel remained stubbornly tight-lipped and unavailable.

"We're all in the dark," Nakir whispered. "I've told you countless times, Zoey, I have no idea where they are. Only Leo does, but he's made himself scarce."

"Then, why don't you go after Leo and force him to give you the information?" Zoey snapped. "You angels are so secretive."

Nakir raised his eyebrows at that. She'd finally irritated him. Cruz was relieved that Zoey had voiced her frustration. Some angels were just dicks.

The archangel's eyes scanned the rain cascading from the stormy skies, his jaw tightening. "You've seen the havoc demons can wreak. We need to prepare ourselves for the worst. Your focus on training is vital for your survival. It's your top priority."

"You've been avoiding us on purpose." Zoey released a deep sigh and looked up at the ceiling. "Why do you seem so troubled? Something's wrong, and you won't tell us what that is. It's maddening."

"Yes, my sword is in the hands of the enemy," he said through gritted teeth. "I *am* deeply troubled."

"You're not searching for Ikari. Cor is probably out

there alone, and instead of helping Peter, you're skulking around here, watching us. It's completely unnecessary. We don't need *your* protection—"

Before Zoey could finish the sentence, a loud BOOM reverberated through the space, jolting everyone into silence. The acrid smell of burning rubber instantly replaced the crisp scent of rain.

Cruz found himself rooted to the spot, unable to tear his gaze away from the captivating spectacle unfolding above. Angel grace surged, growing stronger by the second. A shimmering portal materialized above them. Something came hurtling out, barreling straight toward Cruz with incredible speed—

Cruz was shoved to the ground from behind. He hit the bamboo hard, the wind knocked out of him. He slid away from the portal just in time to avoid a figure landing right where he'd been standing moments before. The sound of the body hitting the floor was awful. The shield around Cruz's neck heated against his flesh. He struggled to rise, gasping for breath, his training forgotten. He frantically scanned the area for Zoey.

There she was—the corner of the dojo, where she'd grabbed a staff, holding it at the ready. The ring on her finger pulsated a warning against a demonic presence.

The portal suddenly closed. Cruz's necklace's pulsating slowly faded. Without hesitation, Nakir rushed to the fallen soul's side. Strange blue rivulets seemed to evaporate from the figure's skin. Which meant this was an angel, *not* a Shade. But why did Cruz's medallion give a warning?

The form lay in the fetal position, letting out low moans. Their hair was spiky black with green tips. It was unmistakably Ikari's, the missing angel.

Cruz made his way over to Nakir and collapsed onto the floor. His limbs felt heavy as the adrenaline started to wear off.

Ikari writhed in pain, his face contorted. He clutched his stomach tightly. He wore all black, and his footwear was distinctive—with divided toes. Nakir's hand emitted the brilliant glow of the immense grace flowing through him as he gently pried Ikari's hands from his abdomen.

Zoey let out a gasp. She was leaning on the staff she'd snatched earlier, and her complexion had turned pale. She trembled from head to toe, her lips a deep shade of purple.

"*Heavenly Father ...*" Nakir whispered, bowing his head.

A jagged cut went straight through Ikari's gut. The gash glowed a supernatural red, like blood.

Blood. Angels didn't bleed. They weren't flesh like humans, but the Chornobyl red was undeniable.

"Oh no." Cruz breathed, fisting his hands by his sides. *This is his fault,* he thought. *Cruz said it felt like home here. Zoey told Nakir they didn't need protection. Cruz jinxed them.*

"*Rimmon ...*" Ikari said with a choking, ragged gasp.

The room was instantly filled with portals, each one spewing out angels, one by one.

Soon, the space was overcrowded with celestial beings. Wild gusts made Cruz's hair fly in all directions. The hot, oppressive air just intensified the chaos.

Suddenly, Leo was there. He placed a reassuring hand on Cruz's arm and led him toward the open doors. "Let's make some space."

Cruz seethed, wondering if the distant rumble was thunder or the physical manifestation of his fury. *Finally, they decide to show up.*

"Where the hell have you been?" he spat.

Corinth was beside Ikari, and Nakir muttered under his breath, grinding his teeth in frustration. "That *demon* used my sword."

Time seemed to warp. Events alternated between fast and slow, and Cruz struggled to focus. His vision blurred.

Corinth clasped Ikari's hand. He exerted pressure on the wound with the other, his palm emitting a radiant light. "What happened?"

"Rimmon ... lured me into ... a trap. He held me prisoner," Ikari panted. "Ran me ... through with ... an angel's sword. Coward ambushed me." Ikari's body shuddered as he half-laughed, half-cried out in pain. "Maybe I shouldn't have ... taunted him." Despite the efforts of multiple angels tending to Ikari, blood seeped from his nose and mouth, his face ghastly pale.

It wasn't looking good for Ikari. Cruz stared anxiously at Zoey, who appeared horrified.

Leo clenched his fists.

"You can't heal him?" Cruz asked Leo quietly, already knowing the answer.

Leo shook his head. He took a few steps closer to Zoey, clutching the staff, and gently led her toward the doors.

"Ikari, stay with me," Cruz heard Corinth implore, as he worked on the injured angel.

Cruz refused to leave. He had to see this through—he needed to understand the horror a demon could perpetrate.

Corinth turned to Nakir, voice tinged with fury and torment. "It was your sword that ran him through. You need to fix him, Nakir. Now."

"His duty has been fulfilled." Nakir's expression darkened as he shook his head. "There's nothing more we can do for him except reciting the angel's prayer."

"Are you kidding me?" Corinth snarled. "*No.*"

A sense of acceptance had settled over the fatally wounded angel. He seemed content. "It is my time," Ikari whispered, gazing up at Corinth with peace and love in his eyes. "Please don't mourn, my friend. I will be reunited with my wife and son."

Wife and son?

Cruz had no idea the angel had been married and had a child.

Corinth struggled to hold back his tears. "Please don't go, Ikari. I need you to stay with me. Keep fighting. I can't handle this without you."

Ikari shut his eyes and then opened them again. "Corinth. Rimmon … he said he's coming for you." Ikari's gaze shifted to Cruz. "Zoey and Cruz—you must keep them safe."

Cruz could hear the loud thud of his own heartbeat in his eardrums.

Keep us safe.

Samyaza and Tamiel stood on either side of Ikari, their eyes closed in deep meditation. The air around them hummed with a powerful energy as they chanted in an unfamiliar language. Ikari's expression gradually softened. His hands dropped down by his sides as his form slowly shimmered and faded until he completely vanished.

Corinth let out a piercing cry. He collapsed onto the mats, his features contorted in pain.

Nakir had always exuded a calm demeanor, but Cruz could feel the archangel's deep anguish and see it etched on his face.

Outside, Cruz observed the rain cascading down in torrents, as if the heavens were shedding tears in solidarity.

35

NAKIR

After Zoey and Cruz were declared safe, the angels and Larna, Corinth, and Alastair gathered in the guest cottage.

An overwhelming dread settled over Nakir. Ikari's death had been *his* fault. *Stronghold* had been used to dispatch Ikari.

Nakir surveyed the room. Still struggling to accept Ikari's death, Leo was conspicuously absent from their group. Tamiel and Samyaza glowered at Nakir from behind the couch, their fury so intense that it seemed they might resort to physical violence.

He couldn't blame them for feeling that way.

With his head in his hands, Corinth sat beside Larna and Alastair on the couch. After a while, he glanced up at Nakir. "How was a *demon* able to wield your sword?"

"Because the one who wielded it is Fallen," Nakir said. "Demons are still spiritual beings. They are also enemies of God. When Satan fell from heaven, Rimmon was among the one-third who followed him, destined to serve until their ultimate demise."

Alastair's hand rested on Corinth's shoulder, his touch a silent acknowledgment of their bond. Nakir could feel the lingering struggle within Alastair. It was a reminder of the immense pain—physical, mental, and spiritual—that had accompanied his departure from his vessel.

Corinth's irritation seemed to grow. "You do realize that *your* sword, just like my dagger and shield, was designed with angelic properties to prevent its use by evil forces? What happened?"

"Was Angela able to wield *the* holy Lance?" Nakir retorted.

Corinth's eyes narrowed to tiny slits. "How do you know about Angela?"

"I have been keeping tabs." Nakir ran his fingers through his hair and sighed. "It's not always as straightforward as *good* and *evil.* But if Rimmon is indeed one of the Fallen, we might have worse problems than retrieving my sword."

Samyaza turned to Nakir, speaking urgently in his distinctive accent. "Do you think we should make preparations for the worst?"

Nakir held his hands up. "If we stop Rimmon, we stop impending doom."

"What do you mean by impending doom?" asked Corinth, his voice low and full of suspicion. "What are you hiding from us?"

"If Rimmon is not stopped, it could destroy humanity," Nakir finished.

"Oh, is that it?" Larna shot to her feet, her eyes widening.

Alastair's gaze remained fixed on the floor, his blonde hair obscuring his face. Nakir could sense that Alastair was disgruntled, but he cautioned Alastair that returning to his body and Earth would pose significant challenges.

Meanwhile, Corinth's demeanor still appeared impassive. But his chest's rise and fall hinted at the turmoil he felt upon hearing the news.

Alastair's fists were clenched against his thighs. "We're always dealing with *impending* doom. So, nothing new there. Something tells me Pete has more to do with this than Leo is letting on. I sure hope Leo knows what he's doing."

"Al's right," Corinth said. "We've got work to do. Sam and Tami, find Rimmon. Stay together—now that we know Rimmon can wield that sword." He turned to Larna, Alastair, and Nakir. "You three stay here and closely watch Zoey and Cruz. After that cryptic message from Ikari, we need to be more vigilant than ever." Rubbing his chin, he added, "I'll check in on Mom, Dad, and Jimmy and follow up with Gabriel Stanton. He always has a finger on the pulse. And trust me, Leo *will* fill me in on Pete—y'all leave that to me. I'm getting to the bottom of this one way or another. Rimmon will pay for what he did to Ikari. Time to ruffle some feathers."

Nakir gave the Nephilim a quick side-eye. "Corinth Taylor, I must retrieve my sword. You can stay here and care for Zoey and Cruz, and *I'll* talk to Gabriel Stanton … again."

"Could you clarify what you mean by *again*?" Corinth demanded.

"I visited Stanton's place in New York, but he denied knowing the whereabouts of my armor and sword," Nakir explained.

Corinth was about to speak, but Alastair beat him to it. "Hold on a minute. You told *Stanton* that your armor and sword are missing?" Alastair rolled his eyes at the ceiling. "Now we know who'll be hunting for those relics. That moron is *obsessed* with anything related to the immortal. He may be working with Rimmon as we speak."

Nakir stood tall, folding his arms across his chest. "I've already dealt with Gabriel Stanton."

"No one *deals* with Gabriel Stanton," Larna interjected. "He is incredibly persistent and doesn't give up when it comes to getting what he wants."

"Don't forget that Stanton doesn't *always* get what he wants," Corinth retorted. He snapped his fingers. A bolt of lightning brought forth his holy blade; the hilt crackled with fire as he tightened his grip around it. "While you're with me, you're under my command, Nakir."

"I am under God's command, and His command only, Nephilim," Nakir said in a whispered threat.

Corinth looked remarkably unfazed by Nakir's words.

"Fine," Nakir relented. "I will stay here to watch over Zoey and Cruz, but only if you promise to inform me when you receive news about Rimmon."

Corinth nodded. "Of course.

36

ZOEY

Leo had taken Cruz and me away, leaving us in shock and struggling to process what had just happened.

That's how we found ourselves in the company of the burly blacksmith, Vinson, of all people. Vinson led us to a secluded cabin tucked away amidst the vibrant surroundings' thick foliage and creeping vines. We'd overlooked this place several times. Intermittent clanging interrupted the solitude, and the air was thick with the scent of iron, sweat, and after-rain.

Nothing smells quite like Earth after it's been through the rinse cycle.

Except today, the stench of sulfur followed us.

I did not feel like confronting Nakir or Corinth. They would only lie.

Instead, I distracted myself from the horror of the day's events to study Vinson. Salt and pepper lined his wild beard and unkempt ponytail. He wore a thick brown leather apron with gloves and long-sleeved clothing.

Vinson was a man of few words, but his presence was

highly intimidating. Why did Cor trust him? We sat perched on the edge of a wooden fence, watching Vinson work from a few feet away. His aged face was covered with protective goggles as he stood before a giant anvil, hammering heated metal that looked like the beginning of some cutting instrument. The steel was unlike anything I'd ever seen, radiating a bright, almost blinding neon.

Mechanically, I spun my ring around my finger. I realized this must be where it had originated. Vinson had forged it—for me.

Ordinarily, that would have been all I could think about for a while, but my mind was dragged back to Ikari dying. That gnarly wound. The blood. And then it morphed Ephrem's hand protruding out of Peter's sternum. *Rimmon said he's coming for you, Corinth. Zoey and Cruz—you must keep them safe …*

I was so startled I nearly lost my balance on the fence. Cruz quickly reached out and caught me before I could fall.

"Are you okay?" he asked.

"No," I replied, not elaborating further.

He gently placed his hand over mine.

I wished I could give him a reassuring smile, but I couldn't. Training—maybe hitting something—would help me clear my mind and release built-up tension. Rage running.

Cruz was intensely focused on Vinson and his metallurgy. The chain around Cruz's neck was exposed through his thin shirt, and I could see the outline of the shield. I wondered if he'd figured out the same thing about his relic that I had.

"Do you always feel like this, Cruz?" I whispered after a moment.

Cruz glanced at me. "What do you mean?"

"Furious." The word left a bitter taste in my mouth. "I think I get it now."

"Anger is cleaner," he murmured. "In its raw state, it prevents you from feeling even more painful emotions ... I guess maybe that's why I get so mad all the time."

His words hit me deep, and we fell into a heavy silence again.

Pound, pound, pound.

Cruz nudged my shoulder.

The atmosphere was thick with intense emotions. When Cruz assured me he wouldn't leave me in the demon realm, I trusted him completely. Despite the opportunity, he didn't abandon me in that dreadful dungeon. It was incredibly comforting to rely on someone who believed in me and to reciprocate that trust. His bravery amid danger was a true reflection of his character.

Pound, pound, pound.

A bead of sweat sprang up on Vinson's forehead, trickling down into his eyes. He halted for a moment to clean his brow.

"Screw it." I hopped off the fence to see what he was working on. The coal burned red hot inside the furnace, and I could feel the heat from where I stood. Surprisingly, it didn't feel unbearable.

"*Zoey*," Cruz hissed from behind me. "What are you doing?"

Vinson paused, his eyes slowly shifting to mine as if he'd heard us. I held his gaze, my heart rate increasing. Those dark irises were soul-crushing and black.

"Your kids," I said, pointing toward the sound of giggles near his cabin. "They're cute."

Cruz quietly approached from behind me. It was evident that he was as eager as I was to learn more about Vinson and the magic created before our very eyes.

Vinson struck the glowing green iron again, causing a spark to fly off it. The sudden movement made me recoil. I floundered backward onto the tip of Cruz's toes. He let out a yelp and instinctively reached out to grab my waist, preventing me from falling. The sudden contact sent a warm, tingly sensation through me.

Cruz cleared his throat and stepped back, settling beside me.

"You're not scared, are you?" I mouthed to Cruz before returning my attention to Vinson. "I get it. You don't like small talk. Neither do I, to be honest. But what you're doing, is it like a combination of alchemy and metallurgy?"

"You are a lot like Corinth Taylor." Vinson paused before lifting his hammer again to take another strike. He spoke in a thick Russian accent, "I never believed in magic until I met your brother."

"I don't know about that," I replied. "Corinth is too talkative."

Vinson snickered, or maybe it was a grunt. I couldn't be sure because his face didn't move. It was like the guy had permanent Botox.

"I'm Zoey, and this is Cruz." I gestured at Cruz, who hesitantly greeted Vinson with a soft "*Hi.*"

Vinson carefully set his hammer aside, then removed his gloves and goggles without acknowledging our presence. He seemed entirely indifferent to social cues. Walking over to the corner of the forge, he approached a shaky table and picked up a canteen. He took a long, satisfying sip.

Cruz leaned in and whispered, "Didn't Corinth warn us *not* to talk to this guy?"

I shrugged, then opened my palm to reveal the ring I had removed, showing it to Vinson. "Did you make this?"

Vinson dabbed his mouth with his sleeve before setting down the canteen. He stayed quiet.

"I'm intrigued," I prodded. "What did you use to forge it? Corinth claimed he used a part of his blade to create the shield and my ring."

Vinson pursed his lips and pivoted, striding into the obscurity of the forge. *Great.* I'd upset him. I wondered if he'd come back.

A moment later, he appeared, clutching a sharp, jagged metal object as big as his forearm.

"Thanks to Corinth, we've formed what you see before you," Vinson explained.

"Wow, Fulgurite!" Cruz piped up excitedly. "When lightning strikes sand, it creates temperatures hotter than the sun's surface, causing the silt to fuse and turn into glass."

I glanced at Cruz and gave him a thumbs-up, thoroughly impressed by his knowledge.

Vinson maintained his poker face as his eyes locked with Cruz's. "This is crafted from discarded angel armor and a sliver of Corinth's dagger. Sadly, our supply is running dangerously low."

"Thank you," I murmured. Vinson tilted his head, and I continued, "I appreciate the ring and Cruz's shield. They truly saved our lives."

"Saving lives is exhausting," Vinson grumbled, wiping sweat from his brow.

"I guess we Taylors have a knack for getting into trouble—"

"And Saldivars," Cruz interjected.

"And Saldivars," I echoed.

Cruz shot Vinson a mischievous grin. "So, can I have a go with that hammer now?" he asked eagerly.

Vinson glared down at the object, his expression sour. He muttered something in Russian that sounded like a curse.

I felt a twinge of disappointment; I'd been eager to take a turn at it myself.

37

ZOEY

Vinson vented his anger on the molten metal while my fear and frustration continued to mount. Cruz was near the hearth, fiddling with the fulgurite. He seemed captivated by Vinson's strong, silent presence.

As much as I enjoyed Cruz's company, I felt a strong need for solitude. Lately, I found myself grappling with overwhelming anxiety.

We'd been waiting for news about Ikari for hours. None of the angels seemed willing to let us in on what happened. Who knew who would be next if even the angels could be so easily harmed? Cor seemed to be carrying the world's weight on his shoulders these days, his face permanently etched with pain and anguish. It was a stark reminder that despite his otherworldly nature, he was not immortal; I had seen him possessed and injured.

Whenever I closed my eyes, the memory of Corinth's cruelty in the demon realm flashed across my mind. Panic clawed its way up my throat.

It occurred to me that I couldn't remember the last time I'd eaten.

As I hopped off the wooden fence, a wave of unease washed over me, making my head spin. I turned toward the cottage to head back.

Suddenly, I heard Vinson's voice calling out from behind me. "Hey!" he shouted. "Where do you think you are going, *malen'kiy*?" Ignoring the question, I started jogging down the narrow path that wound through the dense woods, glancing back at Vinson. With a quick gesture, I indicated that I was unwell and shouted, "I'm not feeling great. I have my watch!"

Once out of his sight, I bolted. All I could think about was not throwing up in front of an audience.

Please don't follow me.

I stretched my limbs to their limits.

With each passing second, my breaths grew heavier, and my heart pounded against my chest as if desperate to break free. Soon, I found myself panting heavily, gasping for air. The discomfort felt oddly soothing. I pushed myself to go even faster, trying to outrun my emotions. Anger was cleaner. The wind was relentless, whipping my braid into my face.

Run faster. Run further.

After pushing myself to the limit, I finally took a much-needed break next to a colossal tree, my legs on the verge of giving out. I leaned over with my hands on my knees, gasping for air, feeling immense relief as I saw no sign of anyone following me. If they were, I had miraculously outpaced them.

My watch was beeping a warning. I looked at it. My heart rate was at 150 beats per minute. *Crap, that's fast.* All the grief, sorrow, and rage building up burst forth in a guttural scream. I punched the dirt until my knuckles hurt, and black filled my nails.

Leaning against the tree, the rough bark pressed into my flesh. It was an anchor to the present, to help me forget the soreness and exhaustion weighing me down. My body ached from the intense trial, and I realized I hadn't taken care of myself properly—no sleep, no proper meals. I closed my eyes, took a deep breath, and tried to clear my mind.

A sudden jolt brought me out of my stupor. Fighting to open my eyes, I realized something soft cushioned my head.

I gazed upward and found myself staring directly into Nakir's face. His coppery hair cascaded over one eye, allowing me to see his mesmerizing bottle-green irises with their tiny golden specks. A sweet aroma surrounded him. I couldn't tell if it was lavender, licorice, or maybe a blend of both.

"I didn't mean to wake you," he whispered.

I sat bolt upright and wiped my nose on my hoodie. "How long have you been there?"

"Only a few moments. You looked peaceful, but it was chilly. So, I thought I would sit beside you."

A rush of warmth engulfed me as I moved away from Nakir. Our conversation had been sparse since I learned he'd deceived me about Peter.

"I'm still furious with you, Nik," I muttered, unapologetic about the fact that I had been practically drooling on his shoulder. He had it coming.

"I understand," Nakir replied, absently picking up a damp leaf and twirling it between his fingers.

"Why didn't you tell me about Peter?" I inquired, my anger boiling back to the surface.

"For your safety. Peter is not the same person you once knew," he murmured. "He's a Shade, and as a demonic entity, he's unpredictable and dangerous. If you were to seek him out, he would only drag you into harm's way."

"I understand if you find it hard to believe, but I know my brother," I said, frustrated. "But I appreciate your honesty."

Nakir released the leaf from his grasp, dropping it near his booted foot. Despite his silence, his piercing gaze remained fixed on me, revealing an impossible intensity. As much as I tried to ignore it, I couldn't help but acknowledge his striking presence.

"When Alastair was your vessel, I saw your true self," I began. "The way you looked at me and intervened to save my life … It was an odd but reassuring feeling," I trailed off, coughing to break the intensity of his stare.

Nakir stayed unmoving as if he were carved from stone.

"I shouldn't have said anything." I started to get up, wiping off my pants. "Never mind—"

"I felt it, too."

His unexpected words struck me like a bolt. I spun around to confront Nakir, my jaw dropping in disbelief. A surge of emotion caught in my throat.

"So, that's why I couldn't go through with killing Corinth," he murmured.

Nakir had spared my life, but at the same time, he had attempted to take my brother's.

I hesitated, then exclaimed, "Honesty again? I can't believe it." My smile widened as I took a moment to look at him. He stayed quiet for a few more seconds, and I couldn't help but ask, "What's the significance of this?"

Nakir shook his head, his gaze shifting to the sky. The faint silhouette of the sun on his face enveloped him in a warm glow and softened the contours of his features.

"A sign," he said in a calm but barely audible voice.

A hush fell between us until I mustered the courage to ask the question weighing on my mind. "Do you feel threatened by Rimmon?"

"Yes," he replied. "And while I'm being forthright, there's something else you should know."

"What?" I asked, curiosity and fear lacing my voice.

"Rimmon can wield my sword and has the power to revive Ephrem."

My fists clenched instinctively. A rush of terror surged from deep within me, and I wondered if knowing the truth was worth it.

38

LEO

Leo found himself standing in the middle of the desert, his armor gleaming in the sunlight. In the aftermath of Ikari's death, he was torn between seeking solace from his brother, Corinth, and the fierce desire to unleash his temper and pain. The internal conflict, a storm of emotions, raged inside him, urging him to seek catharsis through destruction—like finding and ripping Rimmon apart.

Standing over the vast chasm, Leo let out a primal scream, his voice echoing off the towering cliffs. Sunlight glinted off his greaves, a spark that could catch the dry landscape on fire.

Far below, jutting auburn-colored rock formations and a meandering river snaked around massive mountains in the distance. Leo felt a deep connection to this place, understanding why Ari liked it so much.

This has to end, and he will be the one to end it.

Leo held tightly onto the accursed Lucifer's horn that Ari had given him. Even though he knew the thing was vile, it was an exquisite piece of art. Its surface was as smooth and polished as a black diamond. Its color resembled an oil slick—dark and mysterious, while a unique, jagged gold crack ran down its center.

Ikari would have appreciated its beauty. He would have said something like, *It's like Japan's ancient art of embracing imperfection—the joining with gold. For the Japanese, it's part of a broader philosophy of embracing the beauty of human flaws.*

Leo hesitated, overwhelmed by indecision.

Finally, he lifted the horn to his lips and blew into it, producing a low, eerie wail that sounded like a demonic French horn. The unnerving silence stretched into what felt like an eternity. Leo's mind raced. His senses heightened as he thought the Shade had arrived. A creeping dread filled the air, along with the acrid scent of sulfur.

A sharp voice shattered the silence. "You better have a good explanation for calling on me."

Leo's hold on the horn slackened. He dropped it, his sword magically appearing in his hand almost instantaneously. He pointed the angelic blade at the Shade. "Did you set Ikari up?" His tone was challenging and cold. "Am I next, Shade? Did you save me so you could report back to Rimmon? Is Corinth next? How about Zo?"

Ari's pitch-black eyes shifted when he heard Leo say *Zo.* Was anger flaring in them? Maybe Ari cared about his siblings' well-being after all. But most likely, he did not.

The Shade donned a cloak that seemed to be from the medieval era. The hooded cape covered the top half of his body, while black trousers and boots completed the rest of his outfit. He almost looked like a character from a Western.

"Wow, things must look pretty bad if you're decked out in full armor, including a breastplate. That looks heavy," Ari observed coolly.

"It belonged to Ikari. I wear it in honor of him," Leo snarled. "I'm unsure if I can trust you any longer. Did you know about Ikari? It was Rimmon who killed him. He held him prisoner."

"Yes, I knew about Ikari's death," came Ari's terse reply. "Are you planning on running me through with that sword?"

"I should," Leo retorted. The Shade's absence of hesitation, explanation, or concern unsettled him. Leo no longer cared if Ari was Corinth's sibling. This wasn't Corinth's brother. Its voice was utterly devoid of emotion.

"I'm trying my best not to attract attention, Leo." Ari flashed him a thin-lipped smile. "I had no idea they would ambush the angel. I only found out *after* it happened, and I wasn't present when they captured Ikari, or I would have given you a heads-up. I thought we had a plan. Do you not wish to stick with it?"

Leo took a deep breath before he spoke again. "How did Rimmon get Nakir's sword?"

"They fought side by side together before Rimmon decided to follow Lucifer," Ari explained. "The sword went to Rimmon as soon as Nakir vacated his vessel."

Hearing that, Leo took a faltering step back.

"We might want to prepare for an unpleasant reunion when those two cross paths again." Ari scratched his nose. "Look, I have to work my way up the ranks. It's difficult, considering I have to keep sneaking away to meet with you every time you bello—"

"So, you *are* going behind my back."

Leo felt a presence behind him. He turned swiftly, his sword poised for action. "*Corinth.*" Leo dropped his weapon back down to his side. It vanished in a swirl of blue flame. "How did you find me?"

For a long, drawn-out moment, no one moved or spoke.

Corinth's face contorted with intense betrayal, his complexion turning an angry shade of red. He gripped his crackling blade with a fierce determination. "Did you honestly believe I wouldn't do whatever it took to find my brother?"

I'm sorry, Corinth, Leo told him through their telepathic link.

Corinth lowered his dagger, the lightning gradually fading as it evaporated into oblivion, sheathed back at his thigh.

Not forgiven, Corinth shot back.

"I specifically instructed you *not* to divulge my whereabouts to Corinth." Ari's countenance darkened significantly as he spoke. "What part of our pact did you fail to comprehend, Leo?"

"I didn't invite him." Leo shrugged. "How did you track me down, Corinth?"

"Humans have a few tricks up their sleeves that even angels lack." Corinth retrieved his cell from his back pocket. "I put a tracker on your armor."

"Clever," Leo said, impressed. It was almost a relief that Corinth was here. Leo hated lying to him. Perhaps this would be for the better—all their cards on the table.

Corinth drew closer to his brother, who backed away, inching nearer to the precipice.

The Shade didn't want Corinth to see its face.

"That's close enough, Taylor," Ari said, putting a hand out to stop him. "My name isn't Peter. Call me Ari."

"Only if you stop calling me *Taylor*. I know what you're doing; you're trying to distance yourself from me, Pete, and I'm not buying it," Corinth said.

"This was a mistake—" Ari spun, his body beginning to splinter and dissolve into black sand, signaling his intention to flee.

"*Please!*" Corinth shouted. "Okay, okay. Have it your way, *Ari*."

Corinth's cry of *Ari* stopped him from leaving. The Shade looked up, slightly taken aback as he rematerialized. "What do you want, Corinth?" Ari finally asked, his voice hardening around Corinth's name in a way that turned Leo's stomach.

Corinth paused, took a deep breath, and said, "I only wanted to make sure you're … okay."

Ari tilted his head to one side and released a strained, detached chortle. "I'm a Shade, so no, *not* okay."

"I can help you," Corinth pressed. "All you have to do is come home. I can fix you … we can figure this out together—as a family. Just like we always do. Zo misses you—"

Ari bared his teeth, growling. "*Fix* me? What makes you think I want or need to be *fixed*?" he snarled. "You can't *fix* everything. This is what you get." He gestured at himself. "A nasty-looking, cold-hearted monster." The Shade threw his hood back, revealing its bald head and the supernaturally polished onyx skin with gold streaks running down its cheeks. *Gold*, not silver, Leo noted.

Corinth flinched. It was fleeting, but the damage was done before he could rectify it.

A cold smile crept onto Ari's face. "You see, even my *brother* can't bear to lay eyes on me."

Leo studied Ari more closely. *Brother*, Ari had said. The word lingered in Leo's mind.

Corinth ran his fingers through his coifed hair, his voice low and thoughtful. "Zo told me about what happened in the demon realm. She said you saved her life. I can see that you're different—just like *I'm* different. I'm half-angel; you're half-Shade. And I know you're decent, and that means something."

"Half-Shade?" Ari laughed. "Thick-headed idiot."

"Let him go, Corinth," Leo urged.

"I'm not giving up on Pete. *Never*," Corinth hissed. "I'm his older brother."

"Do you see what I mean?" Ari barked. "Corinth just can't accept that I'm not who I used to be. This is why I said to keep him away from me. Taylor, don't expect a friendly welcome if you show up again. I'll be in touch, Leo."

And with that, Ari vanished, leaving behind a scattering of black dust and things left unsaid.

39

ZOEY

I was in my bedroom after a call with Mom, Dad, and Jimmy when Cruz walked in and caught my attention. Keisha had been messaging me continuously, so I planned to text her next. But Cruz picked at his fingernail and stared at me like something was on his mind.

"Out with it, Cruz." I threw my phone on the bed beside me.

"Hey, are you all right?" he asked, genuinely concerned. "I got worried when you ran out of Vinson's forge."

"You keep asking me, expecting a different answer." I stretched my sore ankles. Cruz shook his head slightly as I continued. "Everything's just so messed up right now. I miss home, and the thought of Ephrem returning makes me more than troubled."

I was so tired.

"I get that," he said slowly, giving me a sideways glance.

"What else is there to talk about?" I rolled under the covers, hiding the burgeoning emotions threatening to surface again. My chest felt tight, and my breathing was shallow. Maybe I was getting sick.

Cruz's watch and phone buzzed, indicating that someone had texted him. After a few minutes of silence, I threw the covers back. He had a goofy grin on his face as he stared down at his phone, dimples on display.

"It's nice to see *someone's* happy," I said sullenly, clutching my chest and grimacing.

"Oh, it's just my mom wishing me a happy birthday—"

"It's your *birthday*?" I bolted upright, ignoring the fresh aches in my thighs, back, and arms. "Why didn't you tell me? Now I feel doubly awful for ditching you." I tapped on my phone's screen to check the date. I had almost forgotten what month it was. "It's April 30th. You just turned eighteen, didn't you?"

"I didn't want to make a fuss. My mom likes to celebrate more than I do. I'm sad I won't have her *tres leches* cake, though."

"Wait, are you going to graduation or prom?" I asked.

"That's really not my thing. Besides, I like it here." Cruz lifted one shoulder, letting his voice trail off before adding, "Back home, I'd be working."

I swung my legs off the bed and ran my fingers through my braid, hoping to make it look more presentable. "Let's go get cake. It might not be *tres leches*, but we'll get whatever's available in town." The idea of an unplanned adventure filled me with a sudden exhilaration. When I went to stand, though, I got a headrush. Little pockets of stars popped across my vision.

"Hey, are you okay?" Cruz was beside me instantly, his face scrunched up in concern. "Do you really think that's a good idea? Especially after …" he gulped. "Ikari. Aren't we under house arrest or something? Besides, you don't look so hot."

I rubbed my temples and gulped. "It feels like the walls are shrinking in around me. I don't really like being inside anymore."

"Uh, that sounds like a panic attack," Cruz murmured. "Come on, let's at least go for a walk."

I nodded, thinking that fresh air might do me some good. Slowly, I went to my dresser and rummaged through the top drawer. "Let me grab my jacket and shoes." After a brief search, I found gloves and a fresh hoodie hidden at the bottom. I knew I'd need these for our walk, with the weather still chilly and cloudy.

Cruz went to his open luggage and snatched his parka from its depths. His spicy cologne wafted over to me as he slipped it on over his workout clothes and zipped it up.

The memory of wearing it in the demon realm suddenly struck, and cold washed over me at the vivid recollection. I must have looked even worse now because Cruz bit his bottom lip. The look on his face made it evident that I must have seemed troubled.

The ring Vinson had made with Corinth's lightning glowed brilliantly, reassuring me that everything would be okay. Cruz strode over to me and grabbed my hand in his, and suddenly, the world didn't feel so small, and the walls weren't closing in around me.

Cruz and I strolled along the road toward town, leaving behind the cottage and the pastures dotted with grazing sheep. We had no destination in mind. The peaceful beauty of the undulating hills starkly contrasted the flat terrain of Texas—the sky a canvas of deep charcoal. Heavy clouds loomed overhead, ready to unleash their watery payload. There was nothing more miserable than getting soaked in cold rain. I silently pleaded with the heavens to spare us from such a fate because I was starting to feel slightly better. The farther we walked, the more unburdened I felt.

Dense black curls were neatly brushed to one side of Cruz's head, held together by a heap of gel. All the workouts we had been doing had paid off, as he looked lean and fit. Having recently experienced the difficulty of running and exercising, I had a newfound appreciation for the effort required to stay in shape.

Cruz's eyes were locked forward as he asked, "Does the darkness still get to you like it used to?" He attempted to sound casual, but I detected his hesitation to ask.

I chewed on the inside of my cheek, thinking. "Sometimes, yeah," I admitted.

After a prolonged silence, Cruz held up his scarred hands for me to see. They looked like tiny snowflakes traced on by a silver marker.

"I got into a fight at work the night those Shades attacked me," he admitted.

Cruz suddenly appeared hampered by guilt.

"What's wrong?" I asked softly, leaning in closer to him.

"I had a run-in with some guys I'd had issues with before," he explained, his tone growing intense. "I didn't start it, but the temptation to strike back was too strong. I mean, look at what happened with Nakir. Grabbing that sword and going after an angel was reckless and impulsive. What was going through my head?"

"Are you going to tell me that your bloodlust is too much to handle, and you're going to turn into a werewolf at the full moon?" I grinned at him. "I'm sure those guys had it coming."

Cruz let out a soft snicker. "They did."

"What was the run-in about, anyway?" I asked.

"I didn't like how one of them treated his girlfriend, so I spoke up about it ... and when he didn't like that, I broke his jaw."

I rubbed my chin, my eyes widening at that. "You ... broke his jaw?" As I pondered Cruz speaking up for a girl he barely knew, I was reminded of what he'd done for me in the demon realm. The thought prompted me to pull my hoodie over my head and tighten it. He was impulsive and rash, but he was also brave and selfless.

"Honestly, I think you're much more levelheaded than you give yourself credit for," I finally said.

Cruz's rigid posture eased, and he straightened to his full height as if a weight had been lifted from his shoulders. "I appreciate you saying that."

I nudged his arm, and he flashed me his thousand-watt grin. What a difference a smile can make.

Up ahead of us, as we strolled along, I noticed a lone figure standing near a wooden fence post. I tensed, lifting the hand with my ring on it—until I saw curly amber locks and a bronzed complexion. Nakir. He leaned against the post with arms crossed lazily over his chest, waiting for us to get closer.

"Surprise, surprise," Cruz whispered out of the side of his mouth.

When we got within earshot, Nakir pushed off the fence, striding toward us. "I heard that."

"Angels and their supernatural hearing," Cruz muttered.

Nakir filed in line beside us, his arms still crossed. "Would either of you consider turning back right now … you know, because of the threat of *demons*?" he asked. "Or should I just portal you both away without your consent?"

Cruz glanced around the desolate road. "Unless these demons are possessing the sheep, I think we're out of harm's way for the moment."

I snorted.

"You're *never* out of harm's way," Nakir snapped.

"Come on, Nik," I said, exasperated. "I needed the fresh air. We may have gotten a little carried away with how far we walked—"

"What's so important?" Nakir demanded.

"Well, this is Cruz's eighteenth birthday. It's a *huge* milestone. Would you consider joining us for cake and hot chocolate? We won't have to worry about demon attacks with you there to protect us."

Appease his ego. Did angels have egos? Undoubtedly.

"Zoey was having a panic attack," Cruz blurted out.

I shot Cruz a look, and Nakir pressed his lips together as if he were going to say *absolutely not* but then thought better of it.

But Cruz cut in first. "Come on, it's my *birthday*!"

"I don't think it's a wise decision," Nakir muttered, "but who knows how many birthdays you have left, Cruz … so let's go."

40

CRUZ

As Cruz, Zoey, and Nakir strolled through Crieff in Scotland, he was immediately struck by the lively atmosphere of the town square. They had been here for over a month, and this was their first visit to town—the square bustled with life and energy, far more than he had anticipated. Cruz quickly realized it was also a hub for various storefronts and pubs. Among the quaint shops were an antique store, Jackson's Fine Wines, a toy shop, and several gift shops. The cobblestone streets and historic buildings added to the charm, which starkly contrasted with the modern, vibrant streets of Mexico City—the only other place Cruz had visited out of the U.S. It was a stark difference that was both refreshing and intriguing.

Crieff felt lazy and relaxed. Wandering without a destination was nice. A break from not training, running, and schoolwork was precisely what the doctor ordered. He would have been much happier if not for the third wheel—Nakir, who was totally killing the vibe.

The archangel kept a wary eye out as he scanned the area.

Zoey, walking beside Cruz, was a picture of pure excitement. Her face lit up as she gazed at the various buildings. She looked adorable, her blond braid peeking out from under her hoodie and her cheeks rosy. Cruz wished he had more time to talk to her alone.

As they strolled to the end of the street, a few bikers passed by, and Cruz caught sight of a greenhouse filled with plentiful fresh produce and plants.

Zoey gestured toward a sign with the words 'Tea Garden.' "That looks like as good a place as any to stop."

The café nestled in the heart of a deep valley, surrounded by vibrant greenery. Every outdoor table was occupied, and the air felt chillier, like the temperature had dropped.

Stepping inside, Cruz was greeted by a comforting warmth and the tantalizing aroma of freshly baked dough. The place was packed, and most people were waiting to place their orders. The food selection ranged from tarts and paninis to pastries and cakes.

Nakir looked stiff and on edge as he gestured to a recently vacated table at the back. "I'll grab that table for us."

Cruz knew the archangel was inspecting the place for any hint of demons.

"Do you want anything?" Zoey offered. Nakir looked perplexed, so she added, "You know … to blend in. It would be awkward if you sat there looking miserable and stiff."

Cruz suppressed his laughter as Nakir replied, "I'll have whatever you're having."

Zoey mock-saluted Nakir. "Yes, sir," she said as Cruz followed her to the end of the queue.

"Did you catch that Nakir *conveniently* forgot to chip in," Cruz remarked.

"Don't worry about it. I'm buying," Zoey said. "And as long as he's on bodyguard duty, I don't mind. I've been saving up some money for a special occasion."

With a playful shove, Cruz said, "I won't say no to that." His stomach grumbled as they neared the front counter, his mouth already watering at the sight of the pastries and desserts on display. They had walked a long way to get here, and the journey had burned off his early breakfast.

As the line thinned out, Cruz could hardly contain his excitement.

Zoey pointed to various cakes and tarts. "These all look delicious," she said, licking her lips.

A girl with short flaxen hair approached from behind the counter. "How can I help you?"

Cruz noticed her heavy accent when she spoke—*can* sounded like *kin*.

"Two hot chocolates and two strawberry tarts, please." Zoey glanced at Cruz, indicating that it was his turn to order.

"Make that three," he piped up.

The employee informed Zoey of the price in pounds. Cruz realized he only had American dollars on him and glanced at Zoey. However, she was ready for this and produced the required amount in pounds, handing the money to the lady.

"Good thing *you* were prepared," Cruz told her.

Zoey flashed him a sly grin, her eyes sparkling mischievously. "Cor gave me some for emergencies, but you know what? I think this qualifies as an emergency."

"Oh, this definitely counts," Cruz agreed as his stomach rumbled again. "I'm about to die of starvation."

The lady returned and handed Zoey the hot chocolates and desserts on a tray.

"It's nice to be on the other side of the counter for once," Cruz pointed out as he took the tray from Zoey.

The room buzzed with animated chatter, laughter, and the gentle clinking of silverware. Nakir stood out as he sat brooding at the back of the dining area, casting suspicious glances around him. Cruz noticed Nakir had strategically positioned himself with his back against the wall.

As they arrived at the table and put the tray of goodies down, Cruz swiftly pulled Zoey's chair out for her before she could sit. She rewarded him with a smile and sat to Nakir's right.

"If you were any stiffer, you'd be inside a coffin," Cruz noted, shrugging off his jacket and draping it over the back of the chair. The restaurant had rich, antique wooden furniture. It gave off a polished scent that mingled with the comforting aroma of toasted bread. The dim lighting added to the atmosphere, especially with the gloomy weather casting spooky shadows across the room.

Zoey removed her gloves, pushed up her sleeves, and wrapped her hands around her mug.

Nakir lifted an eyebrow. "I only care about your safety."

"*Only your safety*," Cruz mocked back. "Whatever you say, Terminator."

Zoey chuckled as she blew on her drink and took a small sip. Her eyes rolled back. "*Mmm*, that's good."

Nakir gave Cruz a stony look, and Cruz immediately backed down. "Okay, okay, I'm kidding. We appreciate you looking out for us." He took a drink from his mug. "This is the best hot chocolate … ever."

"Do you not want your drink?" asked Zoey, looking at Nakir's untouched hot chocolate.

Nakir hesitated before confessing, "I've never had it before."

Zoey's eyes widened, almost bulging out of her head. "Do you not eat or drink?"

Cruz dug into his tart, the rich sugar immediately perking up his taste buds.

"I do not need food or water to survive, but I can eat or drink whatever I wish," Nakir whispered, ensuring no one could hear their conversation. "Don't worry; I will do my best to fit in."

Cruz looked around, but nobody appeared to take notice of them.

Nakir hesitated for a moment before lifting the mug to his lips. After a slow, deliberate sip, he set the cup down and announced, "It's quite good."

Zoey grinned at Cruz. "The angel has a sweet tooth for chocolate … I mean, who can resist it, right?"

Cruz sipped his drink and licked the whipped cream from his lips.

"Mind if I ask you something, Nik?" Zoey inquired, her attention now on the dessert in front of her, which she had already begun to sample.

Nakir gave a hesitant nod.

"I was just wondering." She paused before lowering her voice. "Did you fly? What was it like?"

The angel raised his head to the ceiling and briefly closed his eyes. "Once upon a time." For several moments, he remained silent, seemingly lost in thought or memory.

Cruz detected a faint hint of sadness etched on Nakir's face. Suddenly, a vivid image of the angel without his shirt on, revealing his scarred back, came to Cruz's mind. Was that sympathy he felt for Nakir?

Nah.

Nakir spoke in an unfamiliar language, his voice light and honeyed. It was mesmerizing, haunting, and sing-song.

Zoey's voice cracked with emotion. "What does that mean?"

"It can't be translated into your language," Nakir replied with a hint of heartache. "No mortal words can do it justice."

Cruz imagined losing wings was like losing limbs.

"I'm sorry, Nik," She murmured. "It was none of my business."

"No need for remorse," Nakir said evenly. "It had to be done—"

As soon as he uttered those words, the room's temperature plummeted so rapidly that it seemed like an unseen presence had whisked away all the heat. What remained was a chilling frost and unsettling oppressiveness.

Supernaturally oppressive—demonically.

The ruby on Zoey's ring sparked, signaling the presence of evil.

A second later, the shield under Cruz's shirt grew white-hot. The biting cold intensified, seeping into every nook and cranny around them—into the cafe's corners, spreading like spiderwebs. The air even crackled with frost. Several gasps went around the room as Nakir stood so abruptly that his chair hit the floor, causing heads to turn.

Demons.

Nakir scanned the crowded dining hall.

"Rimmon is here." Nakir stared intently at a fixed

point behind Cruz. He lifted his hand to summon angel grace, but only tiny sparks popped off his fingers. "I can't portal us out. The cold is ... messing with my grace." His voice was unsteady. "Zoey, Cruz. I'll hold him off. RUN."

Cruz was startled as he tried to move, only to find his legs completely unresponsive, frozen by an invisible force. His muscles strained, but he was as immobile as stone.

Beside him, Zoey stood in the same uncanny predicament, her wide-eyed gaze fixed on the chaotic scene around them. "What—" she gasped, "the heck—just happened?"

Everyone started dropping their forks, phones, or whatever they held, crying as panic set in.

"I—I can't move," Cruz stuttered, his lips slow to respond. The hot chocolate in his hand turned to icy slush inside the cup. "W-h-hat the ..." he gasped, his fingers curled around the mug turning a frostbitten purple. Cruz released the glass, letting out a shriek of pain as it shattered on the table. The chairs glistened with a thin layer of ice, resembling delicate morning dew on blades of grass. A shiver ran down Cruz's spine as he watched the frost creeping closer and closer. It was as if the icy tendrils were taking hold of everything and everyone in their path.

How could any of this be happening?

Nakir snapped his fingers, trying again to summon his angelic grace, but it didn't work.

It appeared Cruz and Zoey were the only ones frozen in place. The other patrons had started to run for the exits, trampling one another in their haste to escape.

And then the crowd parted around a lone figure striding toward their table.

Shit, shit, shit.

The demon's hand gripped the hilt of a sword, the blade radiating an intense, fiery glow like molten metal. Rimmon's oxblood suit commanded attention as much as the glowing weapon and the polished wing-tipped shoes glinting under the dim light. With each step, the sword left scorching marks on the floor, the trail smoldering behind him as he advanced.

Rimmon's appearance was striking and chilling and almost porcelain-like in perfection—like a demented doll. His eyes were ablaze, flickering from deep, demon-black to a piercing cobalt.

It was utterly terrifying.

Nakir raised his hands and let out a war cry. It finally worked. A shimmering angelic dome formed over their heads, cascading down around them, closing them off from everyone else. The archangel looked the worse for wear, as if he'd used most of his energy to seal them off from danger.

Cruz surveyed the scene before him. The ones who hadn't managed to escape were still seated at their tables, motionless, wide-eyed, and rigid. People's eyelashes and lips were coated in frost, and their eyes were open, indicating the sudden and tragic end they had met. *No.* His heart sank.

This was what Cruz got for celebrating his birthday.

41

ZOEY

My blood ran cold, but at least Cruz and I could move again. Nakir's shield seemed to protect us from the demon—for now. But even under the angel's protection, it was still brutally cold. Rimmon had killed people right in front of us just by passing them. The temperature had been so severe that they'd died instantly.

Our only chance at survival rested on the shield that Nik had produced.

Suddenly, I was trapped in the memories of the demon realm with Alastair, Corinth, and Cruz. The recollection hit me so hard that I felt faint.

I shook my head. *This is what you trained for*, I urged myself. *Fight.*

I gazed at Nik's face, searching for a sign of encouragement. His lips were ashen, and he mumbled something indecipherable. That familiar expression sent a shiver down my spine; it mirrored the one Corinth had worn countless times before. Nik was attempting to connect with other angels telepathically, desperately seeking help.

"*Silver hell,*" Nik snarled, sounding frustrated. "Rimmon is too strong."

Before us, the demon wore a flashy cherry-red suit and matching shoes. His shirt was unbuttoned, exposing his bare chest. His face was a paradox, both youthful and ancient.

Rimmon's hand hovered close to the glittering shield that surrounded us. He tilted his head mischievously, inspecting the translucent dome. His demeanor was unfazed by the barrier. Amusement flickered in those soulless eyes—we were like bugs under a magnifying glass, about to get burned.

A demon as conceited as Ephrem, but unquestionably deadlier.

I tried to press the panic button on my watch, only to realize its face was completely frozen, covered in a thick layer of ice. Frustrated, I tugged my cell phone out of my back pocket. However, a sudden, sharp pain in my hand caused me to drop it, shattering the screen into a million tiny pieces. I cursed, noticing the fiery ruby on my ring sparking, the golden band hot against my skin.

"Hello again, Nakir," Rimmon said calmly. His voice was velvety smooth, like a warm Southern accent (the only thing warm about him). His eyes never left Nakir's.

"Give—me—my—sword," Nakir spat, his voice filled with barely controlled wrath.

Rimmon held up the stolen weapon and addressed Nakir in a friendly tone, showing no signs of fear. "This sword? But it's mine now. It came to me."

The demon shifted his gaze to Cruz and me. His eyes

were unsettling—completely black with no trace of white. Rimmon locked eyes with me for a moment, paralyzing me with terror.

"I guess I'll just have to take it off your corpse then," Nakir growled.

Rimmon stood his ground, unflinching. "I was simply intrigued by those two children. If you agree, I'll release them without harm."

"You killed all these innocent people because of your curiosity?" I spat, my anger boiling over.

Cruz stuck his chest out, bristling. "And who are you calling children, *demon*?"

Rimmon turned to Cruz, his eyes dancing like flames. Cruz hopped back and yelped, knocking over a chair behind him, as Rimmon said, "You *are* children. And these humans, innocent? I hardly think so. They sin. Just like you, Cruz. Always so furious, aren't we? And who could blame you? By my side, I would let you unleash all that pent-up anger on those who truly deserve it."

"Shut up!" Cruz bellowed.

Rimmon's cruel gaze made me remember when Ephrem struck me in the demon realm. The memory of that violent act filled me with an all-consuming rage. This evil had caused so much destruction and pain—to my family. To me. To Cruz.

I refused to be a victim again.

With unwavering resolve, I seized the ring's potent energy, drew a steadying breath, and focused on my needs. Gently, I extended my hand and pressed it against the radiant shield surrounding us, harnessing its power just as Corinth had instructed. A rush of energy surged through my body, causing my head to whip back. *Holy mother of ...*

I can't contain it. Nakir's grace was raw and blistering, and it hurt. Focusing on the task, my ring transformed into a bow with an already-knocked arrow as I pulled my hand away from the glowing barrier. The power surged through me, charring my fingertips. Turning back, I sought Nakir's guidance. His eyes were half-closed from the level of grace he used to keep the shield intact and from me piggybacking his power.

I didn't want to make things worse, but when he nodded and mouthed, "*Do it*," his eyes glimmering with bewilderment.

It spurred me to action.

Rimmon's gaze caught mine, his expression betraying a hint of curiosity. "Well, well, well. What do we have here?"

I pivoted to face the demon, determined not to show any reluctance—an arrow pointed right at his forehead. With a steady inhale, I let the bolt fly, watching it soar through the air ... and then wobble off target.

Amazingly, the golden projectile passed through the shield and struck Rimmon in the shoulder.

Rimmon jerked back momentarily, a flicker of pain and anger masking his face. He yanked on the shaft, pulled it free, and dropped it. The arrow clattered to the floor with a dramatic rattle as Cruz inhaled sharply behind me.

The grace rushed through me—only to drain away just as quickly, leaving me weak and trembling and I sank to my knees. Cruz slid down next to me as my hearing faded in and out, distorted and fragmented.

I uttered in a half-amazed tone as if from far away, "*I hit him.*"

"Yeah, you did." Cruz sounded impressed. "But ... you're hurt."

I glanced down to see my fingertips were red, raw, and smudged black.

With fury blazing in Cruz's eyes, he rose to his feet, shrugged, tore off his necklace, and gripped the shield with all his might. "My turn."

Rimmon reached out and touched the gleaming dome in a dramatic, almost leisurely way. In his other hand, he gripped the hilt of Nakir's sword, as if seeking strength from the weapon.

Suddenly, a shower of sparks erupted from Rimmon, and the stench of burning flesh hit my nostrils. Despite the apparent agony etched on the demon's unlined face, he gritted his teeth and continued to touch the buffer between us for a few more moments. When Rimmon pulled back his hand, it was blackened and burnt. It seemed like he took some twisted power from it.

"You know, Cruz, your mother will be my next visit, I think," Rimmon goaded. "If only you dared to stop me."

I looked at Cruz, shaking my head and trying to catch his gaze, but he refused to make eye contact. His face was turning red.

Meanwhile, Nakir tried to keep his barrier from shattering into a million pieces.

"Don't listen to the demon—" I started to say, but Cruz's medallion expanded, shifted, and morphed into a full-sized shield. He shouted incoherently and sprinted toward Rimmon, the shield held out before him.

Nakir shouted, "No, don't!" but it was too late.

Cruz barreled into the angelic wall, using his shield as a battering ram, unleashing a violent surge that ripped through the place like a raging storm as he struck Rimmon full force. There was the sound of a high-pitched roar as they vanished into thick, black smoke.

A blast wave propelled me in the opposite direction, and a rickety table struck me out of nowhere.

Time held no meaning as I lay sprawled on the floor, my arms trapped beneath me, surrounded by food and debris. It felt like an eternity in that chaotic moment. A low moan slipped from my lips, and white spots clouded my vision. The taste of soot and sulfur lingered at the back of my throat.

Nakir. Cruz.

I blinked groggily, and my gaze landed on Nakir first. He lay still in a crumpled heap near the front counter, his clothes charred and tattered. A fresh cut marred his forehead, and his eyes remained shut.

My heart plummeted like a stone.

Please be alive.

I rose shakily, ran to the archangel, fell clumsily onto my knees, and violently shook him. "Come on, Nik! Wake up!" I cried. He remained still and silent, his eyes closed. "Please, wake up. I need you to wake up *now.*"

Struggling to stand again, I grasped the back of a chair and surveyed the chaotic scene, hoping to spot Cruz. *He's okay. He ran away. He isn't dead.* Amid the tangle of bodies, it wasn't easy to discern who was who, so I searched for any indication of life. My fists clenched so tightly that my nails dug into skin.

"That was fun."

That accent was smooth, silky, and flattering—the demon's pace was unhurried and slow.

My eyes snagged on the flash of red.

Rimmon stood in the hallway to the bathroom, casually wiping the dirt from his pants, his eyes locked on something at his feet. I followed his line of sight to see a pair of sneakers that resembled Cruz's. "Thank your wild temper," Rimmon said coolly, looking down at a prone form.

To my relief, I saw the feet twitch. Cruz was alive, but for how long, I wasn't sure. He was unconscious, lying flat on his back, and in mortal danger.

"Stay away from him!" I shouted.

Rimmon, surprised, snapped his head up. His gaze snagged on me from across the room, and he raised an eyebrow. He slowly crouched down and effortlessly lifted Cruz by his collar with one hand. Cruz's feet dangled like deadweight in the air.

Frantically scanning the smoke-filled room, I searched for anything that could aid me. I had my ring, but where was the sword? Suddenly, a glint caught my eye beneath rubble nearby.

I lunged for the hilt, snatching it up before brandishing it at Rimmon. With a surge of confidence, I taunted, "Hey, demon, do you want this?"

"That belongs to me, child," he said slowly, dropping Cruz. "Now give it back."

"Come and get it!" Warm grace shot through my veins, and my ring pulsed, signifying that my idea was taking shape. Sparks started to fly off my Converse.

I dashed toward the exit, moving at a pace beyond human capability. Determination drove me forward, regardless of the potential consequences.

My hair tumbled down my shoulders as my braid came undone. The wind whipped around me. Adrenaline surged through my veins, making my blood boil and my heart race as I ran faster than humanly possible.

Thank you, ring!

I never felt more alive and freer than in that moment.

As I raced ahead, I saw Rimmon struggling to keep up in my peripheral vision. The sword's weight in my hand felt exhilaratingly light as I outpaced a demon—even faster than Cor and Nakir.

Racing across miles in mere seconds, everything around me turned into a dizzying, maddening whirl. As I pushed ahead, my confidence wavered. The unreal speed and unfamiliar scenery left me feeling discombobulated.

The icy wind whipped against my face, but my hands were slick with sweat. I struggled to keep hold of the sword.

Suddenly, the fierce buzz of my watch came back to life.

A deep, sharp pain lanced through my chest, causing me to screech to a halt so fast that I left skid marks in the dirt behind me. My Converse were on fire. I let go of the sword, feeling it slip from my grasp. I tumbled and tumbled, the world spinning around me until I finally stopped, the scent of damp grass filling my senses and the persistent drone of my watch echoing in my ears.

Stranded in the middle of a field, I lay on my back, completely disoriented and unsure of where I was. I knew I had to get up and run—Rimmon wouldn't be far behind—but my heart pounded abnormally against my rib cage, matching the rhythm of my confusion.

As I lay there, drenched and surrounded by spongy earth, a sheep grazed nearby, chewing obnoxiously on the tall weeds. Its indifferent stare implied that my soggy situation was of no concern.

With my vision blurred, I still caught a glimpse of my watch. The display showed a blinking heart icon.

The world tilted and spun.

I gazed upward at a swirling cloud, feeling a growing sense of urgency.

Rimmon appeared in my line of sight. I fought the urge to vomit.

He peered down at me, keeping the sword just beyond my grasp. "Your doctors would call this tachycardia," the demon drawled. "It means your heart is not filling with blood before it pumps again."

My chest did feel tight, and I couldn't get up, no matter how hard I willed my ring to work—to heal me. But it had to be a lie. I was only sixteen. I couldn't have a heart attack. *Could I?*

"Heart attacks are no joke," Rimmon remarked with a disapproving shake of his head. As I gaped in disbelief, he added, "Did you think your relic could shield you from the repercussions of wielding angelic grace?"

Not like this, a voice at the back of my mind said. *You went too hard, too fast.*

I lay there, my heart pounding as his words sank in.

"You're just a mortal," he continued, "not meant for powers beyond your body's limits. Only angels can handle such miracles. Didn't anyone warn you? Angels, they use you up and then toss you aside."

No—because I'd done it before—by stabbing Ephrem with the Holy Lance.

My pulse raced, the rapid thumping loud in my ears, and I gasped.

The digital heart on my watch flashed the words MEDICAL EMERGENCY. I clutched at my chest, the air becoming more challenging to draw in.

"I can save you." Rimmon's lips tightened as he knelt beside me. "All you have to do is take your ring off."

The last time I fell for that, bad things happened.

"N-o-o—chance," I spat, teeth chattering. *Why would he save me, anyway?*

Rimmon stabbed the sword into the spongy earth, grimacing slightly.

I balled my fingers around my ring.

Rimmon let out a low chuckle. He clasped my fist in his, and a sizzling sound came off his skin, causing him to grit his teeth. "If I wanted you dead, I'd just wait."

Sleep dragged at my bones.

With a firm grasp, the demon examined my hand, turning it over. My fingers were still red and raw from touching the shield. "Fascinating," he mused. Slowly, he started to unfurl each one until he got to the delicate band. "That was very entertaining—you shooting the arrow at me. You show serious promise, child. What a waste it would be to see you dead now."

"*Sc-c-c-rew you.*" I couldn't catch my breath as I struggled to push him away. Rimmon overpowered me effortlessly. In one quick move, the ring was off my finger. He let it slip from his grasp and disappear into the moss without a sound.

The demon pressed his withered hand against my torso. I shrieked in agony as my bones, skin, hair, and muscles burst through me with the intensity of a thousand frozen suns.

Darkness within me stirred, swirling and yearning to break free. And then, a moment later, the sudden, intense sensation disappeared, and I found myself gasping for breath, huddled in pain but alive.

42

NAKIR

Nakir had come to with Cruz shaking him. Saldivar had been burned on his shoulder, and he had soot covering his face, but otherwise, he was okay. Zoey, on the other hand, was not. She had *Stronghold.* The demon had gone after her and the sword. Of all the idiotic things she could have done …

But now, *Stronghold* didn't matter—only her life mattered. Why had Zoey taken the sword? Surely not to save Cruz or *Nakir's* neck. He was supposed to save *her*, not the other way around.

Cruz held his watch up. "It's working again. She's here—"

Nakir seized Cruz's wrist, swiftly acquiring the coordinates, revealing her exact location. Still holding onto Cruz, he opened a portal and hauled the kid through it.

They found Zoey Taylor lying on her back in a field, stock-still, a few hundred kilometers from the tea garden, the soles of her shoes still smoldering.

"She's not moving!" Cruz shouted, stepping up beside

Nakir, a stricken look on his face. A plume of white escaped his mouth.

For an excruciatingly long moment, neither of them wanted to approach her. The sword was gone. It could only mean one thing. *She's dead.* A terrible tremor went through Nakir when he saw Zoey's hands folded across her chest, her face pale. He was too late.

Cruz whispered, "Is she ..."

"Stay here," ordered Nakir, moving with supernatural speed toward Zoey.

"*Hell no*," came Cruz's angry, dwindling retort.

Nakir braced himself for the worst as he sprinted to Zoey's side. He knelt beside her motionless body, cradling her in his arms. His body surged with a healing aura as a searing shock ran through him, and he trembled, detecting the lingering taint of malevolence.

Zoey stirred. To his surprise, he found using his grace on her was unnecessary. Her heart was still beating steadily and gently in her chest.

"Thank God." Nakir's voice shook as he buried his face in her neck and hair, an intense wave of emotion washing over him.

Zoey's wide chestnut-colored eyes snapped open and locked onto Nakir's deep, worried gaze. Her eyes sparked with emotion as she blinked rapidly, their gazes locked as time seemed to stand still. Nakir couldn't bear to loosen his grip on her.

Cruz, who had just caught up, skidded to a dramatic halt beside them. He gasped for breath, his hands on his knees.

"Are you okay?" Nakir asked Zoey, searching her face as she nodded.

"Are *y'all* okay?" she asked, running a hand gingerly over her ribs and across the spot on her chest where her heart was located. "I'm … surprisingly … *not* having a heart attack."

"Heart attack?" Cruz asked Zoey, clearly confused. His pallor was almost the same as hers—white as a sheet. "Did Rimmon do this?"

Zoey could only shake her head.

Something caught Nakir's eye: a red twinkle in the thick grass. He fished the object out of the weeds—Zoey's ring. Bits of dirt and earth still clung to it.

"What happened? Why did you take this off?" Nakir asked.

"I—I didn't," she said. "Rimmon did."

Nakir felt a shiver go through her.

"Rimmon was able to touch your ring?" Nakir asked in rising dread.

Zoey nodded slowly. After a long beat, she said, "My ring gifted me with supernatural speed."

"Cool," Cruz piped up, interrupting her. "Faster than the *Flash.*"

"*Not* cool," Zoey said, shaking her head. "I mean, it was at first. It was awesome! I had the sword and was running faster than Rimmon—but then I got lost, and my heart started racing … and … and then I just collapsed. Rimmon caught up to me and took the sword back and told me the only way he could save me was by me taking my ring off—"

"Wait, *what*?" Nakir looked at her sharply when he heard that. "What do you mean *he saved you*? Did I hear that correctly? Rimmon *saved* you?" Why had the demon saved her? It was bewildering—and concerning. But it made sense because Nakir still felt the chilling effects of malice coming off her.

"Yes," Zoey confirmed, chewing the side of her cheek. "I'm just as confused by it as you are."

"Did Rimmon say anything to you?" Nakir finally asked, deeply uneasy.

Zoey's shoulders slumped as she rubbed her arms. Nakir finally released her.

She spoke, her voice filled with sorrow. "He said I can't use angelic grace like that without facing the consequences," she confessed, tears welling in her eyes as she sat up. "I'm so sorry, Nik. I took the sword to lead him away from you and Cruz."

"I did *not* need your aid. If you are *ever* faced with that situation again, you must choose to save yourself. Got it?" Nakir was perplexed by Zoey's concern for his well-being. He was an angel of the Lord and did not require assistance from a human child. Still, a strange sense of warmth passed over him.

"It looked very much like you needed my help. Besides, I did what you told me to do—I ran." A rush of color returned to Zoey's cheeks as she added, "Nik, you were unconscious and bleeding. Cruz was about to be murdered—I couldn't stand by and watch that happen. I knew Rimmon wanted the sword, so I took it and ran. It was the only thing I could think to do."

"Thanks," Cruz said, his voice low and regretful. "I'm really sorry, guys. The demon got under my skin, and I fell for it. Zoey, you could have died." He ran a hand through his hair, and ash and soot drifted to the ground.

Nakir glanced over at Cruz, tight-lipped. "Even though this pains me to admit, you both were able to bring forth angel grace, which I thought impossible. You inflicted pain on Rimmon. Perhaps the training *is* working. I am grateful you're both alive."

Nakir put a hand to his head, and when he pulled it down, it came back slick with red. He wiped it on his slacks, troubled. It was going to take him longer than he thought to recover. After a moment, he beckoned for Cruz to come closer. "Let me get you both back to the cottage."

Before they disappeared into Nakir's portal, Cruz said, "For the record, I'm *never* celebrating my birthday again."

When they arrived back at the cottage, the darkness of night had already descended. As Cruz and Zoey relaxed in their room, Nakir gathered all the other angels, the Nephilim, and Alastair to share the unsettling news. They were shocked to learn that Rimmon could disrupt their telepathic connections, break through their shields with *Stronghold*, and even touch Zoey's ring.

Everyone was on edge and angry, and Nakir couldn't blame them. Protecting Zoey and Cruz was the new mission, and Rimmon's interest in them was *not* good.

Zoey's brother, Corinth, regarded Nakir with a brutal glare after discovering what happened at the café.

Nakir stood alone in the dimly lit courtyard as night crept in. Lost in thought, he looked up at the deep purple sky, dotted with countless sparkling stars. The sight reminded him of the breathtaking beauty of God's creation—a small glimpse of the indescribable peace of heaven. Despite longing for such harmony, Nakir had never truly experienced it. After all, he was a warrior.

He felt a dull ache where his wings had once been. His longing for the sensation of flying was unrelenting. Nothing could compare to the weightlessness, freedom, and exhilarating kiss of the wind against his face.

As Nakir restlessly paced the grounds, the dojo came into view, light pouring from its open doors. Peering inside, expecting to see Alastair or one of the angels. He was surprised to find Zoey—training.

Alone and focused, she gripped a short wooden sword, her gaze fixed on a training dummy. Beads of sweat ran down her neck, drenching her white tunic. A white sash wound around her waist, and she stood barefoot.

Struggling with the sword's weight, Zoey exerted all her strength to lift it above her head. With a clumsy motion, she brought it down on the left arm of the practice dummy, emitting a deep sigh of exhaustion. Her arms hung limply at her sides as she bent over, trying to catch her breath.

"Looks like you've been at it for a while," Nakir commented, coming inside and taking off his boots. He didn't need to ask why she wasn't sleeping—he already knew why.

Zoey whirled around, brandishing the wooden sword with surprising skill as she pointed it at Nakir. He was impressed by her proficiency—clearly, she had practiced before. As soon as she recognized Nakir, she let the sword fall to her side.

"Hey."

"I come in peace," he said, crossing the room, his steps muffled by the bamboo. "May I join you?"

Zoey shrugged. "Sure."

"Shouldn't you be resting, especially after having a heart attack?"

"I was given the all-clear—medically, I mean," she said.

"Might there be another reason you're in here training

so late?" he asked gently, stopping at the weapons rack and examining it with interest.

Zoey took a deep breath before saying, "I dropped the sword, Nik. It slipped right out of my grasp. You'd have it now if I had retained my hold on that grace *and* the sword."

Nakir furrowed his brows. "Your guilt is unnecessary. What you did was miraculous. Brave, irresponsible, and … clever."

She gave him a small smile, and her posture relaxed.

"I saw the arrow you let loose on Rimmon. Have you trained with a bow before?" Nakir asked.

Zoey shook her head, wiping her brow.

"Impressive you were able to hit him, then," Nakir said, meaning it.

"I could have had better aim."

"You should train with a lighter blade—just until you get a feel for it, and then when your skill improves, you can move up from there." Nakir shrugged off his jacket and picked up a thinner-looking wooden blade. It was a little longer than Corinth's dagger.

"Wait …" Zoey said, her voice trailing off. "You're not planning to train *with* me, are you? Because I'm not on the level you're on—and by level, I mean supernaturally. This is just me working out some—okay, a *lot*—of aggression." She placed her hand over her heart, a shadow crossing her face. "I—I had to be sure … you know, it's still beating. Still working."

"And are you satisfied that it is?" Nakir asked, raking a hand through his hair. "Look, I get it—"

"*Do* you?" Zoey grumbled, glancing down at her bare feet.

Nakir sprang forward with lightning speed, suddenly

stopping inches away, causing her to flinch. Undeterred, Zoey stood her ground, showing admirable courage as she stared up at him. Too long, perhaps.

He cleared his throat. "How about we both work out aggression?" Nakir handed her the wooden sword. She took it, if not reluctantly. "Rimmon has *Stronghold*. And he killed all those innocent people on my watch, and I couldn't stop the demon because I was protecting you two."

"All those people ..." Zoey's face went ashen momentarily, then she licked her lips. "You're going to kick his ass in round two." She paused. "What's *Stronghold*?"

"My sword," Nakir said, starting to circle Zoey, his arms resting loosely by his sides. Relaxed. Calm.

"Cool name. Don't you want to use a weapon or something?" Zoey raised the wooden blade. "To defend yourself?"

He laughed. "I hardly think I need a weapon to do that." Nakir shot her an arrogant grin. "And I won't even use my grace—like strength or speed." He wanted to needle her, to see what she was capable of, as he knew she could already handle herself under pressure.

Zoey transformed before his eyes, shedding her uncertainty and embracing a newfound confidence. She swiftly shifted into a fighting stance, locking eyes with Nakir.

Nakir noted her carriage and poise, which spoke volumes about her training, a skill Alastair had instilled in her. He dipped his head, bowing slightly right before lunging at her.

43

ZOEY

Even without superpowers, Nakir was still too fast. He dodged to the right with sure-footed ease. I tried to counter, mirroring his movement, to hit him with the sword, but he dodged the blade as I jabbed out at him. I flailed back a few steps, almost losing my balance.

Maybe I grazed his shoulder.

Nakir didn't give me time to counter. He spun in one fluid movement, slapping the weapon out of my hand with an impressively high kick. I gasped—more out of surprise than pain. The wooden sword skittered across the mats, resting against a suit of armor a few feet behind me.

Nakir came to a sudden halt, arms crossed. He hadn't even unleashed his grace. I realized he wasn't trying to harm me; he hadn't even made physical contact.

Holy. Crap.

When was I going to get decent at this?

Stupid angels.

Stupid cardio.

Stupid limp arms.

Irritation licked at my insides as I rubbed my face. Nakir bowed, signaling the end of the fight—like it was over before it began. My face flushed, fire igniting inside me.

Stupid Rimmon. Stupid Ephrem. Stupid boys. Stupid fighting.

I hated this, and … in a tortuous way, I also loved it: the utter exhaustion, the burning muscles, the rushing blood in my veins. The complete focus took my mind off the bad.

And the grief was back—all of it.

Then I thought about all those people at the tea garden.

I lost it.

Putting on a burst of speed, I flung myself at Nik, surprising him and wiping that smirk off his face. Barreling into his chest, I took him to the ground, both of us in a tangle of arms and legs—with me on top. Nik grunted.

Larna taught me a neat move, using Brazilian Jiu-Jitsu the last time she was here. I was still getting the hang of it.

And then Nik swiftly turned the tables. Before I knew it, he had me pinned down, leaving me struggling to break free. I screamed up at him in frustration, struggling against his grip, raging, yelling. He only got up when my fury melted, and I went boneless.

"Did I hurt you?" Nik's lips were near my ear as he assessed me for injuries. I didn't have any physical wounds.

I shook my head as angry, hot tears ran down my face.

Nik slid beside me, wrapping a warm arm around my shoulders as we sat up. His scent was a soothing blend of lavender and evergreen.

"I'm sorry," he said, sounding sincere. "I shouldn't have pushed you, not after what you went through with Rimmon."

"I needed the push." I sniffed. "It's not that. I mean, it is. It's everything, I guess."

"When was the last time you slept?" he asked.

"I don't know."

I didn't.

Nakir was silent, letting me blubber into his shirt until he finally said, "Alastair's taught you well. I'm impressed with your progress, even if *you* aren't."

"Why?" I scoffed, unable to accept his compliment. My right arm felt tender, so I started to massage it. Every part of me hurt from the hours of training I'd been doing lately. The blisters on my feet had hardened into calluses.

Outside, steam rose from the chilly morning air.

Nik scooted back, taking some of his body heat with him.

"I mean, I've been taught by Corinth and Larna when she's here, and Cruz, too. Larna graduated me to weight lifting." I glanced away from Nakir's excessively green eyes. "You knocked the sword out of my hand in *seconds.* I'd be dead in a real fight."

Nakir looked down to his right shoulder. I sat up to follow his line of sight. The stitching on his button-down shirt had ripped. "You grazed me," he said, tipping his head.

A healthy dose of pride washed over me. I gazed up at him and chewed on my lip. That flood of power had been addicting, and I wanted to chase that feeling.

"I'm tired of feeling helpless," I admitted.

"You are *not* helpless," Nakir whispered. "You stood up to Ephrem. You stood up to Rimmon. That takes spirit—and foolish nerve."

I let his compliment sink in, swallowing the lump in my throat. "I miss my brother, Pete," I finally admitted.

Nik nodded. "I know."

"Can you help me arrange a meeting with him? I need to find a way to persuade Pete to come home, or at least ensure that he's doing all right ... to some extent."

He cautioned me in a soft, gentle tone. "That would not be a wise decision."

"Corinth has already told me as much. I don't care. I need to see him."

Nik's jaw twitched before he spoke. "I'll see what I can arrange. But for now, Zoey, please make sure to get some rest."

44

GABRIEL

Desperate and impatient did not make for a good combination. Aging was a messy business. Each day that passed, Gabriel Stanton felt the inevitable pull of gravity and time on his bones. Ten years ago, he'd started getting gray hair, creaking joints, wrinkles, and frown lines where he had never had them before. His muscles were waning. Exercising required extra effort. Being alive for almost three thousand years had conditioned him for ultimate control: power, wealth, and vitality.

Control—now he felt it slipping through his fingers like sand in an hourglass. That was why he had been pushing to get his immortality back.

Damn Corinth Taylor.

Gabriel finished the last of his drink and stood, a bout of dizziness washing over him. It was expensive Scotch, and with no food in his system, it left him feeling slightly sozzled.

Clasping his hands behind his back, Gabriel crossed to the ornate dining table, where a red velvet pillow sat. On top of the pillow was a syringe filled with golden liquid. The nectar of the gods. Well, *a* god, anyway.

Gabriel Stanton was about to become ascended—*again.*

Alone in his penthouse, he had ordered all his staff and security out of the room. Privacy was for the best right now. Gabriel didn't hand out trust to anyone. One of his staff would try to convince him *not* to do this. He couldn't chance—or stand—someone else gaining immortality before him. The time to act was now. *Be bold.*

Outside, the setting sun glinted off the Hudson, sparking it like a jewel under light. It was a sign. Endings, beginnings. Gabriel loathed both, but when he put them together, like an ouroboros—a snake eating its tail—it meant there *was* no end. No death. No loss. Only life. Riches.

He was desperate.

Human trials had yet to be successful, but they were *so close* to triumph. Animal testing had shown signs of promise. The scientists had chosen a rodent with tumorous lumps on its skin. When injected with the golden elixir, the old lab rat's white fur had all but changed, especially around its face and neck, turning it youthful right under Gabriel's very eyes. Miraculous. For about ten minutes, the now-brown-furred creature had chittered and run around its cage like nothing was ever wrong with it in the first place. The treatment was considered one hundred percent effective and deemed safe for human use by advanced AI tech the scientists had run it through. There was minimal risk.

Gabriel stood over the hypodermic, not even realizing he'd moved.

It had been a subtle pull. With Rimmon out there, Gabriel knew he had to do something drastic to gain the upper hand.

He plucked the needle up, ripped off the cap, and tapped the syringe to ensure no air bubbles were inside. *This is going to work*, Gabriel thought. *It has to.* He rolled up his sleeve, inspecting the vein at the crook of his elbow. He saw double: two syringes, two veins. No, just one. He shook his head to clear it.

Just do it, the voice inside him insisted. *One jab, and it will be all over.*

You'll be unstoppable.

You won't die.

You'll be young again.

Gabriel wasn't a reckless person. The last time he'd been negligent with his own life was to save Larna Iszler's. It was preposterous that he'd even considered saving someone else's neck besides his own. Over ten years ago, he'd stepped right into the line of angelic fire when Angela had tried to kill Larna. The memory of Gabriel's own burning flesh still haunted him. He wasn't sentimental. He didn't care for people, but Larna wasn't exactly people. She was brave. Brash. Beautiful. One of a kind, and she'd bested him once.

Corinth Taylor, on the other hand, was infuriating. The Nephilim *wouldn't* die. Corinth had changed everything for the worse. What would anyone do to the one who took their life away from them?

Get revenge.

Gabriel's actions were sloppy; he knew it, but he couldn't stop himself. He inserted the needle into his arm, took a deep breath, and pushed down the plunger.

The effect was immediate.

The blood in his veins turned white hot. Incredible vertigo overtook him, and the room tilted on its side. He released the empty hypodermic, collapsed to his knees, and then, a moment later, fell to his hands. The loft rolled. He felt feverish and clammy—

And then darkness engulfed Gabriel, the world swirling into oblivion.

The next thing Gabriel Stanton knew was that he wasn't on Earth. He had no idea where he was. Not in space. He was floating in an abyss of white. All around him, there was only snowy, billowy filament. Gabriel felt disconnected from his body and couldn't adjust to the weightlessness because he wasn't on solid ground.

This was only a side effect. The drug needed time to work. He was fine. It was a trip, perhaps a dream. Gabriel convinced himself of this until someone appeared out of a swirling mist.

That *someone* caused his eyes to go wide. *Bollocks.* He took a sharp breath and reached out, not believing his eyes.

His soul ached—the cruelty.

"This can't be real," Gabriel whispered incredulously, the longing and sorrow in his voice foreign to his ears. He wanted this to be real—more than anything else, more than immortality. Because floating in front of him was ... of all beings he *did* care for ... was his mother, Gaia.

She wore a one-shouldered ivory Grecian dress, cinched by a gold cord at the waist. Her honey-colored skin was toned and unblemished, and a ribbon of gold leaves pinned back her long, flowing dark hair. He remembered she was older when she'd been brutally taken from him, but *now*, she was younger and beyond breathtaking.

Gaia lifted her arms out to Gabriel but did not touch him. "Hello, my son," she said in his ancient tongue. "I have been waiting for you for a very long time."

An overwhelming sense of peace settled over him. There was no tension, no survival mode, only serenity—a sensation he'd never truly felt before. What was happening? What was wrong with his eyes? They were blurry and wet.

"*Mother*," he choked out. Gabriel couldn't say anything else. The lump in his throat was suddenly boulder-sized.

"Shhh, shhh, shhh," Gaia cooed. Then, his mother was in front of him, wrapping her arms around his shoulders.

He felt ten years old again. And for only a handful of times in almost two thousand years, he wept. To feel so much, so strongly, was something he'd been avoiding like the plague. Vulnerability was excruciating, and letting it build up over thousands of years hadn't helped.

"I—I can feel your arms. Smell your hair. How can this be?" Gabriel asked, searching her sky-blue eyes. "I saw you die."

"I do not have much time, Ephialtes, for you are almost gone—"

"What do you mean?" Gabriel whispered. *Oh no.* This had to be part of the angel's plans. "No, no, no." They constantly meddled in everything. He hated angels … and yet, here was his mother, *almost* angelic … divine.

"I have been allowed to come to you to give you a choice." Gaia reached up to gently caress his cheek and wipe away his tears. Her fingertips were warm on his face. Gabriel closed his eyes briefly, consoled by her gentle touch. "You have done much harm in the world, my son, harm that needs repairing."

Gabriel felt the weight of her words. Her disapproval

stung. No! He'd done *great* things—world-changing things. His corporation had made billions, and he'd donated millions. He had evolved—ascended and gained notoriety. He had won awards. He had provided jobs. He had prestige.

And yet, he could see the pain in her eyes—*for* him.

For the first time in Gabriel's long life, he considered *not* pursuing immortality—for a fleeting moment. What was waiting for him on the other side?

Maybe—just maybe—

"Because you have aided Corinth Taylor and other angels of the Lord, you are granted a rare opportunity before you die. Become an angel, a warrior of God, and live in service to Him, or"—she paused—"you will be left to deal with your transgressions, for all of the lives you have taken and disrupted when you were a creature of darkness."

Creature of darkness?

"Ascended being, Mother," Gabriel corrected on impulse. "And I am *not* dying," he argued vehemently, fury rising in him. "I will not be in service to *anyone* but myself." What he did, he *had* to do. For the greater good. "Don't you see, I am meant for so much more?"

"*My child*," she whispered, her voice heartfelt and profound, "so misguided you have been. So full of fear. And that has partly been my fault. My death has warped you, and rightly so. The pain you must have felt, witnessing my murder. But being alive for thousands of years is no longer an option. I am at peace. And so shall you be. We do not have much time. Have you decided to join us, my son?"

It was too much. "*Warped me?* Warped me?" Gabriel cried, unable to process anything his mother had just told him. "Oh, no, Mother, your death has helped shape me into the most powerful ascended being on the planet."

He took a long beat, his head still foggy but at peace.

His mind and body seemed to be fading, his world shrinking. This was precisely why he had wanted to live for an eternity.

Maybe he could, as an angel.

"Ascended?" she murmured. "No, dear child, not yet."

He *was* an ascended being. This was precisely what he'd always wanted. He was being offered unimaginable power. Gabriel opened his mouth to accept, but as soon as he did, he was ripped violently away—and everything went black.

Gabriel Stanton shot up into a sitting position, gasping for oxygen. A hand was planted firmly on his chest—not his hand, someone else's.

It was so cold that it felt like a frozen piece of meat. Gabriel's vision swam in and out of focus before finally clearing. As Gabriel looked around, he discovered he was on the floor of his penthouse, the empty syringe beside him.

He glanced at the pale hand still on his chest, slowly following the hand to an arm and then up to a face. It stared back at him.

Rimmon. The demon. *Holy hell.* He was wearing a glitzy silver suit with red loafers and no socks. *Knob.*

"Ah," Rimmon said, the faintest smirks cropping up on his face. "Welcome back."

"What ..." Gabriel panted. "Happened?"

"You died, and I brought you back." Rimmon shrugged, backed up, and blew on his hand like a smoking gun. "At some cost."

His fingers *did* look like they were smoking and singed black with soot.

And Gabriel's chest *did* hurt.

"Well," Gabriel hissed, "that's unfortunate."

"You might be sore for a few days. I had to fight to bring you back. Both sides want you badly. You have been a very defiant boy."

Boy? Gabriel blinked back at Rimmon, at a loss for words. *What sides?* He raked a hand through his damp curls, feeling out of sorts. "The last thing I remember is injecting myself and then collapsing. Does that mean ... it—it didn't work."

"It didn't work," Rimmon echoed with an exaggerated nod, as if waiting for Gabriel to catch on. *Dolt.*

Gabriel ignored the demon's proffered hand as he returned to his feet, still unsteady. "So, I guess there's a reason you decided to bring me back."

"Ding, ding, ding, what do we have for the winner?" Rimmon said.

Gabriel noted that the creature's tone was as icy as his hand.

"And that would be?"

"Well, for starters, remember that deal we made about the sword and how I said I'd let you keep it if you held up your end of the bargain?" Rimmon asked.

"I have upheld my end." Gabriel raised an eyebrow. "You now have unfettered access to the gateway to the demon realm."

"Yes, yes, you did. However, you won't be getting the sword in return."

He figured it would work out this way. Demons were never to be trusted. "Why is that?" Gabriel asked, straightening his tie back into place, calm and collected again.

"I brought you back, so now I own you. The soul mark on your chest solidifies that."

"What … mark …?" His gaze traveled down to his chest. Slowly, Gabriel unbuttoned his shirt and pulled it aside, afraid of what he might see there. Right smack in the middle of his sternum was a blackened handprint. He licked his dry lips, feeling chillier and more unsettled by the minute. "Does this mean I'll stop aging and live forever? Because that would be worth the blemish."

Rimmon shook his head. "Unfortunately, no, Gabe. But it does mean you're to do exactly as I bid you to do whenever I ask."

Gabriel squashed the curse on the tip of his tongue. "I don't do *anyone's* bidding but my own."

Rimmon snapped his fingers. Gabriel immediately fell to the floor, his knees hitting the expensive hardwood. The demon's voice boomed inside his head like surround sound: *Don't make me hurt you to prove my point—because I love hurting people* and *proving points.*

The pain was agonizingly tortuous, all-consuming, and boiling.

Gabriel shivered as his teeth chattered. He rubbed his arms in a futile attempt to generate warmth. The cold's icy grip seeped into his bones, the coldest sensation he'd ever experienced.

When he finally mustered the courage to open his eyes, he found himself curled up in a fetal position, trembling uncontrollably. His hands were still pressed tightly over his ears.

Rimmon had vanished, leaving him alone in the frigid darkness.

45

ALASTAIR

Alastair stared ominously at the Devil's horn on the marbled kitchen countertop. The damn thing was an obnoxious shiny onyx with a crack down the center filled with gold. It gave him the willies.

They were in the angel's cottage, trying to strategize. Was it late—or was it early? Last Alastair looked at the time, it was four in the morning. The problem was that being one of the only humans in the room, he was the only one who needed rest. Exhaustion started to take hold. His ankle, the mangled one, hurt like the dickens.

With his hands behind his back, Corinth paced the cramped living quarters. A cottage true to the name, the place had large white logs on the walls and a vaulted ceiling. Generally, this would give the place an open, airy feel, but not this day. How was Alastair supposed to consider bringing a child into this world if it might come to an end?

A fire was roaring in the hearth, and the space was well-warmed. All around them, on every surface, were old tomes, scrolls, Bibles, charts, maps, and ancient and dusty-looking relics. Leo was perched on the edge of a counter near the kitchen, squinting down at a piece of parchment resting under a pane of glass. It looked like it was about to shrivel up and disintegrate on the spot.

"What are you looking for?" Alastair yawned as he moved to stand beside Leo, wishing he could do more. He had always been the boots-on-the-ground type, but that had flown out the window after his injury. Now, he was the researcher. *Blech*. He'd been much more academic and patient with scholarly stuff when he was a vampire—when there had been oodles more time.

"I'm still looking for any mention of Rimmon," Leo answered coolly, without looking up. "Which is what you should be doing."

Alastair looked down at the rolled-open scroll. He was one of the only ones, besides the angels, who could read and speak multiple languages. "My ancient Hebrew is rusty," he whispered over Leo's shoulder. And it *was* rusty, but that wasn't the problem. The holes, rips, tears, and faded ink prevented him from making any of it out. Maybe he needed glasses. Not to mention, all of the dust from this stuff was wreaking havoc on his sinuses. "I've been trying for hours."

Leo's hand flickered briefly as he snapped his fingers. The proximity to the angel was enough to send a current shooting up Alastair's arm. He jumped back as Leo removed the glass covering the parchment and planted his glowing palm against it.

The tattered scroll started to levitate.

Astonished, Alastair watched as the holes mended, and the script became legible again. Even the ink looked wet.

Alastair sucked in a sharp breath. "Why in heaven's name didn't you do that in the first place?"

Leo glared at Alastair as the scroll floated back down to the bar top.

They'd both perfected that smart-alecky glower. Alastair noted that it made Leo look *exactly* like Corinth.

"Ancient relics like this should be preserved as is, but in this case, even *I* was starting to go cross-eyed trying to make it out," Leo grumbled. "And I think I found something."

"What?" Corinth came up beside Alastair and Leo, his hands fisted inside the pockets of his black trousers. Alastair noted Corinth still had on his trademark colorful purple Converse. Some things never changed.

"I found a reference to a place called Rimmon and a Syrian deity named Rimmon—a false god. Rimmon is mentioned in 2 Kings 5:18: *But may the Lord forgive your servant for this one thing: When my master enters the temple of Rimmon to bow down, he is leaning on my arm, and I have to bow there also.* The meaning of the name Rimmon is *Exalted*, or the *spring of the pomegranate*. I found very little about a fallen archangel, though."

"To the Semites, Rimmon is the god of storms. Ice storms," Nakir said softly from the couch. Everyone turned to look at him. He had his head buried in his hands. "I fought alongside Rimmon once upon a time. He is formidable."

Alastair almost felt sorry for the angel. *Almost.* "What made him turn to the dark side?"

Nakir rubbed a hand across his jaw. "The same thing that turned them all. Jealousy. Greed. Power. They hate humans and Nephilim alike. God's attention has always been on humanity, and Rimmon doesn't like it."

After that, no one said anything for a while. Alastair

digested that information before Corinth finally said, "Storms, did you say?" His voice was menacingly soft. "I'm pretty good at wielding storms, too."

The charge in the room tripled, causing Alastair to pat his hair back down. "Easy, Cor."

Corinth blinked several times before he realized his hands were sparking with grace. He shook his head. "Sorry, but these demons keep messing with my family. What about Pete? Has anyone gotten word from him?"

"Family is God's gift to you, as you are to them. They are the first essential cells of human society. And I ask that you not call on Peter for that reason," Nakir interjected.

"Why?" Corinth turned to stare at Nakir before he continued. His suspicion was growing, adding to the tension in the room. "This isn't really about family, is it?"

Nakir's eyes didn't shift from Corinth's questioning gaze. "It's *always* about family. Deceit, betrayal ... it hurts the most when the people we love turn on us."

Corinth squinted at Nakir. "What's your point, Nik? And be careful here because I know Pete will never betray me."

"The longer we wait for Rimmon to make a move, the stronger he will get," Nakir explained. "We can delay no longer. We must gather our forces and take the fight to them."

"Forces? What *forces*?" Alastair raked a hand through his hair, mussing it up. "We need to wait for Pete ... Ari ... to contact us. Patience is required, not fighting."

"You're putting all your faith in a *Shade*?" Nakir raised a brow. "How do you think Rimmon found Zoey and Cruz in town? It wasn't by chance."

"You think Pete is working with Rimmon?" Corinth

spoke in a whisper-soft voice, an edge in his tone. "Like you said, you don't get to choose your family. Demon or not, Pete's still my brother, and I'm giving him the benefit of the doubt." He let the sentence trail off as his gaze met each person's in the room. "If you don't trust Pete, that's fine. But trust *me*. Please. I have an idea."

That piqued Nakir's interest. He sat up straighter. "I'm listening."

Corinth pursed his lips, then asked Leo, "Where exactly does this place reference Rimmon?"

"It's near the Jordan Valley," Leo said, twisting around on the barstool to face everyone. "I planned to check it out. Do you think the demon could be there?"

"There's a good chance," Corinth said slowly.

"Nik," Corinth said. "I need you to stay with Zoey and Cruz."

Nakir was shaking his headful of curls. "Not this time, Nephilim. This is our first big clue as to where Rimmon might be located. If he's there, you're going to need me. You're going to need *all* of us."

"Nakir's right, Cor," Alastair cut in. "We need all hands on deck. Contact Samyaza and Tamiel. They'll want to be involved, too."

"I don't think I like the two of you on the same side," Corinth grumbled. "Okay, Nik, you're with us. Can I count on you to protect my sister and Cruz while we're gone, Al?"

Alastair placed a hand on his chest, offended. "Come on, brother. You shouldn't even have to ask."

46

CRUZ

Cruz found himself standing at the anvil in Vinson's forge, sweat dripping onto the molten metal. His goggles were flecked with tiny droplets. Crafting a weapon out of a chunk of metal was taxing, but somehow, Cruz had convinced Vinson to let him swing the hammer.

He regretted it now because his arms were sore. Cruz had woken up much earlier than usual and ran until completely worn out.

Forging would help him build muscle, become tougher, and learn a new skill—and maybe, *just maybe*, the dark thoughts wouldn't creep in if he kept his mind occupied. With renewed determination, Cruz pounded the flat side of the iron with his mallet, exerting all his strength to mold the cutting edge of a dagger. Trying to perfect his technique, he made minor adjustments with each strike.

Vinson watched Cruz, occasionally offering a few words of advice when he noticed him making mistakes (which was often).

Cruz wore earplugs, so the only sounds he could hear were the hammer and his heartbeat. He was wholly absorbed; the cathartic rhythm of hitting the steel lulled him into a trance-like state.

Pound, hammer, heartbeat, repeat.

Pound, hammer, heartbeat, repeat.

Pound, hammer, heartbeat, repeat.

The memory of the Shade's attempt to gouge out his eyeball crept back in. *Mierda.* Cruz's heart started beating faster. Then the image of the Shade morphed into Rimmon … the demon who froze all those people in a single breadth.

Cruz imagined the metal was Rimmon's head, and at the same time, he felt a tap on his shoulder. He whirled around, raising the hammer to defend himself—

Vinson lashed out, grabbing Cruz's arm, halting his attack mid-swing. Effortlessly, he snatched the weapon out of Cruz's sweaty grasp.

"Sorry, sorry!" Cruz shouted, making a mental note of how much strength Vinson possessed. "I'm a little on edge." He drew the plugs out of his ears, willing his pulse to come back down.

Vinson set the hammer-turned-weapon on the table behind him, remaining level-headed despite having just been attacked.

"A little?" Vinson furrowed his bushy brows.

"Okay—maybe a lot," Cruz admitted, scratching his forehead where the goggles left an indent. "I was so caught up in work… I forgot you were even here … and then I thought about …" He shook his head. "Never mind. It doesn't matter. I promise I wasn't trying to take your head off."

Vinson studied Cruz quietly for a long time before he nodded. "You're not half good at forging."

"Don't you mean not half *bad*?" Cruz asked.

Vinson blinked back at Cruz. "No."

After another long, awkward beat, Cruz returned the goggles to Vinson. He couldn't seem to do anything right—this guy was a ghost—but Cruz liked something about Vinson.

"Next time," Vinson said, "focus on tapering both sides of steel. Hammer out flat edge to shape bevels. Beveling will form the edge on either side of blade."

"Next time?" Cruz asked, a hint of excitement in his voice. "You mean you're going to let me come do this again?"

Vinson barely lifted his chin. Was that an answer? Cruz was going to take that as a *yes*.

Suddenly, the hairs on Cruz's neck stood on end. The air vibrated. An angelic portal opened a second later, and a tall, slender form bounded out.

Cruz backed up and gasped as the figure landed lithely beside Vinson, who never flinched.

Tamiel was Samyaza's War chief. She was over six feet tall, with short, curly black hair and a dark complexion. She wore full armor and a broad sword sheathed at her back. The angel looked fierce, primarily when she evaluated Cruz with sharp, feline-like eyes, determining whether he was a threat.

"Mama, Mama, Mama!" Shouts of glee emanated from the path nearby.

Vinson's son and daughter ran toward the forge's entrance, but Tamiel quickly blocked them from entering; the fire inside was still burning hot.

What?

Protective and motherly ... which was weird from an

angel in full armor, Cruz thought. The children hugged Tamiel's legs, and she smiled, patting their backs, her face softening. "Hello, my little angels," she cooed in a thick, unfamiliar accent.

"*Wait*," Cruz blurted out. "Does that mean?" He pointed at Vinson. "It means ... Corinth is no longer the last remaining Nephili—"

"Don't—finish—that—word," Vinson said sharply, cutting Cruz off.

Nephilim.

"Why?" Cruz glanced at Tamiel and then looked around, searching their surroundings. No one else was nearby, but the giant angel gave Cruz a stern look, instantly making him uneasy.

It was worse than one of Vinson's looks.

Corinth had told Cruz that his kind—Nephilim—were nearly wiped out by angels who believed they were superior to humans. Were they afraid history would repeat itself? Cruz could see it in the way Vinson and Tamiel squinted at him.

"Promise me you won't breathe a word of this to anyone. It's not safe," Vinson cautioned severely. "Do you understand?"

Cruz nodded, wanting to avoid getting on the wrong side of these two. He was itching to ask them a million more questions, but they wouldn't talk anymore. They'd already set off with the little ones toward home.

Zoey, barefoot and dressed in a gi, twirled a training sword in her hand. She searched for an opening to stab Cruz. How could someone be so sweet and aggressive at the same time? What a world of difference a few weeks could make.

"Why are you giving me the evil eye?" Cruz asked, exhausted from the intense wind sprints he had done earlier. "Haven't I already been punished enough today?" Following a strenuous morning of forging, his arms felt heavy and unresponsive.

"Do you always whine this much?" Zoey slashed her sword back and forth, looking for an opening. "And Sensei Alastair would say otherwise."

Concentrate, Cruz scolded himself.

Zoey was wiping the floor with him.

He struggled with the graphite bo. Despite its lightweight material, it was almost too much for him to handle because of his floppy arms. Alastair wanted to train them with a wide range of weapons. They had been learning to adapt to various martial arts styles. *At least we're using weapons*, he thought, trying to get himself to focus.

Lately, it seemed everyone had been too hard on Cruz and Zoey. It was all so grueling. Ugh.

"Because you're not giving me anything to work with," Zoey yelled, diving at Cruz again, gaining ground as he fell back a few steps. "Are you even taking this serious—"

Cruz darted right in the nick of time as a delirious giggle bubbled out of him.

"It's not funny," Zoey rebuked, ducking past one of his half-hearted attempts to knock the sword out of her hand. "Are you even trying?"

"I'm trying *not* to be struck by a wooden sword," Cruz grumbled.

All he yearned for was his bed, to bury himself under the covers and drift away into a peaceful slumber. Cruz's mind started to wander again. Was Corinth aware of the Nephilim kids? He likely was, because they had all decided to remain off the grid. Things were starting to click into place: Cruz and Zoey weren't the only ones being looked after. *Vinson and Tamiel have kids.* He found it peculiar that an angel and a human were paired up. Of course, those two together made a ton of sense. What did they talk about, though?

Zoey sprang at Cruz, shouting.

And she nearly got him that time, but Cruz managed to dive to the ground, roll to the left, and shoot back to his feet, staff in hand.

"Stop running," Zoey said, clearly enjoying herself. Her wheat-colored braid cascaded down her back.

"You've been practicing without me," Cruz gasped, floundering back a step. She was better than he was today—more centered. And because her smile was so disarming, he found himself slow to react when her wooden blade came down with remarkable force, knocking the bo out of his hands and sending it skittering somewhere behind him. "*Ouch*," he gasped, narrowly avoiding her blade's back strike.

Cruz tried to regain his balance—he really did—but it was too late.

Zoey sent him flying to the ground with a kick center mass. He landed hard on his back, his arms flailing out beside him. He panted out a soft expletive as the tip of her blade went to his throat.

Zoey let out a loud whoop, turning to see if Alastair had caught her moment of triumph.

A lightning bolt of anger struck.

Oh, hell no. Cruz hooked his leg behind Zoey's calf and

tugged. Her sword hit him hard in the gut as she dropped it. At the same time, Zoey lost her balance, yelped, and fell to her knees beside him on the mats.

"*Ow*," she said.

"*Oof*," Cruz breathed as the air left his lungs. He curled onto his side, the sword tumbling to the floor beside him. "I deserved that."

Clapping came from nearby, but it didn't sound like admiring or respectful applause. It sounded mocking.

Cruz barely lifted his head. Alastair stood over them frowning, his arms folded tightly across his chest, far from amused.

"Both of you, take a knee." Alastair looked between them, his lips pressed together into two thin lines. "First off, Taylor, great job—you took down your opponent." Zoey grinned. "But your opponent was only defeated because they were so *distracted*." He raised a finger, signaling for them to remain quiet, making eye contact with Cruz before exhaling.

Great. That was disappointment ... for sure.

"You would both be dead if this had been a real fight. Zoey, you can't afford to take your eyes off your enemy, not even for a moment, especially when the enemy is hard to eliminate. Treat Saldivar like he's a demon or Shade. Always stay vigilant. You gave Saldivar the upper hand when you looked back at me for approval. You should never let your guard down. Taylor, you practically handed your weapon to your adversary. Do you think that would have stopped a demon?"

Zoey's delight over beating Cruz vanished instantly. She lowered her gaze. Cruz noticed the tips of her ears turning red.

"And Saldivar," Alastair began.

Oh no.

"What were you thinking? You were so unfocused that Zoey beat you in mere moments. If she had been serious about harming you, you would not have been given a second chance to defeat her."

Cruz felt his face flush.

Alastair was right, and Cruz knew it, but he couldn't help feeling annoyed. That surge of heat was back in his belly. "I'm beat. I can barely raise my arms, man. Can we call it a day? This isn't fun anymore."

Cruz hadn't intended to say it like that, but it was already too late.

Alastair's eyebrows shot up in surprise, indicating he couldn't believe what he'd heard. "Fun? *Fun*? This isn't meant to be *enjoyable*, Saldivar. And when you're on this mat, it's Sensei, *not* 'man.' Am I clear?"

Cruz clenched his jaw, suppressing any snide remarks that might escape. He nodded and hissed, "Yes, *Sensei.*"

"Look," Alastair began, his voice tinged with displeasure—and distress? "I know you're both being pushed to your limits. You're tired. We've been at this every day for weeks on end. But you need to focus on training harder than ever. This isn't a vacation. It's survival. There's no time for games. You should be giving it your all—and then some, understood?"

Cruz felt uneasy and a little guilty hearing Alastair express discontent. This was only an off day. He had seen Alastair give his all to protect them, and he knew Alastair didn't scare easily—but was that fear in his voice?

"Is there something else we should know?" Cruz asked as his eyes darted to Zoey's.

She tilted her head, also eager for the answer.

Before Alastair could respond, another voice spoke up from behind them. "Y'all should know, Al doesn't give that speech to just anyone."

Corinth emerged from the darkness of the open doors. It was chilly outside, and he wore a black leather jacket and beanie; his wavy chestnut locks poked out from underneath it. The Holy blade was sheathed at his thigh. "He gave the same speech to me when I was your age." Corinth gave them a reassuring yet fleeting smile. "You should be proud. The way you both sparred was nothing short of impressive. I think you two might be ready ..."

"Ready for what?" Zoey asked, hesitating.

"To join us," Corinth answered.

Cruz's heart started beating harder. "Join you?"

"Perhaps. You may want to listen to Al, though," Corinth said evenly, swiping a hand over his chin. "He's *usually* right."

Alastair gave Corinth a slight nod. "I'm *always* right."

A figure appeared behind Corinth. Larna. She was dressed in a dark brown duster with tactical pants and a fitted vest underneath. Her dark hair was slicked back into a tight ponytail, and Cruz couldn't help but feel intimidated by her.

Both looked like they were ready to go to war.

With a noticeable limp, yet without the cane, Alastair hurried over to Larna. His face lit up in a brilliant smile. Their affection was almost tangible as they locked eyes, radiating pure love and bliss. Cruz wished someone would look at him that way. He couldn't stop his gaze from wandering back to Zoey.

Her eyes shifted worriedly between her brother, Larna,

and Alastair. "Y'all are going after Rimmon, aren't you? What about Peter? Do you know where he is? Be careful, Cor. The way he instantly froze those people ..."

Corinth looked between Larna and Alastair, scanning their faces. They nodded slightly as he went on. "You two *are* the future, and while I don't want to put you in danger or pressure y'all, the truth is, you're part of this paranormal world now. You can't avoid it. Trust me, I tried. I wasn't like y'all when I found out I had angelic grace. I wanted nothing to do with the supernatural or angels. You two have embraced it."

Zoey and Cruz beamed back at Corinth with pride.

"Can we come up with a team name?" Cruz asked. "How about *Guardians of the Galaxy*?" He put a hand on his chin. "Or ... Ascended Guardians."

"I kind of like that." Zoey looked at her eldest brother. "But I don't think we're ready for that yet, do you?"

"Maybe not yet, but you will be." There was a brief silence before Corinth spoke again. "We're all proud of the hard work you've put in—you two make a great team. No big decisions will be made tonight. Why don't you both wrap up? The sink is filled with dirty dishes. I can smell them from here." Corinth waved his hand in front of his nose. "After that, I suggest you both grab a shower and get some rest. Maybe throw in some laundry while you're at it."

"Jeez, you sound just like Mom and Dad right now," Zoey muttered, getting to her feet to stand before her brother. She stood on tiptoes and wrapped her arms around him. "Please be careful. This demon is ... scary."

Corinth lifted Zoey off the ground, wrapped her in a bear hug. "I've got this." His eyes were shut tight, and Cruz could sense the depth of his emotion.

As Cruz stood, the creak of his joints reverberated through the dojo. He felt reanimated, exhaustion washing away, replaced by a sense of accomplishment. The challenges he had confronted earlier had been daunting but worth it.

Corinth set Zoey down and gestured to Cruz. "Bring it in, kid."

Cruz rushed forward and threw himself into Zoey and Corinth's waiting, open arms. The warmth of their bodies and the gentle pressure of their hands on his back made his frustrations melt away. He turned and noticed Alastair standing behind them, subtly trying to suppress a grin with his hand.

"Cor, can you tell me where you're headed?" Zoey asked as she drew back, the worry back on her face.

Corinth appeared uncertain about divulging the information. Larna spoke first. "It's probably nothing. We might have a lead on Rimmon's whereabouts, and we're going to investigate. In the meantime, you two keep a low profile. Alastair has agreed to stay and look after you two while we check it out."

"Do you think the information is legit?" Zoey asked.

Corinth furrowed his brow. "With any luck, Rimmon will be in hell by tomorrow."

"Cor, I can't stress this enough: you come home—and bring Pete back," Zoey said.

"What? No arguing? No threatening to come with me? No barrage of questions?" he asked suspiciously.

"Not today," she whispered into his jacket. "Just bring our brother back."

47

ZOEY

Back in the cottage, I dried the dishes at the kitchen sink while Cruz washed them—and complained about his sore muscles. At least he was in better spirits after today's training session. Sheesh, he'd been in a bad mood.

Right now, though, my mind was preoccupied with thoughts of Cor, Larna, Nik, and the other angels. While Cruz and I had conveniently decided not to talk about the elephant in the room, they were going after Rimmon.

"So, I'm not supposed to say anything, which means you're also sworn to secrecy, okay?" Cruz started, barely waiting for me to nod before continuing. "Did you know that Jack and Vienna are Vinson's *kids*—and they're *Nephilim?*"

I almost dropped a slick dish as I turned to him. "Wait, what?" My mouth fell open. "You mean Cor isn't the *last* one any longer?"

"No," he mouthed, glancing around. "Can you believe it?"

"So, who is Jack and Vienna's mom, then?" I asked slowly, thinking.

"Tamiel," Cruz replied eagerly, his brows rising. I saw them all together at the forge. They told me not to say anything because it was dangerous …"

"No way," I whispered. "I did *not* see that coming." I put a finger to my lip. "So, do you think they're in danger?"

"I haven't seen the kids do anything like Corinth yet, so I'm assuming they aren't gifted with angel grace yet," Cruz explained like an expert on the subject.

"Cor said he didn't get his powers until he turned eighteen," I pondered as Biscuit meandered into the kitchen, weaving through my legs.

He hissed, and it sounded like a warning. I glanced down to see his hackles rising.

A second later, Biscuit bolted, disappearing from view. I started to yell after him, but the temperature in the room dropped so suddenly and dramatically that I stopped. That's when the red jewel on my ring began blinking, and Cruz's shield blazed with a white light. Cruz and I shared a knowing look, realizing what would happen a moment too late.

An invisible force slammed into me hard, knocking the wind from my lungs. I skidded across the tiles, fetching up against a leg underneath the small kitchen table, confused and faint. Vaguely, I knew that the same force had flipped Cruz around and pressed his back so hard against the sink that it looked like he was doing a backbend.

Three Shades materialized in a cloud of sulfur, wearing all-black cloaks.

Cruz's face went ashen at the sight of one of them.

The Shades tried to advance. Luckily, Cruz's shield lit up brighter, and they shrieked and fell back slightly.

I risked taking a quick peek out from under the table. My heart plummeted. The one he was staring at was missing an eye. This was the one that had attacked him at his home. *Not. Good.*

A large butcher knife magically soared out of its block, halted mid-air, and aimed right for Cruz. They weren't going after me, so maybe I could get the drop on them.

I pressed the button on my watch. We only needed to buy time before an angel or Alastair came to our rescue.

"I told you, kid, I'd be back. Now, it's time to take that eyeball." The one-eyed Shade threw its hand out, and the knife flew at Cruz.

"No!" I shouted, jumping out from under the table. At the same time, the shield around Cruz's neck sparked, illuminating an ethereal halo that rapidly took shape. The knife ricocheted off the shield with a loud clang.

The Shade cried out as the invisible force holding Cruz released him. Cruz fell to his knees, ducking behind the fully formed shield, pressing himself against the sink and making himself as small a target as possible. Biscuit flew at one of the Shades, biting its ankle as it turned toward me. It hopped up and down before trying to attack my cat.

Hell, no.

I kicked out, sweeping the Shade's leg out from under it. Its body gave a vulgar-sounding *plop* as it hit the floor on its back, a stinking mass of oily flesh. It whipped its head around, its neck snapping, to glare at me, giving a shrill, irritated shriek.

Those dead, solid-black eyes.

My ring burst into a gold knife with a ruby hilt. Screaming at the top of my lungs, I dropped to my knees, aiming for its center mass, and stabbed down. The dagger sank in, and the thing scattered to a million pieces, black sulfur and dust flying everywhere. I fell on my face in the spot it had occupied, panting, and covered my head.

Adrenaline pumped through me like a steam engine.

Getting to my feet, I witnessed the one-eyed Shade staring at the remnants of its dying companion. It directed an ear ear-splitting howl at me. My world turned wonky as everything muted, and my stomach gave a nauseating flip.

Cruz jumped up and slammed into the one-eyed Shade with his shield. Its flesh sizzled, smelling like burnt popcorn and rotting eggs.

"You have to be stronger than that, *kid*," the Shade taunted Cruz, but it was whimpering.

Wait, there were *three* Shades, weren't there?

Where was the third?

Alastair's words echoed back at me from earlier: *Zoey, you can't afford to take your eyes off your enemy, not even for a moment, especially when the enemy is hard to eliminate.*

Something stung me in the back, but I ignored it as I darted toward Cruz to help—

My knees went weak, and I staggered against the sink, barely catching myself and turning around. Little pops of white burst across my vision. Behind me, in the entryway near the den, the third Shade flashed a wicked leer, licking its slick, blackened lips. They looked like jelly.

Clumsily, woozily, I thrust out at it with my ring-turned blade. But there was a disconnect from the brain to the body, and the dagger crackled and burst back into a ring. It slipped from my hands and slid across the floor, resting partially under the stove, the gem no longer twinkling.

My gaze flickered over Cruz. His face was so full of

rage as he pounded his shield into the one-eyed Shade's chest, legs, and torso, beating it senselessly, wholly absorbed in the task. "You—threatened—my—*madre*!" he shouted with each strike.

Looking back at the Shade before me, it gave me a little finger wave, silver veins on its neck standing out as it strolled back into the kitchen. "I shall watch your rite of passage happen."

There was a flash of movement. A blurred body came out of nowhere from the hallway. I couldn't discern what happened until the Shade's eyes bugged out of its head. It unleashed a terrible moan before exploding into a torrent of black dust. Once the ash dissipated, I saw who had come to my aid. Alastair. He was holding a shiny black horn. The gold crack down the center seemed to shine with ghostly brilliance.

Cruz had pinned the one-eyed demon to the opposite wall and was slugging it when Alastair moved, agile as ever as if Alastair had never been hurt in the first place. He spun, using the sharp end of the horn to pierce the monster right through the back of its neck. It fragmented in a torrent of black soot, obliterated.

Cruz floundered back a step, his breath leaving him in loud, ragged rasps. He seemed stunned that he hadn't been able to finish the job himself.

Alastair's chest heaved. "Are you okay?" His face had gone white. A pained grimace crossed it as Cruz nodded, his eyes still wide.

A nagging ache throbbed down my legs and then shot up into my chest. I gasped, clutching it. My legs gave out, and I started to sink to the ground. Alastair hurried over, reaching me just before I fell, and guided me to a nearby chair.

Worry etched on his face, he scanned me for any sign of injury. "Where does it hurt?" he asked urgently.

"Everywhere," I breathed. Energy drained out of me in strange pulses. "M-m-my back," I stuttered.

Cruz was on my other side, gripping my hand in his. I focused on the glimmering shield between his scarred knuckles. At least all the threats were gone.

"It's not that bad, is it?" Cruz said with a sob, turning to Alastair and then to me. "You're gonna be alright, Zo."

"Stay with me," Alastair commanded, his fingers sliding under my shirt. My head fell forward, and I gasped sharply as I heard him growl, "Not on my watch, no way." He seemed genuinely concerned.

Cruz's grip on my hand tightened. "Call Corinth," he urged, his voice filled with anxiety.

"I tried. They're not responding," Alastair replied, his voice strained.

A tear rolled down Cruz's face, leaving a trail on his soot-streaked cheek.

"What's wrong? Why are you crying?" I murmured, hoping my words made sense. I just wanted to reassure Cruz that everything would be okay. Like delicate spider webs, silver lines snaked up and down my arms.

Oh, now I understood.

Alastair winced slightly as he declared, "Only one person can help now." Determined, he raised the ancient-looking horn to his lips and blew softly. It emitted an odd, haunting sound.

I couldn't shake the feeling that someone or something was watching me, but no matter how hard I looked, I couldn't see anything. The feeling was compelling, almost electric, and I let out a soft, involuntary moan.

As the room plunged into darkness, a foreboding presence began to manifest. Slowly, a shadow materialized, taking on an eerie, spectral outline in the dim light.

Biscuit jumped onto my lap, purring.

I pointed at the strange shape near the doorway. "C-c-can you see that?"

Cruz shook his head. "See what, Zo?"

The presence turned into a pillar of sand before solidifying into a Shade.

Cruz's shield began to pulsate and glow white again under his shirt. "More Shades," he croaked.

Just as Cruz was about to spring to his feet, surprisingly, Alastair swiftly pulled him back down. "Hold on, this one won't hurt you."

The Shade solidified, leaning against the doorjamb with an air of indifference, arms crossed. Its skin was a grotesque shade of ichor, with deep black eyes. But what set it apart were the glistening veins of gold, not silver, running up and down its neck and arms.

Fear didn't consume me, even though it probably should have.

"Cruz, back off with that relic. Trust me, it'll be okay," Alastair said calmly.

My ring was still somewhere near the stove.

"This better be good," the Shade said, sounding bored.

I hadn't heard that voice in a long time and was sure I would hear it ever again. The Shade's penetrating gaze met mine, and its name slipped out of my mouth: "Peter?"

48

NAKIR

A mid a moonless night, six figures formed a tight circle: Corinth, Larna, Tamiel, Samyaza, and Leo. Nakir stood on the outside of it. Petra sat in the mountainous region near the Jordan Valley. The necropolis of ruined temples and artificial caves was carved out of the red sandstone cliffs.

As soon as Nakir stepped from the portal, a sinister tingle spread through him, signaling they had arrived at the correct location.

It was a good thing they were prepared for a fight—because he was assured there would be one. "Thanks for the sword," Nakir told Tamiel, who only nodded in response. She didn't like him, but that was okay. They only needed to fight together, not get along.

The Bedouin farmers had set fires far below them. A few donkeys and a flock of goats surrounded their campsite. The night appeared peaceful, but Nakir knew it would be far from it.

"Being human has disadvantages." Larna fished a small

torch from her pocket, switched it on, and directed its light around. Her mouth fell open as she gazed at the rocky outcroppings and quarry above and below them. There were smoothed, eroded holes in the cliffs. Caves. The mountains towered so high they couldn't see where they began or ended.

"I now understand why they call this place Red Mountain," she murmured. "In the dark, at least for me, these will be dangerous grounds to traverse. Why do angels always pick the worst locales to fight in?"

A grimace crossed Corinth's face; clearly, he felt the portentous presence. "Let's pray it doesn't come to fighting."

Leo glanced around. "We're in the right spot. I can feel it."

"I know," Corinth said, facing his half brother. He ran his hand over his forehead, pulling back his beanie.

"Cor, how much coffee have you had?" Larna asked Corinth, shining the light near his jittery feet.

Corinth shot her an annoyed glare that clearly said she knew him too well. "Not important." He met Leo's steadfast stare. "Proceed as planned."

"There are miles and miles of caverns," Larna said. "How do we search them all?"

"We split up," Nakir answered before anyone else could.

"Agreed," Corinth cut in. "Larna and Nakir are with me. Sam, Leo, and Tami start low. We'll begin in the areas that are harder to access by human means—"

"Hey," Larna whispered, holding up her wrist and exposing her watch. "I lost signal. If something happens, I won't be able to alert any of you to it—which means we won't be able to contact Alastair or the others back in Scotland either."

She sounded worried to Nakir. He, too, was troubled by this news. He feared for Zoey, Cruz, and Alastair. What if this was a trap or a diversion?

"I don't like it any more than you do, but we have to trust Alastair has things handled." Corinth pressed his lips together, adding, "This might be our only chance to catch Rimmon by surprise."

"I doubt that," Nakir whispered. "He probably knows we're here already."

"Let's hope not," Corinth murmured. "Keep your heads on swivels, everyone."

They all nodded and headed in their agreed directions, the angels transporting themselves closer to the valley below them. Nakir caught three distinct flashes, indicating that angel portals had opened up.

"All right. Larns, you're with me since I know you can handle heights." Corinth clasped his hands, and they ignited, blue coils of energy coming off his body like vapor. "Nakir, there is an entire cave system on the other side of the mountain, toward the peak. There are no ladders, so the only way to get to different locations is by portaling. We might end up in different spots, but the caves should all connect back up eventually. Stay in contact through telepathy in case we get separated, okay?"

Nakir gave a quick nod. *Got it*, he replied telepathically.

Corinth seized Larna. Together, they plunged into the churning vortex he'd opened, disappearing into the darkness.

For a fleeting instant, Nakir felt weightless as he passed through his portal, as if soaring before he emerged on the opposite side.

Landing, he whirled around and brandished his sword,

scanning his surroundings. The cave appeared deserted. It looked like this had once been a place of residence, as evidenced by the rock wall carvings, the sand beneath his feet, and an old firepit. It felt far removed from everything else up this high on the mountain.

Corinth? Nakir said. *Where are you?*

In a tomb that looks like it used to be a temple. There are winged cats near an altar. It seems like there's an entryway and worship area with columns. It's a tiny space for a temple. Larna and I are going to look around at the support buildings. We'll try to link up with you as we search. Hang on—

The connection was abruptly severed as an ear-piercing screech echoed through his mind. He staggered to his knees, relinquishing his sword, and frantically clasped his hands over his ears. *Ahhh!* When he recovered somewhat, Nakir returned to his feet shakily and grabbed his weapon.

What happened?

No reply.

Corinth? Tamiel? Leo?

Silence.

It's a trap! Nakir tried to warn as he dashed toward the opening of another cave. As soon as he did, the unshakable presence of malice prickled his neck. He pivoted, sprinting to another cavern—only to find it filled with more demons and Shades. He wheeled around, desperately attempting to open a portal to flee to Corinth.

However, the cave was swiftly flooded with ominous, shadowy figures materializing in clouds of smoke and sulfur, hemming him in from every direction. Their numbers were overwhelming, crushing his very breath.

A shadowy figure lunged at him.

Instinctively, Nakir's body lit with lightning as he

gripped his sword. He swung it at the Shade and struck it down. The thing hit the ground with a terrible screech and disintegrated.

Another dark shape lunged at Nakir, snarling and brandishing a jagged spear. With lightning speed, Nakir raised his shield, deflecting the deadly blow. In one swift motion, he spun around, driving his sword into the thing's chest and felling the creature.

Nakir fought with all his might as Shades and demons closed in on him from every direction. Despite his best efforts to unleash his power, they just kept coming. He struck down four incredibly quickly, but ten more emerged for every four he took out. Bodies pressed in around him from all sides, and he knew he was in for the fight of his life.

49

GABRIEL

Gabriel Stanton had done many despicable things in his lifetime, but this ... this was the lowest. Reduced to serving Rimmon for the rest of his life. The mark on his chest weighed him down like a ball and chain. But there was no fighting it. Not with the all-consuming darkness being lorded over him. He would be severely punished if he didn't do exactly what was asked of him. That blackened handprint was more than superficial—it was a shock collar.

Deep within the dark recesses of the quiet hollow, Gabriel waited alone, perched on a rocky outcropping overlooking the dark expanse outside.

Suddenly, he faintly heard pebbles and stones shifting underfoot. Someone was approaching, moving carefully and trying their best to remain silent. Gabriel saw the flicker of a torch, its warm glow casting strange and shifting shadows across the rough-hewn walls. It was otherworldly—no, it was Netherworldly.

And then, just as he had expected, he saw her—*Larna.*

She emerged from the darkness and passed within inches of his hiding spot, her eyes fixed firmly ahead. Corinth was behind her, glancing around, searching for any hint of danger. The Nephilim's blade did not warn them about Gabriel's presence, even with the darkness attached to him.

I'm right here.

One of the worst aspects of being forced to carry out heinous acts against his will was that Gabriel had to inflict harm upon someone he cherished, the only individual he held dear in this world.

At least her death would be quick, by his hand.

Corinth, Gabriel could care less about—karma had always been nipping at the kid's heels.

Gabriel walked out onto the landing of carved stone stairs and inhaled deeply. Below them was at least a hundred-foot drop down the cliff. Stepping out of that suffocating cave felt like a breath of fresh air. The lingering scent of Larna enveloped him—an irresistible mix of vanilla with a hint of cinnamon.

Corinth whirled around in an impressive blur, his blade arching with grace, pointing right at Gabriel's throat before he could even say *hello*.

Larna was right behind Corinth, her eyes laser-focused on Gabriel and a katana in her grip, also pointed at him.

Gabriel slowly lifted his hands and smiled.

"Gabe, not exactly the demon I hoped to find tonight," Corinth snarled. "Why do you always show up like an unwanted guest at the worst possible time?"

He has no idea how right he is.

"What the *hell* are you doing here?" Corinth pressed.

"You can put that blade away, Taylor," Gabriel all but purred. "I'm here to help."

"Help?" Larna scoffed. "Help how?"

The suspicion was as clear as day in her voice, and he smiled inwardly as she put the flashlight right into his eyes and flinched.

Larna Collins was a brilliant one. It's why she had been the one to use compulsion on him—and won. A pang of sadness hit him.

"I know where Rimmon is. He's not far. I can take you to him," Gabriel whispered, looking around, trying to sell it. "But we *must* hurry—he's about to depart the caves to return to the demon realm."

"The demon realm?" Corinth said quickly. "But I destroyed it."

"Keep up, Taylor. He's rebuilding," Gabriel said with an exaggerated sigh. "Rimmon came to me, asking for help getting back inside."

"Why didn't you come to me, then?" Corinth asked, doubt coloring his voice. "I don't like this ..." he started to turn to Larna.

Gabriel knew he was losing the Nephilim. He hoped the kid would wake up and leave.

I'm not going to do it. I won't kill Larna. I won't bring Corinth Taylor to you.

As soon as he thought it, a sharp pain lanced his skull, and he shuddered.

"I couldn't." Gabriel hissed, tilting his head and glancing around. "Rimmon prevented it. I pretended to be in league with the demon until he finally trusted me enough to give me breathing room. I have to get rid of the threat before the threat gets rid of me. Right? Why would I be in league with this demon? He will bring Ephrem back, and if he does, you know what will happen to Zoey ..."

Taylor's eyes lit up as he took the bait and lowered the blade slightly. "Not if I kill Rimmon first."

The kid's weakness—it's his friends and family.

"Come with me now," Gabriel urged. "We won't run into any Shades until we're closer. You can't use a portal—it will give us away, and he'll flee."

The Nephilim shut his eyes for a brief moment, then snapped them open. "Dammit. Nakir's not responding. I have a feeling he's going solo."

"Try the others," Larna said, sounding concerned. "I don't like this, Cor. We can't trust Stanton. We should reconvene."

"Standing right here," Gabriel muttered through clenched teeth.

"I know," Larna retorted right back.

She's always been brighter than Taylor.

Corinth furrowed his brow, deep in concentration, his eyes darting back and forth beneath his closed eyelids. "I can't contact anyone. I suspect Rimmon is interfering with our links."

"I'm getting a bad feeling about this," Larna interjected. "It's time for us to leave."

I'm not going to do it. I won't kill Larna. I won't bring Corinth Taylor to you.

Pain struck Gabriel again; his vision went black, and he gasped.

"Gabriel?" Larna asked, concern in her voice. "What is it?"

Gabriel was going to lose them, and as soon as he thought it, pressure started building in his chest, and a voice invaded his head: *Don't blow this.* "Migraine. Look, this is our only chance at stopping the demon," Gabriel insisted.

"*Please*," he begged. He didn't know who he was begging—Rimmon or Corinth. "If you don't follow me now, Rimmon will open the gates of hell."

After a long pause, Gabriel thought Corinth might not go for it, but then Corinth said, "Lead the way, Gabe. No surprises. We'll call in the cavalry—"

"No!" Gabriel said quickly. "Too many angels will give us away. It has to be just us, Taylor. Stealth mission."

Corinth pressed his lips together before finally nodding.

They crept along, both Larna and Corinth at Gabriel's back.

He did *not* want to obey the demon, and that thought was enough to kindle the fire in his gut, to fight the malicious entity taking up residency inside him.

I'm not going to do it.

Eventually, Gabriel's pace slackened, his every step evolving into an arduous feat, until he found himself clutching his stomach, breathless, in excruciating agony. His body throbbed with pain. They weren't far now.

I won't kill Larna. I won't bring Corinth Taylor to you.

"What's wrong, Gabe?" Corinth asked, coming up beside him. The kid trusted Gabriel too much. There was a hesitation; the lightest hand was at his back, and a healing warmth started spreading through Gabriel. For a moment, he thought it might work, that he'd be freed from his bondage. But then dark agony enveloped him, clawing at his soul—his heart, his insides. *Damn this kid for caring. Damn this kid for being inherently decent.* How Gabriel hated Taylor.

Corinth fell to a knee, gasping, his voice trembling with urgency and pain, and Larna came up beside him. "Corinth, what's the matter?"

"I don't feel right," he answered softly, weakly. "There's s-s-s-o-o much darkness inside him … I'm freezing."

A dribble of saliva slid out of Gabriel's mouth, and the world tilted on its side and went black. He clawed desperately at his chest as if he could dig the evil out. *No.*

"*Gabe! Gabe!*" Corinth shouted, sounding frailer by the second.

Amidst the overwhelming anguish, Gabriel caught the distant echo of Larna's concerned voice.

Then, the oppressive sensation vanished in a blink, and Gabriel became a mere observer in his own body. He sprang to his feet, unequivocally consumed by Rimmon, his metamorphosis hidden from everyone else.

Larna stood behind Gabriel. Corinth was on the opposite side, returning to his feet, having recovered slightly.

They partly blocked the entrance to the tomb where Gabriel was meant to hand over the Nephilim.

This is the end of the road, kid.

It was funny, but now that Gabriel had the strength to kill Corinth, he discovered he desperately did not want to. Taylor's emotions were his downfall, and the entity inside Gabriel knew it.

Unable to control his body, Gabriel spun, kicking Larna with enough force to send her flying against the outer wall to the stairwell. Her arms flailed out before she toppled backward over it, falling—

Gone. Just like that.

Larna's distant cry reverberated around the bluff, forever etched into Gabriel's memory.

Corinth's anguished cry reverberated across the

mountaintop, his eyes widening in disbelief and shock. And then his face contorted into one of the most terrifying expressions, as his entire being ignited like a solar flare. Corinth was going to try to save Larna, but it was too late. Rimmon, occupying Gabriel's body, now possessed supernatural strength and speed (oh, the irony.) And the fact that Rimmon *also* occupied his own body meant he could be in two places at once now.

Gabriel kicked out at Corinth, who managed to counter, impressively blocking his assault with his leg. The attack was only meant to distract the half-angel long enough for Rimmon to step up behind him.

It worked.

Rimmon seized hold of Corinth from behind and dragged him down into the tomb.

The unmistakable swift burst of demonic energy solidified over the doorway, trapping them inside before he could escape.

The Nephilim looked ready to explode as he glanced around, sizing up his enemies. Gabriel knew Taylor couldn't use his angelic energy to portal out or communicate with the others—he was limited in strength inside the tomb. It was how they'd captured Ikari.

Corinth fought anyway, striking out quicker than lightning, punching Gabriel in the jaw. Gabriel floundered back as Corinth lifted his holy blade, which had magically appeared in his grasp, and aimed it. The hurt and betrayal were etched into every line and crease on the kid's face.

Rimmon, behind Corinth, brought the hilt of *Stronghold* down hard onto Corinth's skull.

Corinth collapsed in a crumpled heap, out like a light.

Standing over Taylor, Rimmon had a look of pure glee on his face.

Corinth awoke to find himself strung up like a slab of beef in a meat market—dangling by a chain, wrists cuffed with ancient restraints, scrawled with demonic inscriptions to keep his powers at bay.

Back in command of his body, Gabriel had done all the dirty work.

Now, he held Corinth's lance, waiting on orders from his master. *Bollocks.* How could he get out of this?

You can't, the voice answered.

"*Larna better be alive,*" Corinth stressed shakily, his head sagging and bare feet barely dragging the stone floor. His dark brown locks were damp with sweat and blood, but the Nephilim's stare was fierce and unrelenting. "If I don't kill you, Alastair will. You're worse than dead, Gabe."

"Very noble." Rimmon stepped forward, holding Nakir's sword and wearing the white helmet he'd taken from Gabriel. "Oh, little Nephilim, it wasn't *Gabriel's* choice to kill Larna. I did it by possessing him. Believe it or not, Stanton had a soft spot for Larna, and vastly surprising to me—he still holds a soft spot for *you*, Corinth. I saw the truth in his mind."

Corinth ignored Rimmon's snide remark to glance at the holy blade in Gabriel's hands. He gave Gabriel a curt nod, a strange look crossing his features. The kid wasn't angry that Gabriel possessed it. Odd. Corinth's eyes lit up as they peered straight into Gabriel's soul—and he had been sure he didn't have one.

"The dagger *chose* you, Gabe," Corinth said with as much poise as he could muster, considering how limply he hung by his wrists. "It's yours now." A trickle of blood ran down the side of his neck.

The Nephilim sure did have moxie.

Gabriel furrowed his brows.

What?

Preposterous.

But what if …

"No, it's not. And no, it didn't." Rimmon barked out a laugh. "That vile *thing* holds no power here, and neither do you. You're as helpless as a human child. Why do you think I hauled you down here? Well, that, and to have a little fun."

"You killed Ikari." A dark shadow passed over Corinth's face as his flashing eyes locked on Rimmon. "*Demon*, I won't think twice about cutting you down."

"Such violence." Rimmon glanced at Gabriel, one side of his mouth curling up. "Gabriel, you never told me about this side of the half-breed. I like it." The demon shifted his gaze back to Corinth as a slow, cruel smile spread across his lips. "Angela and I knew each other long before you killed her, Corinth. She was too preachy. I'm glad she's gone. I think you and I might have been friends in another life—pity yours will end now."

"Some way to treat your friends," Corinth sighed, the pain evident in his voice as he tugged at his restraints. His gaze locked on Gabriel again, but Gabriel averted his gaze from those intense eyes. He knew Corinth was looking for a way out. Or maybe he was signaling Gabriel in some way. The blade was just a blade in Gabriel's hands—nothing more. Right?

They'd been in this position before, and Gabriel had stepped in to help.

Not today, kid.

"Mr. Stanton can't help you right now, Corinth," Rimmon murmured, catching Corinth's glance. I did save your sister," the demon continued, inching closer, Nakir's sword clutched in his grip. Don't I get credit for that? Tell me you don't hate me, and I'll consider lopping off your head to make it quicker."

"Never mention my sister," Corinth snarled, "*ever— again.*"

"You're quite sensitive, aren't you?" Rimmon's eyebrows shot up. "Ephrem will soon be by my side. But you, you're all mine."

"Ephrem and Gabe may be your loyal mutts," Corinth said, his voice steady as he shot Rimmon a steely gaze. "But I am not and will *never* be yours to claim."

Rimmon strode purposefully toward Corinth. His grip was tight on the sword as he raised it high above his head, his intention unmistakable. "Your time is up, Nephilim."

50

NAKIR

More demons pressed in around Nakir. They sparked and fell off his glowing shield like insects. He slashed and hacked at the surrounding horde of Shades, his breath coming in ragged gasps as another barrage flew at him. They came in relentless waves, forming an impenetrable wall to keep him boxed in. The hissing was unbearable. The angry cries and taunts were worse, adding to the cacophony.

This was about Corinth. Rimmon was going after the Nephilim.

Nakir should have seen it coming.

The stench of sulfur filled his nose as a Shade came out of nowhere, screamed, and then fell dead at his feet—a small victory amid chaos.

The demons were counting on his need to fight. To destroy every last one of them. Nakir dodged out of the way of an incoming spear. As he did, he spied a narrow opening ahead of him, past many bodies. The odds were overwhelming. He wouldn't make it, though. There were too many of them. But Nakir, fueled by his willpower, refused to give in.

A faint smile formed on his lips. Nakir wanted their heads. He abruptly halted his advance, a sudden change in strategy that caught the demons off guard. They stopped momentarily.

Nakir squeezed his eyes shut, endeavoring to rip open a portal with every ounce of strength, leaving himself vulnerable without his shields.

As he screamed in defiance, a sharp rip tore through his side, and waves of pain coursed through his body. The demons closed in on him, stabbing, clawing, and biting. It was a good thing he had armor; still, the unarmored spots on his body screamed in pain.

The wind howled, and thunder roared. Suddenly, a rupture in the fabric of space exploded open with cataclysmic force, instantly obliterating the surrounding Shades and demons. The remaining creatures recoiled in terror as Nakir leaped into the swirling vortex and vanished, thinking about Corinth's location.

Instantly, he stood on the edge of a cliffside terrace with a looming staircase.

It was quiet. Too quiet. An evil presence, thick and smothering, lingered heavily in the air.

To Nakir's left, a red light emanated from another opening a few steps down. It looked like an entrance to a tomb. Didn't Corinth say he was inside a tomb?

A faint, wounded cry came from nearby. Nakir tensed, listening.

A moment later, the shout came again. He ran to the top of a stone staircase, gazing down the sheer drop-off and listening.

"*Help!*"

Nakir leaped through another portal he'd conjured without hesitation and landed on a rugged outcropping.

He scanned the surroundings until he found the source of the cry.

Larna. Her fingers clung desperately to the rugged rockface, her strength fading with each passing moment. A deep gash marred her brow; its crimson streak ran down her face, a testament to how much she'd struggled to hold on. Her duster hung in tatters around her waist. Every line etched on her face mirrored the intense concentration required to stay alive.

Nakir realized Larna couldn't see in the dark to scale the wall.

"I got you," he told her.

As soon as her gaze caught Nakir's, relief washed over her features. "Corinth, you have to help him—" she started to say, but her hands slipped.

She lost her grip and plummeted into the dark.

Nakir dove headfirst after Larna, freefalling. He caught her around the middle as he opened a portal below them, and they plunged through it.

51

ZOEY

I sat slumped in the kitchen chair, Alastair's supportive presence beside me. Still casually leaning against the wall, Peter fixed me with his intense, all-black gaze. This was precisely what Nik had cautioned me about. It was clear that part of Peter was missing something fundamental, something vital—his soul.

Cruz nervously paced a few feet from us, keeping his medallion away from Peter. His eyes darted to me as he chewed on a fingernail. The shield around his neck emitted a strange glow, heightening the nervous atmosphere.

"Pete," I said thickly, giggling and half out of my mind. "You're bald." A part of me didn't believe my brother was standing there. He had to be a hallucination. "You've looked better."

Peter let out a low snicker. "You too, Bean Pole," he said, approaching and squatting beside me. This close, I sensed alarm and urgency coming from him. *He does care. He is in there. He does have a soul.*

"If this were all it took to get you here, I would have done it sooner," I said weakly.

"Yeah, sure, kid." Peter turned his gaze to Alastair, seeking his approval to touch me.

Alastair gave him a nod, and Peter's ice-cold hand touched my lower back. I gasped as a burst of silver exploded behind my eyelids, almost making me black out.

"Hold on, Zo," he whispered.

Things happened in loopy, distorted increments after that.

The darkness tried to hook in, refusing to give up its hold over me, like a leach being forcibly removed. I screamed and struggled as someone held me down. My mind was consumed by the shard writhing inside me, refusing to leave its new host.

I heard Cruz whispering a prayer and focused on his words, even though they were in Spanish. Little by little, the pressure started to disperse.

Eventually, it was gone, leaving me frail and drained.

Demon attacks were no joke.

Pete sat on the floor beside the bed I lay on. My hand dangled off the side, and he wound his fingers through mine. Cruz was on his own bed, watching us, legs crossed and still looking upset. Biscuit purred beside me, enjoying my body heat.

Alastair had gone to tell Cor and the other angels. I tried not to think about how worried I was for my brother. *Dear Lord*, I prayed, *please bring Cor back home safely.*

"You saved my life ... again," I murmured, sleep dragging at my bones. "Thank you, Pete."

Pete had pulled the hood of his cloak back onto his

bald head, refusing to make eye contact with me. I reached over, and he flinched. Slowly, I tugged his hood back down, revealing his face. "You don't need to hide from me."

He thumbed a hand toward Cruz. "It was more for his benefit."

My eyes sought Cruz's, and he shrugged as if to say *facts*.

I smiled at that. "I knew you were still in there," I told my brother, faint and sleep-deprived. "I'm glad you're not … you know, dead."

Pete didn't say anything to that, only squeezed my hand.

"Will you help Cor?" I asked. "Jimmy and Mom and—" I started to say, but Pete released my hand and stood so suddenly that I immediately missed his presence.

"I can't … stay. I only wanted to make sure you were okay before I left. Please don't seek me out, Zo. The life we once shared as a family is …" he paused. "Over."

Tears sprang to my eyes and leaked down my face. "Pete, don't say that—"

"My name is Ari." His voice broke. "*Please*, Zo, you have to let me go." The pleading in his voice had me crying even harder. This sucked. *Screw it.*

"No," I said firmly, trying to sit up. But I was too weak to do it alone, and the covers held me in place.

Cruz had this haunted expression plastered on his face, like he felt sorry for me.

Pete vanished in a whirlwind of black ash and dust. Cruz's eyes met mine as he hurried over to my bed, helping me to lean back against the pillows. My entire body hurt.

"Easy now," he said. "Pete's just trying to keep you safe, I think. I saw the hurt on his face."

I couldn't hold back the tears. I sobbed uncontrollably. Cruz embraced me tightly, and I rested my head on his chest, feeling the warmth of his shield against my face.

52

GABRIEL

There was no more banter as Rimmon charged, *Stronghold* aimed directly at Corinth's heart. In that split second, Gabriel knew, without a doubt, that the half-angel wouldn't escape.

Corinth's lightning-filled eyes met Gabriel's—and held his stare. Infinitely. Time didn't exist in those eyes. Gabriel could not look away. Compulsion or something else was being forced upon him. Damn, that angel was powerful. Perhaps, in Corinth's final act, he planned to free Gabriel from possession. But then, many jumbled-up memories struck him all at once. His entire three thousand years passed before his eyes in a myriad of beautiful, overwhelming pandemonium.

One image rose to the surface above all the others: his mother. Warm, kind, and gentle, her embrace was all he craved. Suddenly, he heard her voice: *My child, so misguided you have been. So full of fear. And that has partly been my fault. My death has warped you, and rightly so. The pain you must have felt, witnessing my murder. But being alive for thousands of years is no longer an option. I am at peace. And so shall you be. We do not have much longer. Have you decided to join us, my son?*

It was a memory that had been wiped from his mind. He was sure of it.

Join us?

Gabriel's fingers curled tighter around the hilt of the holy dagger. He *did* have a choice. He always had a choice. *This* was *his* life. A divine and glorious peace settled over him at that realization. *Peace.*

And then something inside him fissured. Warmth flowed in, loosening the dark entity's tight hold over him. And Gabriel was free—if only momentarily, as grace overcame him, stealing his breath away.

Don't think.

The blade in his hand sparked to life, trusting him to do what needed to be done.

One selfless act.

Very unlike Gabriel, in one last desperate, thoughtless, absurd act, he teleported right into the path of the oncoming sword—which pierced his heart instead of Corinth's.

The holy blade exploded in a blinding array of light, blasting Rimmon backward and sending the demon crashing through the unholy barrier. It shattered into a tiny million rubies, sizzling away into the night—a breathtaking sight. Gabriel dropped the sacred blade. He watched in awe as the lightning and fire dissipated.

The manacles around Corinth's wrists broke. He fell to his knees, his body blazing with grace, wings ablaze at his back. The miraculous display blinded Gabriel.

His vision cleared for what could have been an eternity or a few seconds. He found himself lying on the cold, hard stone with Corinth crouched over him. Gabriel's eyes moved down his torso to see what he hoped wasn't there. The sword stuck out of his chest. He knew it; that glorious feeling of peace had been a lie. Gabriel grasped the blade's hilt and heaved up on it, pulling it out with one final grunt. It clattered to the ground beside him.

Astonishingly, Larna was on Gabriel's other side, clutching his hand in hers. "Gabriel, you idiot. Why did you do that?"

Gabriel blinked stupidly back at Larna.

She must be dead. *He* must be dead. "I suppose you're here to take me to the afterlife?" he slurred. "Fitting."

But now that he was studying Larna more closely, he saw a large gash over her left eye. Through a ripped hole in her sleeve, he saw a nasty-looking laceration on her forearm. Her fingers were swollen and bloodied.

Gabriel scanned the darkened corners and spotted the archangel, Nakir, gazing steadfastly back at him with a pitying expression.

Gabriel was not dead, but he would be soon.

"You'll want your sword back, I suppose." Gabriel laughed. Blood bubbled on his lips as his eyes traveled down to *Stronghold*. At least he couldn't feel the wound. "I thought I'd killed you, Mrs. Iszler," he said numbly, squeezing her hand. "It's nice to see I didn't."

"You have to try harder than that, Stanton," Larna said gently, her eyes forgiving, her hand in his warm. "It was a good thing Nakir swooped in at the last second. I'm glad I climb on my days off."

"I'm sorry," Gabriel murmured. "It was not my … intention to … harm … you, my dearest." A trickle of blood slid out of his mouth. "I tried to stop … it."

She nodded, her gaze filled with remorse, grief, and, surprisingly, tears. "Corinth told me."

Corinth said, "You saved my life, Gabe. I tried my hardest to repay the favor, but there's too much damage … the sword …. I … I tried." He hung his head as his voice cracked, then grasped Gabriel's other hand. "I'm so, so sorry."

Gabriel's eyes widened. The tiniest, inconsequential bit of … non-annoyance appeared on his face, as a smile. "Oh, for fuck's sake, kid," he said feebly. "Don't look so miserable."

The Nephilim let out a sad chuckle, wiping his eyes. "Why save *me*? You hate me, Gabe."

"It turns out—I don't," he said softly, his vision starting to slide in and out of focus. He was just so tired. Sleep sounded good.

Blessed, peaceful sleep.

53

ALASTAIR

When all the angels had returned, Tamiel, Samyaza, and Leo looked like they had been in a horrendous battle. But as soon as Alastair saw his wife, her coat slashed and face swollen, he checked her for injuries. If she had any, the angels had healed her of them. The fire in his belly wouldn't go away. He was livid.

Breathe, Alastair, breathe.

Larna squeezed his hand as if sensing that he needed the reassurance, which he did.

Alastair had been so worried when they'd lost contact. *Never again*, he vowed. *This can't happen again.* He could have lost her. She was his soul, his everything. If Alastair lost Larna, he'd lose it all.

Nakir's blade, *Stronghold*, was back at his side, where it belonged—but at what cost?

Corinth looked shell-shocked.

Alastair could still see the guilt written all over Taylor's face.

It would never leave the kid; he knew this from

personal experience. The sacrifice was heavy. It's always too heavy.

While Cruz and Zoey slept off the aftereffects of the demon attack, everyone else sat in front of a huge bonfire they'd built in the field near the guest cottage. It was cold, but the blaze felt good. Alastair needed the crisp air on his skin. He was proud of how Cruz and Zoey had handled themselves against three Shades—more than proud.

Cor had been *unhappy* to discover that Zoey had gotten infected with a shard. Thankfully, Ari had saved her, and everyone was grateful. Even the other angels, skeptical about working with a Shade, were indebted to him. Alastair knew it wouldn't be the last they'd hear from Ari. The Taylors always seemed to show up when you least expected it.

"Gabriel Stanton. I can't believe it." Alastair rubbed his sleep-tired eyes and exhaled. He felt, of all things, sad. "Stanton is … is *dead*. I was starting to go from hating him to disliking the jerk. That is, until he kicked my wife off a cliff. But in the end, the billionaire did the right thing. He jumped in front of *Stronghold*, sacrificing himself. Cor, I'm glad you're okay."

Corinth only shrugged as he sipped his coffee.

"Will there be a funeral for Stanton?" Alastair asked, not unkindly.

"We called his security team, and they took his body to make arrangements for burial," Larna answered thickly.

Nakir lounged in a worn-out lawn chair, its fabric struggling to hold his weight. The crackling fire cast dancing shadows on his face as he leaned in, seeking solace in the warmth. His gaze shifted from the flickering flames to Corinth. A blend of determination and an inscrutable emotion Alastair couldn't quite decipher shimmering in Nakir's eyes.

Samyaza, Tamiel, and even Vinson gathered around the fire. All looked equally uncomfortable. Vienna and Jack were asleep, but Tamiel tilted her head, using her superhuman hearing to listen for any sounds or threats.

Nakir locked eyes with Corinth. "You showed true fearlessness going after Rimmon. I owe you my gratitude for … well, for everything. I underestimated you, Corinth Taylor. In the coming days, consider me by your side if you ever need anything, ready to offer my help as a friend."

Corinth nodded, seemingly unable to find the right words. Gabriel's death had left him shaken. The billionaire had always seemed superior and unpleasant, yet he had somehow wormed his way into their hearts.

Alastair threw a glance at Nakir. "Thanks for rescuing Larna."

Nakir inclined his head. "I owed you."

"So, what's your next move, Nakir?" Corinth finally spoke up, breaking his silence. "Because you're welcome here."

"Search for my helmet, armor, and the rest of my gear," Nakir said. "Care to join me?"

TO BE CONTINUED.

JOIN THE ADVENTURE

Join the adventure for the latest book updates and freebies and to support your very grateful author.

Sign up for our mailing list to keep in touch: http://www.eepurl.com/dg029j

Join me on Discord for an online book club—I often pop in and chat, and I'd love to see you there, too. Come say hi at: https://www.discord.gg/UYGXNTJ.

Do you Love this book? Please consider rating or reviewing it. It means the world to me to hear from you.

ACKNOWLEDGMENTS:

This book has been a *long* time in the making. *Phew!*

I apologize to everyone who patiently waited for me to finish it.

Dear reader, please know I agonized over this book for countless hours—that turned into years. Many obstacles happened while trying to complete *Halo & Horn*, including my brain taking a vacation, burnout, attempting to finish another book (unsuccessfully so far), working full time, and so on. The little goblins in my head often tell me my writing is never good enough, so it means the world to me when y'all keep reading.

Anyway, if you happened to have finished this book and loved it, please consider dropping me a line or rating/reviewing it.

Thank you to my editor, Salima Alikhan, for your time, experience, advice, and grace in working with me. An editor is worth their weight in gold.

Thank you very much to my cover designer, Mark Reid, and book formatter, Lorna Reid, who have both been with me from the beginning. You two are incredible and instrumental in my success, and I wouldn't be here without you.

Thank you to my family, who constantly uplifted me and encouraged me to keep writing.

Let me say that again, only louder: THANK YOU TO MY FAMILY, WHO CONSTANTLY UPLIFT AND ENCOURAGE ME TO KEEP WRITING. Thank you to Becky Pruitt, my manager and big sister, who does majorly heavy lifting on my behalf.

Thank you again, Juan Arriaga, for inspiring the character of Cruz Saldivar. Thank you also to my travel companion, Michael Smith, and my twin, Christy, who always reassures me that I'll get through this. Thank you to Misty Spitzer for being my hype girl and Stephanie Hancock for never giving up on me. There are so many people to thank that I can't list them.